The Sun in Horus

MARIANA VILLA-GILBERT

The Sun in Horus

HAMISH HAMILTON
London

First published in Great Britain 1986
by Hamish Hamilton Ltd
Garden House 57–59 Long Acre London WC2E 9JZ

Copyright © 1986 by Mariana Villa-Gilbert

British Library Cataloguing in Publication Data

Villa-Gilbert, Mariana
 The sun in horus.
 I. Title
 823'.914[F]   PR6072.145
 ISBN 0–241–11720–8

Phototypeset by Input Typesetting Ltd, London
Printed in Great Britain by
St Edmundsbury Press, Bury St Edmunds, Suffolk

To the memory of Norah Smallwood.
With my thanks.

Contents

'Q'

'Nor was that all,' Mrs Hemery said. 'For the lad – he'd been up her place, see, and was riding that wretched motorcycle thing – raced out onto the road and was struck by a single vehicle speeding past. Mr Quigley, who was in the field across, saw it all. He was thrown, he said, from one side of he road to the other. The driver didn't even stop. When he got to the wire, young Hook was hung from it like a rag doll. Killed outright, Mr Quigley reckons.

'Mrs Harding? – ah, she went back to town when everything was settled. I was sorry, too. She was good to me while she was here; a really nice lady. Goes to show though: there's some as gets up to all kinds of things on the quiet.

'No – it must have been terrible for her. Even if she was quite calm about it after. Sounds wicked perhaps, but – while, in a sense, both he and the lad got what they probably wanted – she alone, in some strange way, seemed unaffected by it all. It was the shock perhaps . . . who's to know?

'But this was how she always struck me – it was like, no matter what he done, she could be happy in spite of him. He never really knew her, of that I'm sure. Never really knew what she was thinking. And it was this as made him so resentful. She was a curiously complete sort of person – easily satisfied. It was little things as made her happy. Quite out of this world, she was. And it was this as brought them – to tilt at her, like Sancho Pancho (she meant, of course, Don Quixote) at his senseless windmill.

'Still, like I said – who's to know? There's not one of us as truly knows another.'

But then he would wonder. How was it he'd allowed the situation to so deteriorate it had become for him an everyday nightmare? To so master him he was little more than a slave? He was in all other respects a reasonable man. Tolerant to a fault. But, with her. . .

He began by suggesting she might prefer to live in the country. (Life in town, where she was the object always of an admiring eye, had become for him unbearable.) She was fond of the country: the air would do her good.

Her pure, her pale face.

'But – permanently?'

Could she not do then without her many admirers?

Her large, violet-grey eyes were like a freshly painted watercolour. Diffuse, yet startling. She'd that totally feminine, timeless quality. Was neither fashionable, nor unfashionable, but just herself. Mostly, she wore her hair up. In either a French pleat, or a plait. A rich brown, it contrasted well with the true ivory of her complexion.

She called him Leonard. He called her Alexandra. Any diminutives of which would have been unthinkable.

And so, as seemed now inevitable, he'd secured her here in the old house in which he'd lived as a child. Not that this was a complete success. For – as in town – he remained convinced she'd manage if she wished to deceive him.

He never spoke about her to anybody. Among his friends there were two sorts of stories in circulation. That she'd been a humble company secretary. That she was the errant wife of an emigratory Polish aristocrat. Neither of which tales was likely ever to gain factual credence. Her past – her present even – was his closely guarded secret. And must remain for them a mystery.

She was herself mysterious. A creature of myth, who reminded him always of a sort of latter-day Persephone.

Denizen with him of some darkened underworld all blackened by his deadly breath. Her beauty alone was a fact. And the admiration it drew. A burden – if indeed it was a burden – she apparently bore without concern. His rapidly tightening grip on her served only to increase her elusiveness. His wife of almost a year, she was as much a mystery to him still as to his friends.

He'd enter unexpectedly . . . to find her alone. But was sure someone had been there. Her patient replies to his carefully worded questions only made him more suspicious. He took to arriving home at all times, hoping to catch her out. But no.

He stopped her next from going into the village. Anything she wanted could be sent up – or the woman must go instead. He forbade her even to ride her bicycle: a minor accident provided him with the excuse for which he was waiting. If she wanted a walk, she was to go with him. Certainly not alone.

'Where's your wife old man? – doesn't she come up to town at all?'

Questions like these produced in him a terrible guilt. Which he carried as far as his front door, where he again convinced himself any such guilt was unnecessary. She was as vulnerable as a priceless gem. As open to covetousness. She must be constantly watched. Or, if she could not be watched, then she must be made totally inaccessible.

A slave to routine, as to some demon god, he'd play these little games with himself. If, for instance, the 'phone stopped ringing before he could grasp the receiver – if so-and-so didn't happen by such-and-such a time – then she was with someone. And he must get back at once. He'd find, on replacing the receiver, that the sweat stood on his forehead.

All this was telling on him – of which he was well aware. But was quite unable to help himself.

'Women,' he once told a colleague, 'are by nature duplicitous.'

His confidences, however, were few. He was not normally given to laying himself open to speculation.

'Everything here,' he said to her on the one occasion he

was able to refer to – or, rather, to hint at – his obsession, 'is perfect. Only I am imperfect.'

She was silent.

He was suddenly wildly afraid.

He wooed and wed her in as quick a time as he was able without altogether frightening her off.

She had seemed, he remembered, surprised when at last he'd made his feelings known to her. He'd no way of ascertaining whether or not this was a genuine reaction. But she surely must have noticed that his eyes acknowledged her every movement. . . ?

Even so, she was never quite sure of him. He knew that. And remained, still, doubtful as to whether she'd done the right thing. He'd attempted earnestly to reassure her. She'd wanted to be convinced. But, of course, he was only as good as his actions.

'How would you have me?' she cried out once in exasperation. 'As a passionless puppet, more dead than alive?'

Terrified by this near collapse of self control, this glimpse of her humanity, he'd only stared. She mistook his silence perhaps. Prepared for some terrible anger. It was the only time she'd raised her voice with him, or given him any hint as to her feelings.

He entered the room. It was early afternoon. The French windows were open: the net was drawn gently out, fell gently back again. The air was sweet with honeysuckle: the decor – whose soft greys, whose pastel hyacinth with its hint of carnation and rose so pleased him – appropriately unobtrusive.

She too wore blue. Seated on the sofa, an open book beside her, she was listening to the Monteverdi Vespers. (Not too loud: he could hear the clock tick.) The whole of which tableau achieved in his eyes a near perfection. Here was a beautiful woman engaged, during her hour of idleness, in a suitable occupation. . . He wanted to kneel down before her. To say to her:

'Alexandra, dearest, are you happy?'

But daren't. For she'd feel, then, obliged either to lie to him or to remain silent. Each, in its way, as afflictive as the other. Instead, like one who stands before a particularly striking portrait, he only looked.

Until, at last:

'You didn't expect me. . . ?'

'No. How should I? – you didn't say.'

But suppose she lied? Or spoke only half a truth? Was the whole thing not a trifle too contrived? A trifle too deliberate? Was she not perhaps doing this only because she felt it to be expected of her?

Abruptly he changed the subject.

'How,' he asked, 'would you fancy a dinner party? Oh, yes: I'm sure you would – you haven't seen anyone in ages.'

She smiled faintly.

'Since you've already answered for me, what am I expected to say?'

He stared.

'Well, it would for instance have been nice if you'd said no, you'd rather spend the evening alone with me . . . '

'Well, all right. I'd rather spend the evening alone with you.'

'You're laughing at me!'

'No, Leonard.'

'And what are you thinking now? – anything for a quiet life?'

She shook her head.

'No. Not at all.'

He looked blankly at her a moment. Went then to the window. The air on his cheek was like a balm.

'It was not necessary for you to say anything. I know exactly what. . . '

She waited for him to finish. Then, when it was apparent he didn't intend to:

'Who are they? – who's coming to dinner?'

'Jamieson, Hill and Carter – with their wives, of course.' He turned suddenly. 'And a man called Pfeffer – hopefully, we'll get that deal through at last. Really, it's a business rather than a social occasion. But Jamieson thought it'd be a good idea to wine and dine him first at a rather more domestic level – the Jerries being especially susceptible to that sort of thing.'

'It'll be a change, I suppose.'

'A change? A change from what?'

She looked directly at him. But nothing. No hint at what she was thinking. It was this open expression of hers which so infuriated him. She whom he'd virtually imprisoned was no more a prisoner than the breeze which came in at the window. That for which he reached, at which he hopelessly grasped, was no more substantial than a dream.

She closed her book. Rose quietly, and left the room.

The place was actually nothing like a prison. For a start, it was nowhere near so imposing. It was little more than a largish, part collapsed country cottage. Built of stone, it seemed every year to subside a fraction further into that same soil from which originally it came. To submit, somehow, a degree or two more willingly to the exuberance of growth with which it was surrounded. Tall trees, creepers – wistaria, and damp ivies – which adhered hungrily to its irregular façade. The front was somewhat untidy. And – were it not for her own diligent efforts – must have succumbed already to neglect.

There'd been a gardener. (More than one over the years.) He'd fired him in anticipation of her arrival. The only servant here now was a part time cook-cum-housekeeper – a woman from the village who put in a few hours every morning, and whom he already suspected of acting as a secret accessory to his wife's amours.

At the back was a beautiful little garden. To this, she gave her full attention. It was perfection in miniature. There was a largish lawn – irregular, like the house itself. More or less in the centre of which was a pool with a small ornamental fountain. There were irises, and aquilegias, and fuchsias, and several shrubs. It had a marvellous ambience, a still serenity. Beyond – partitioned off by an old brick wall in which was a rusting iron gate – was a wilder area, untended now for a number of years. Here were dark-leaved rhododendrons, tall

Japanese anemones which stood at dusk like the pale beacons of some magic land, a number of old trees, and the odd, equivocal, weather-worn statue. Which last, when evening fell, achieved a personality of a kind which – since childhood – had filled him with a sort of superstitious dread.

Here indeed, locked away behind the postern gate, was the whole agonised world of his childhood. When at the cottage he'd spent most of his time here, quite alone, since it was his only escape. The only place in which he could in a limited sense relax or let off a small amount of steam without inadvertently annoying his formidable father.

He was brought up by a nurse. His mother, soon after his birth, died from what remained for him still an unspecified illness. His father, who'd loved her deeply, suffered a nervous collapse from which he never fully recovered. As a result of which his small son's every act was rigidly controlled, his every move safeguarded, his every thrust at self expression effectively stifled. Nor was he often allowed out of his father's sight. And, when he was, so feared his all-seeing eye, his corrosive displeasure, he rarely risked a false move.

His father, for his time even, was anachronistically severe. He was also something of a contradiction in terms. Physically, he was tremendously powerful with a terrifyingly huge and dictatorial voice. But was subject to alternating moods of frightening euphoria and black depression. A covert psychopath, he waxed and waned with the moon in all her several phases.

Heavily bearded, fatally handsome, he was a man of violent temperament and insatiable sexual appetite. The existence of which last in others roused in him a frenzied disgust. He was shocked, appalled, and infuriated – without once recognising the fault for his own. His ego was equally insatiable. He extorted flattery shamelessly. Quick to take umbrage, slow to forgive, none dared contradict or criticise him – least of all his son, at whatever age.

He'd gone in fear of his father until the day of his death – and feared his memory still. The self-confessed inheritor of some – though not all – of his father's faults, he blamed him remorselessly for his own psychosis. The monster should never have been allowed to breed.

But this garden, this wrecked memorial to his childhood, was of course the ideal place for a secret tryst. . .

All around were only woods and fields, and a meandering secondary road, and the odd farm or two.

The atmosphere was rather different, however, a few nights later when the narrow way before the front gate was all but blocked by a Mercedes estate, a beautifully kept E-type Jag, Jamieson's Rolls and a company car or two.

'So who are your friends here, for goodness' sake?'

Carter. To her.

He watched carefully for her reaction to this. She did not, however, look at him. Did not seek to betray him with an accusing stare, for which loyalty he was momentarily grateful. Till shame crept in. Then rage. This black-frost anger for which he'd no explanation.

'Oh, I don't know,' she said. And smiled suddenly. 'My cat, I suppose. I have a darling cat – he's an absolute character. You'll meet him later, no doubt. He spends all his time in the garden at present. But we do, of course, have neighbours. . . '

'But Alexandra my dear, this is ridiculous. In fact, shameful. Leonard old man: what are you doing, hiding her away like this?'

Still he didn't take his eyes off her. But couldn't fault her. From her expression, she might just as easily have been deciding what to have for dinner. Pfeffer, however, now took an interest in the conversation. He looked curiously at her, his head a little to one side. He'd the bright, acquisitive eyes of a greedy eater.

'She has only to say when she is bored. I thought it would make a change for her – you like it don't you, my dear?'

Again she smiled. But there was no secret, no subtlety in her smile. It was clear, bright, and open.

'But of course.' And, to Carter: 'You know, there's plenty for me to do here. I love gardening, for instance. The garden

— you must see this too — is entirely mine. The fruit of my labours.'

It was not yet twilight. The windows were open. Somewhere beyond, a blackbird sang a jolly, rollicking song. The mingled scents of honeysuckle and jasmine perfumed the still, slightly moist air. It had threatened all day to thunderstorm: there was a hint of it still, though the cloud had lightened toward evening.

On the table, the tall candles were starting to make their presence felt. Seen, rather. And were palely reflected in the darkening pool of the large, rectangular glass over the mantel. Likewise the several faces conceived of their illumination. At the centre of which her own stood serenely suspended like a pale planet upon some mythical horizon. There was a faint aroma of beeswax.

'No,' she added after a pause. 'One loses one's taste for London here. Hard to imagine sometimes it's only an hour's ride away.'

'What about Leonard? — you'd not give it up so easily, I bet.'

He was annoyed.

'Well, of course, as a businessman. . . I don't know though: there are times when I'd like to. My health isn't —'

Jameson looked quickly.

'But my health isn't bad, considering. And no businessman wants to retire before his time.'

They never, Carter guessed, discussed these things. It was only when — as now — he spoke publicly that she'd any inkling as to what was in his mind.

'Well, you've another fifteen years to think about that,' he laughed.

'And you, madame?' Pfeffer suddenly interrupted. 'Will you be content to continue with your gardening all this time?'

Embarrassed, she glanced suddenly in his direction.

'Why, yes. I think so. . . '

He looked interestedly at her.

'How strange.'

Carter, who'd caught something of the stiffening atmosphere, laughed again.

'She has green fingers, you know. The seasons are because she is.'

But was looking at her too.

Was weighing, perhaps, the pros and cons of the twenty years difference in their ages – she and Leonard.

Later, going out, she saw them in brief conversation.

'No,' Leonard said. 'Certainly not.' And: 'There was a gardener. I didn't trust him. I was forced to give him the sack.'

'He'd his eyes on you,' he accused, all evening.'

'Who. . ?'

'Pfeffer!'

She seemed surprised.

'Well, if he did, I wasn't aware.'

'You must have been. Everyone else was.'

'Leonard, I assure you. . .'

'Why? Why can't they keep their damned eyes off you? Every time it's the same. I'm sick to death of it.'

'Leonard, please. I'm tired. I'm going to bed.'

'No. This time I want to know. This time I'm going to find out.'

'But, for goodness' sake, what is there to find out? What can you possibly suspect me of? All I've done is to sit at table and play hostess to your friends.'

'Ah! – but this is a rôle I have imposed on you. Had I not been there, you'd have ended up in bed with that fellow! I might prevent you, my dear, from revealing your thoughts. But I can't prevent the thoughts themselves. All I've ever done, let's face it, is suppress you.'

'Leonard, if you've any quarrel with Pfeffer then please tell him so. I don't know the man. Nor am I likely to see him again.'

She went quietly from the room. Left him staring after her.

He made no mention of it to her, but was forced into an appointment with the firm's doctor. Jamieson missed nothing.

'Well Harding, you're not of course getting any younger.'

'Meaning what?'

The medic calculated swiftly. Then:

'Just what I say. It's your heart I'm worried about. I think you should see a specialist. Who's your doctor?'

'Chambers. Harley Street.'

'Then I suggest you get along there and see what he says. He'll no doubt arrange for you to see a specialist.'

'My heart. . .? I've never had any trouble before.'

'Are you under pressure at all? — other than at work perhaps? Any personal problems, that sort of thing?'

'Not at all. No.'

'Take my advice anyway. See your own doctor and get him to fix an appointment for you.'

'Yes. I'll do that. But really, I've never felt better.'

The room was empty. She'd been here, however. Her writing things were out still; the escritoire open. But writing to whom. . . ?

There were flowers. Delphiniums, larkspur, and large hybrid aquilegias. A small green caterpillar worked its way slowly round the rim of the cut glass bowl. There were a few fallen leaves on the blotting pad. A word or two in her handwriting on an otherwise clear sheet of paper leapt suddenly up before his eyes.

'Dear Q. . . '

But nothing more.

She came quickly down the stairs.

'Is that you Leonard?'

He stared still at the sheet of paper.

'Yes. Of course.' And, as she entered, but without turning: 'To whom are you writing?'

'No one.'

'No one?'

She came slowly across.

'I've decided,' she said, 'to keep a diary.'

'And shall I be allowed to read it?'

'Certainly. If you wish. It'll be a record of my daily

doings, that's all. More a notebook than a diary. A gardener's notebook.'

'I see. But "Q". . .?'

Her patience both humbled and irritated him.

'A fictitious friend. I thought I'd do it in the form of a daily letter – the sort of thing we used to do at school.'

He looked at last carefully into her eyes. Feared he'd find some hint of duplicity, or at the least a tell-tale embarrassment, but met only a controlled exasperation. (For the same reason he questioned her always as tactfully as possible: had never, for instance, dared inquire too deeply into her past. He knew only that she was married, and widowed within a year.) He was ashamed briefly. But was almost immediately suspicious again.

'It seems a funny sort of thing to want to do. . .'

'Leonard, be sensible please. Were I inclined even, who is there here?'

He said nothing. But was stung by this reference to inclination. It was, he felt, a revelation – though certainly not a deliberate one.

He went again into the hall, collected his post. Among the half dozen or so envelopes was one from his doctor. He tore it quickly open. It gave the specialist's findings in full. There was evidence of a minor attack – two perhaps. A third was certainly not desirable. He had made a second appointment for –

He crushed the letter quickly into a ball and slipped it into his pocket.

They took their evening meal in silence. Those last words of hers – 'Were I inclined even, who is there here?' – seemed branded on his brain.

He couldn't sleep. Had not, he remembered at one point, destroyed the doctor's letter. Must do this first thing in the morning. . .

He was struck then with equal ferocity by a further thought. His near neighbour was a farmer named Quigley. A man somewhat younger than himself with black eyes and very white teeth whom he disliked intensely.

He'd a wife – a dowdy sort of woman, who appeared a lot older than she actually was. But had a reputation, too, as something of a philanderer. Old Quigley – his father, from whom he'd inherited the property – had been a good man, well liked. But his son was different altogether.

Quigley. 'Q'.

'But we do, of course, have neighbours. . .'

'Dear Q. . .'

No. It was impossible. Ridiculous. Surely –

God, this heat. He'd not sleep again tonight, that much was certain.

Because – yes, he was sure of it. She was writing to him secretly. In compliance, perhaps, with his request for a tryst; or in agreement to some suggestion.

Tomorrow, as soon as he got back, he'd pay Quigley a visit. He'd sort this thing out once and for all. Suppose he caught them together – God!, no. It didn't bear thinking about. He'd kill her rather than see her submit to another. . .

Yes. He'd go there tomorrow. Get this thing sorted out.

The farm was two to three miles from his own place.

There was a largish Jacobean brick house backed up by sprawling outbuildings. The house faced north, and appeared somewhat forbidding. This impression accentuated by the shrubbery which, though kept in check, seemed to dominate the frontal view. The soil here smelled furtively damp; God alone knew what viscous creatures crawled among the rot there, copulating smoothly with their own sex, blitzed suddenly by a bright eyed thrush or – at night – by a lumbering hedgehog.

He left his car outside. Walked up the drive. His heart was hitting his ribs like a cloth-wrapped hammer. His head throbbed with the torrent of illogical thoughts and images dammed up behind his brow, but he'd no real idea what he was going to say. He could not of course refer at once to what he believed had taken place between them, would have first to feel his way.

He went up the three or four steps and rang at the classically formal front door. He waited a minute or two before this was at last opened to him. It was the woman Quigley employed as a housekeeper.

'Sir?'

'Quigley: is he in?'

'He's here, sir. But not in the house. He'll be round the back I expect. Shall I call him?'

'No. Don't bother. I'll go round. Thank you.'

There was no one in the yard except Quigley's rough, resentful, dumb young hand. This youth had at some time deserted the Navy and was released finally on the recommendation of a service psychiatrist. He'd heard this, and other tales besides – none of which was difficult to believe as, glowering, the wretch got up off his bike and kicked down the stand. This machine – on which he rode round the estate while repairing fences or digging ditches – had the appearance of an enraged charger, the front fender standing wildly high and splashed with filth. Small but robust, he wore a flat, angry expression. In contrast to his stocky build his full, sulky lips were those of a petulant girl.

'The master – where is he?'

The youth stared. Then:

'Mr Quigley! – someone to see you.'

Seconds later, Quigley came out from the barn. Smiling, as usual, from ear to coarse red ear.

'Harding! – what can I do for you?'

Confronted with the man himself, he felt strongly the flimsiness of his argument.

'Ah, Quigley. We were wondering. . . Perhaps you'd care to come over for dinner one night – the wife too, of course.'

'Decent of you. Yes, thanks very much. We'd like that.'

'I thought perhaps my wife might have dropped you a line. . .'

Quigley, he could see, didn't quite know what to make of this.

'No. We've had nothing. Unless it went – '

'She hasn't got round to it then. Only I was passing, and I thought. . . Thursday: at seven. Will that do?'

'Suit us fine, yes. We'll look forward to that.'

Not, he knew, entirely true. But, though the trip had proved a little embarrassing, he was enormously relieved.

'Quigley,' he said, 'is coming to dinner Thursday.'

Watched for her reaction.

'Quigley? – oh, over at the farm?'

'Dipper's Pool. Friend of yours, I thought.'

'I wouldn't know. I only met him once.'

'You surprise me.'

'I don't understand. I've not been outside the house – the garden rather – more than half a dozen times.'

He felt a stab of guilt.

'You've been to the village. . .'

'Twice, I think. I wouldn't say I got to know anyone there.'

'The mountain, however, came down to Mohammed. . .'

She looked blankly at him. Took up her needlework at last and resumed sewing.

It was nearly three in the afternoon. It was very hot. The house was still. It was so quiet she could hear – not only the lazy tick of the old case clock on the wall – but the unhurried investigations of a bumble bee outside the window.

She returned to her book. But, after a minute or two, her eyes wandered again from the page. It was simply too hot to concentrate. She watched the net at the window for some sign of a breeze but it barely stirred.

She looked awhile. Listened.

Put her book to one side at last. Got up and – impelled as by some soundless flute, some sweet pipe which acted not on the ear but on the heart – went to the window.

She stood a moment on the threshold and gazed into the garden. Back-lit at this hour, there were large areas of shade cast both by the intersecting wall and by the trees beyond. There was an atmosphere of sleep, of suspension. Very little moved. There wasn't a bird to be seen. What sunlight now managed an entry here shifted slowly, but perceptibly across the green. Glittered in the darkened surface of the pool, in the water which came hurtling suicidally down from the bowl of the fountain. The air was softly scented with jasmine, honeysuckle, and – from somewhere over the wall – with a wild fragrance of rambling rose.

She walked slowly out across the grass. The postern way, with its wrought iron gate, was like a tall stained glass window. Beyond was a blaze of greenish light which filtered in through the leaves of the trees. It must, she thought, be very beautiful there. Rather like a church. There was nothing to be heard at present. Except – suddenly – a blackbird's startled cry. The air was briefly charged with tension. There was a breathless silence, followed by an agitated upward flight into the branches of a tree. If she hadn't known better, she'd have suspected an intruder. She'd this sense suddenly of having fallen asleep and of passing – not without reluctance – over the perimeter of a vaguely unpleasant dream.

She stood a moment by the fountain. A welcome coolness came up off the water. The aquilegias, pierced through with light, appeared almost painfully fragile.

Became aware, in this same instant, that she was watched.

There, at the gate. Someone looking into the garden. Nor did he attempt to hide himself from her, to escape her gaze.

Her sense of dream deepened. Shot through with sudden fear. She'd seen him, hadn't she, somewhere before. Was sure she knew him. Knew his face, rather. Yes, of course. It was that boy of Quigley's. He'd not taken his eyes off her all the while they were there. Nor, strangely, had Leonard noticed this.

She mastered her fear, crossed quickly to the gate.

'What do you want? – there's no entry this way.'

He said nothing. With only the gate between them, she saw him quite well. His corn coloured hair, which stood up raggedly all over his head, seemed to blaze against the light. But was struck particularly by his eyes. They were a deep grey-blue. The extraordinary intensity of their colour offset by the soft brown of his flyaway brows, his oddly negative expression. He reminded her of one of those punky girl pop stars – or he was Jean Genet's boy prisoner: a bruise-eyed, pale faced, bed-wetting orphan. He was probably, she now realised, older than he looked. But his gaze had an odd, diffuse quality. Like that of an innocent girl. His face was dirty, with barely a trace of beard.

She thought suddenly of Leonard. Was terrified.

'Did you want something? If not, then please leave.'

He'd something in his hand. Which he thrust now through the gate.

A rose.

She was at first astonished. She then felt desperately sorry for him. Her heart warmed. Burst suddenly open. Her entire person seemed filled with music: a great orchestral climax by Richard Strauss perhaps – shamelessly romantic. She at once regretted her anger; looked again into his wide set, uncertain, yet strangely powerful eyes.

'A rose. . .' And then: 'For me?'

He nodded. Staring all the while.

She reached slowly out and took it from him, afraid it might be a trick. She half expected that, like some callous schoolboy, he'd snatch it away, delighting in her embarrassment.

But no.

Watched only for her reaction. Holding at the same time onto the bars of the gate he was, with his blunt and blackened fingernails, like some hungry prisoner. Or some poor creature caged in a zoo. She may, perhaps, have given him a similar impression: of a creature caged, deprived of freedom.

She put the flower to her nose.

'Thank you,' she said. 'It's beautiful. . .'

But he'd gone.

They sat at breakfast.

'Is there,' she asked, 'a key to the postern gate?'

His mahogany eyes fixed firmly on her own.

'Yes. Why?'

'I'd like to go in – have a look around. Mrs Hemery says the roses were lovely there at one time. People used to – '

'Yes. But not now. It all wants seeing to. You couldn't possibly put that right on your own.'

'I shouldn't want to. I'd like to see it as it is.'

'Why the sudden interest? – it's just an odd corner. There's really nothing to see.'

'It's not,' she said, 'a sudden interest. Mrs Hemery was speaking to me and – '

He shook his head.

'The place has literally gone to seed. It'd want a whole army to sort it out.'

'But, like this even, it must have a beauty all its own. And it's full of birds. I've seen jays there – squirrels too.'

He stared.

'Haven't you enough to interest you here?'

'Why, yes. Of course. But that, really, isn't the point.'

'No? As far as I'm concerned it is the point.' He knew that he was unreasonable, impossible perhaps, but was reluctant to allow her a wider horizon – on so small a scale as this even. Besides, someone. . . 'I'm sorry my dear, no. I'm not opening it now. Sometime, when I've a moment, we'll go there together. You'll see then what I mean.' And: 'Apart from which, I don't like the place. I left something of myself there. Died there in a sense. . .'

She hesitated.

'When can we go there together? – you're so seldom here.'

He glanced at his watch, carefully folded his napkin. Outwardly calm, he began to feel that he would choke.

'We'll discuss it another time. I'll not get up to town at this rate.'

She approached the gate and looked out through the bars.

The day was overcast: all beyond was still as a picture. The rhododendrons – their blossom gone – looked in the pale light which filtered down from above like their leaves had been waxed.

It was very hot still. Thunder rumbled intermittently in the distance.

But realised, with something like a sense of shock, that the gate was open. And, looking down, saw that the catch was away from the lock. Someone had tampered with it. But who? Lord!, if Leonard had seen it first he'd have sworn it was her.

She pushed it slowly open. But, about to cross the threshold, froze.

His body bare except for an old pair of jeans and scruffy canvas boots, his eyes a deep slate blue in the even toned light, he came it seemed from nowhere.

She stepped quickly back. Tried to shut the gate on him.
But he forced it from her grasp and thrust his leg into the
aperture. Again she tried to close it, but saw that she was
hurting him.

'No, please! You don't understand. My husband – '

He'd the small but brittle voice of a peevish child.

'Ah, c'mon. I want a kiss, that's all.'

She looked helplessly at him a moment. Shook her head.

'No. You don't understand. . .'

'I love you.'

His wheedling tone with its hint of hidden violence broke
her resolution. She knew in that instant that there was no
escape. She saw her frail craft slip out into the torrent, herself
with it, and knew there was no way she could ever again
get back to where she was before. All, in the space of a few
seconds, was changed. She was swept helplessly out upon a
sea whose surface glittered invitingly but whose still depths
were set with hidden snares.

But allowed him to kiss her. . .

He licked first at her upper lip, like a cat. Pushed with his
tongue and forced an entry.

Her life, it seemed, began now. Nothing that had gone
before was of any consequence.

This was all that mattered. For her, for him, this was the
one experience. Irrespective of whether or not either had felt
this before.

'When can I come. . .?'

'I don't know. I don't know.'

Took his beautiful, his very strange face gingerly into her
hands.

'It's so difficult for me. . .'

But was appalled to hear him reason now with the terrible
clarity of a child who plots against his parents or an
unpopular relative.

'I'll fix it for ya. Keep 'im busy for a bit. . .'

'Yes. But. . .'

The first drop of rain fell shatteringly upon a nearby leaf.
Followed at once by countless others – all equally blind,
equally forceful. The leaves, the branches even, bent before

their onslaught. Each sounded to her extraordinarily loud.
A slap in nature's face.

'Look my dear, the damned car's packed up on me. I'm a
few minutes walk from the railway: there's a train due
shortly, I'm told. Fortunately I was near a garage. They
expect to have put the trouble right by this evening – or
they'll lend me a vehicle they said. So I'll get a train back
here to Stealer's Hatch, then drive myself home.'
    'Yes. All right. But do take care. . .'
There was an awkward pause. Then:
'What about you? – will you be all right?'
'Me?'
He was unable to conceal his agitation.
'I'll be a little late, no doubt. What will you do?'
'I'll do,' she said, 'what I always do. Read a book.'
'Good, yes. All being well then, I'll see you around seven.'
'Don't worry. I'll have everything ready for you.'
She put down the 'phone. Looked at it a moment.

She stood at the window. Felt that her fear would over-
whelm her.
    He appeared at last as arranged at the postern gate and she
went out to meet him.
    He put the key he had himself cut carefully into the lock.
His apparent facility for this sort of thing – for what was
after all a criminal act – disturbed her.
    Words from her childhood: 'He who'd steal a pin. . .'
    But when the gate was open and he threw himself on her
she no longer cared.

They lay together on the large old-fashioned sofa with its
broad floral motif in muted shades of hyacinth and rose. The
room was full of the scent of flowers; the movement of the
clock comfortably slow. Time, it seemed, stood still for
them. The afternoon hummed leisurely to a halt.
    'Darling . . . tell me your name.'

He hesitated.

'Mick,' he said.

She smiled. Smoothed the hair back from his forehead.

'That's nice. But I shall find a secret name for you – a name known only to ourselves.'

He didn't of course see the need for this. Briefly, she was afraid.

'Remember, we must be very careful.'

'Sure.'

She listened again to the clock. Until:

'How long have you been coming here?'

'Coupla times. You know the rest.'

'It's funny – I'd a feeling sometimes that someone was watching me.'

'Yeah?'

She kissed him quickly.

'Yes. You.' And: 'You knew about me already?'

'Yeah. Princess in a tower they call you.'

'What do you mean?'

Again he hesitated. Then:

'It's talk, innit? Down the village.'

'Is it?'

'Yeah. 'Bout you an' 'im. 'Bout what 'e's doin' to ya.'

They were right, of course. But she resented this coming back to her through someone she hardly knew.

'No: my husband is a very busy man. He has to go up to town every day. Or he'll stay, perhaps, overnight. And, naturally, it worries him when he must leave me on my own for any length of time – you'd feel the same I expect.'

'That's not what they say down the village. . .'

'No. I don't suppose it is. Not that they know anything about it.'

He smiled slyly at her.

'It's what 'e does talks loudest. Not what 'e says.' And, before she could reprimand him for this: 'You got any lovers 'cept me?'

She looked at him a moment. She ought, she felt, to be angry. To scold him for this. Instead, she spoke frankly. Could no longer deny herself the need for this.

'Not now, no.'

'But before?'

'What – before Leonard? Yes. One or two.'

Like moths to the flame. Unbidden. Were as soon destroyed. Through no fault of hers, but through their own suicidal persistence.

'But you – I know nothing about you at all. Only that you work for Quigley.'

'Yeah.'

'What did you do before that?'

'I was in the navy.'

'A sailor? – yes, I can imagine. For how long?'

'Just over eighteen months.'

'What happened? Or did you just decide you didn't want to be a sailor any more?'

He was silent a moment. Then:

''S right.'

'And then you went to work for Quigley?'

'Yeah. After a bit I went to work for 'im.'

'And you've been there ever since?'

'Yeah.'

She smiled.

'You've a wonderfully expressive vocabulary.'

'A what?'

'No, it doesn't matter. How old are you now?'

'Twenty-two.'

'Darling. . . You don't look that even. You remind me of an orphan. Were you happy as a child? – are your parents still alive?'

'Yeah. Reasonably happy. I was one of five. Me dad walked out one day: I don't remember much about it. Me mum's all right though. She lives out Eltham way.'

'You're from London. . .?'

'Yeah.'

'What made you want to work here?'

'I wanted to get away, that's all. I'd 'ave tried anyfink.'

'What about your mother?'

'She's still got two at 'ome – me sister, an' me youngest brother.'

'Do you prefer it here?'

'Dunno really. Get's a bit lonely sometimes. 'F you fancy a scrap, there's no one to scrap wiv.'

'You mean a fight. . .?'

'Nah!, not really. 'F I've 'ad a few on a Saturday night maybe. . . But not really, no.'

'What sort of things do you like doing?'

''Avin' a few on a Saturday night!' He laughed. 'Nah. Best of all I like ridin' round on me bike. She comes in 'andy on a place as big as Quigley's.'

'What sort of machine is it?'

'Two-fifty cc. What's called an off-road bike – she'll go anywhere. But she's street legal an' all: so you get, like, the best of both worlds.' He played a moment with the front of his trousers. 'I always wanted a bike, but me mum was against it. You know 'ow it is. . .'

'Everything comes, they say, to he who waits.' And, after a minute or two: 'I don't suppose you care much for music?'

'I do though.'

'What – popular music?'

'Yeah. I like the Stones. An' Bowie – Bowie's God. Oh, an' Bow Wow Wow. But they've split now.'

Again she smiled.

'That wasn't quite what I meant.' And: 'What am I going to do with you?'

'Dunno,' he answered.

A sense of panic rose suddenly inside her like a storm whipped wave.

'Darling, how will we manage? Suppose he – '

He sat up. Put his fingers over her lips.

''E'll never know nuffink about it – that's a promise.'

She could not, however, help feeling he was probably more afraid than she even. That it was she who was the stronger of the two, and that any responsibility for their affair was borne by herself alone. But what hope was there for them? – constantly under the threat of discovery, of her appalling marriage. That he'd some sense of this, she was sure. His expression proved it. But how clearly did he see into the future? Had he any real sense of consequence?

He reached for his cigarettes, lit one.

''E come over the other day – asked for Quigley. Mad, 'e

was. I dunno what it was all about: but like 'e was gonna kill 'im. I reckon 'e's – '

'No, please. Don't talk like that. He means well. In many ways he's an exceptional man. The trouble is he's a perfectionist.' And, as if contradicting herself: 'I don't know what it is. I. . .'

'What is 'e – fiftyish? Speaks for itself, don't it? 'E's scared you'll run off wiv a pretty fella like me.'

She had to laugh.

'And I was told you were inarticulate!'

He stared momentarily. His expression was that of a part psychotic child.

'What's 'at?'

'What's what?'

'What you just said.'

'Inarticulate? – unable to speak one's thoughts, to express oneself.'

He grinned, flicked the ash off his cigarette.

'It's them I don't wanna talk to says that.'

She kissed him gently on the forehead.

'Ah! So, really, there's more to you than meets the eye?'

His expression flickered somehow.

''F you want, yeah.'

He crushed out the part smoked cigarette, threw himself on her suddenly. Took her nipple between his teeth and teased it with the tip of his tongue. The skin of his features drew smoothly taut across the bones beneath: his lashes battened down as for sleep.

'No – come along. You'll have to go in a minute or two.'

'I've only bin 'ere 'alf an hour!'

'Add three full hours to that and you're nearer the truth.'

'I'm not goin' till you've fixed up about next time. We can't give 'im too many breakdowns or 'e'll start to wonder.'

His casual manner disturbed her. It was something she tolerated only reluctantly.

She took his face in both her hands.

'Look my darling – we must be very careful. For his sake, if not for mine. I shan't be able to see you anywhere near as often as I'd like. We must be very discreet. Have you got that into your pretty head?'

'Yeah, okay. 'Ow long then before – '

'You see, the difficulty is that Leonard has taken to turning up when I least expect him. He'll get it into his head that I'm up to something here on my own and dash back on the spur of the moment. So . . . leave it to me. But how shall I contact you? How shall I let you know when it's safe to come? I can't leave the place – he won't even let me go beyond the postern gate.'

'See whatcha mean, yeah.' He scratched his chest a moment. His youthful limbs were as smooth almost as a girl's, with just a trace of yellow hair on his thick little forearms. His nipples were like two tender buds. ''Ere! – what about a dead-letter drop?'

'What on earth is that?'

'You know – like in some of these spy things. It's a place for leaving messages. Might be a 'ollow in an old tree – anyfink like that. There's a brick loose on that wall down there. I'll pick out the rest of the cement then all you'll 'ave to do is shift the brick, stick your bit of paper in be'ind an' slip the brick back in again. Come wiv me now, an' I'll show ya.'

He got up. Fastened his jeans and went to the glass.

'Too good lookin' that bloke – that's 'is trouble.'

'Little peacock!' But then: 'What's that tattoo you have on your back?'

'Which? – down 'ere?'

'There, between your shoulder blades.'

'Oh.' And: 'I 'ad that done one shore leave. Good innit?'

'I don't know – I don't like it at all. It looks like some sort of demon from here.'

He came back to the sofa. Grabbed his T-shirt and pulled it quickly on, gave her his hand.

'C'mon. I got a knife 'ere in me pocket. It won't take a minute. I'll check the dead-drop every night. So, if you leave a message, gimme good time.'

She rose, put her things to rights.

'Are you sure it will be all right? It seems a little risky somehow – rather childish.'

'That's what's so good about it. 'E'd never fink of summink like that.'

He was right, of course. Leonard thought along very complex lines by comparison.

She kissed him again on the forehead. Smoothed his hair.

'Your English is appalling. I'll have to teach you to speak properly.'

'What – like 'im? No fanks. It's them types what got me down when I was in the navy.'

She patted his cheek.

'I'm sorry about that. It's rather a narrow way of looking at things. Still, you're only young yet. It could come, with time.'

'We don't get out there an' get this thing settled 'e'll come an' all, an' our goose'll be cooked.'

She smiled.

'Yes darling. I'm coming. But oh my God, wait a minute: I can't leave that cigarette end there. . .'

They sat down together at table.

'Would you like a light? Or shall we have the candles?'

He looked a moment at his plate. It was nearly nine, and just starting to get dark.

'I think the candles. No: don't get up. I've matches here in my pocket.'

He applied a lighted match to each in turn. Each came uncertainly to life. Wavered, bowed, then rose rapturously tall. Watching, she was reminded of her lover. . . (Mick Hook! How sweetly his name escaped the frantic lips of her mind! Over, and over, and over.)

He sat down again. Spread his napkin across his knees. She noticed that he looked terribly tired. It must have been a dreadful day for him. Yet, strangely, she felt no guilt. Had in fact felt more uncomfortable on many a previous occasion when all she'd done was help Mrs Hemery, read a book, or make ready for their meal. Nor did he submit her to the usual barrage of questions. He seemed preoccupied, though no less aware of her.

'It must,' she said, speaking her thoughts aloud, 'have been a dreadful day for you. . .'

'Yes. It was a bit of a mess-up. Thankfully, it's all right

now. Puzzles me though. As you know, I'd a complete overhaul on the car just a short while ago.'

'What would you like – French beans, courgettes, or both?'

'A little of each. What was the meat like after all? – you weren't, I remember, so terribly happy with it at first.'

'Well, Mrs Hemery said she thought she could do something with it. And it seems she was right. It's English, of course. Which is why it was so expensive. But I thought it looked a little coarse.'

'Mm. Shall I carve – or will you?'

'You'd better do that. I always make such a mess of it.'

'Very good. You'd like a little off the side here I expect?'

'That'll do nicely, yes.'

They couldn't, she thought, have been more polite to each other had they been total strangers.

'It wasn't, however, entirely unsuccessful – my day, I mean. We've forced that deal with Pfeffer through at last. And, I feel, on very satisfactory terms. Jamieson was over the moon, as you might imagine. He'd have given me anything I asked for, I'm sure.'

She smiled.

'You should have asked for a new car.'

'That wouldn't have been such a bad idea. The old boy was in such a good mood I couldn't have gone wrong. Another time perhaps. What about you – did you have a good day?'

He did not, however, look at her. Was absorbed in what he was doing. She took careful stock of him before risking her reply to this. Nor, apparently, did he sense her hesitation.

'Yes. In fact, something rather wonderful happened today.'

He looked quickly at her. Something, perhaps, in the tone of her voice. But was amazed to discover that, having betrayed him, she was yet able to meet his gaze with the same equanimity as when she was innocent of his accusations. (And to think that, had he not brought her here, she'd never have known the beautiful child!)

'Yes?'

'Yes. The fuchsia – you remember I was afraid it wouldn't

take, let alone survive the winter? – well, it's smothered in buds.'

'Marvellous! And this was the cutting Loretta gave you last year?'

'That's right. We visited here shortly after, and I brought it with me. But I really didn't expect it would survive that terrible cold spell.'

'Nor I. Well, that certainly is an achievement.'

'I think it depends on the variety. Some are hardier than others.' She rose. Helped him to green vegetables and new potatoes. 'How's that?'

'Yes. Thank you. That's quite sufficient. What about you?'

'Oh, there's plenty here for me. I'll have a little of each too, I think.' And, on resuming her seat: 'But the nasturtiums – this is what really amazes me. Have you seen them? It's as though, since we had the rain, they've gone absolutely berserk. I've never seen so many – and all from one small packet of seed. And so large. Really, some of the leaves are as big as dinner plates.'

'Yes, I did see them. All this must be very encouraging for you.'

Again she smiled.

'It's like a rhapsody. The whole garden is like a rhapsody. It gets more beautiful with each day that passes – it's quite a job now keeping it in order. But I love it,' she quickly added, so he shouldn't become concerned. 'And, because I love it, I don't of course find it difficult.'

He looked suddenly into her eyes.

'Do you really mean that. . .?'

'Yes. I do.'

And she did, of course. And he could see that she did. And an expression – if not of happiness, then of something very like, crept across his features. Made him look, in the space of a few seconds, ten years younger. She was suddenly desperately sorry for him. In the same way she'd felt sorry for her lover. But there was not the same attraction. . .

'I do,' she said again. 'And I'm tremendously happy doing just that, doing my garden.'

But now, again, his features clouded over. His eye, like an eclipsed sun, grew dark.

'But why all this? – it wasn't necessary. I – '

'Because,' she quietly reminded him, 'you asked me did I really mean what I said. Leonard, please: if I hadn't replied, that too would have been wrong.'

He looked at his plate.

'I did not, however, ask for a confession.'

'A confession. . .?'

'This was what it amounted to.'

'If those who confess regularly had as little to confess as I, then all priests would very shortly be out of work. Or, at the least, extremely bored.'

They finished their meal in silence. But it was a silence, she sensed, without rancour. Rather, he mused. It was as though he'd something on his mind and sought some means by which to make this known to her without putting it directly.

When they'd eaten they sat a while together on the sofa. Strangely, she couldn't relate this item of furniture to the one she'd known this afternoon. It was as though that had been another sofa altogether – and this another room. But there was no attendant sense of guilt, of having deceived him in his own house. It was as if she were without the slightest effort become two totally different people leading two totally different lives.

He asked would she like to watch TV?

She said not particularly.

They were silent again.

He glanced at a newspaper. She, while stroking the cat, at a book.

Until the cat became suddenly restless and he got up to let it out.

Then, when he returned:

'There's a sky full of stars out there. I was reminded of a picture I once saw of the Virgin.' And, having seated himself again: 'What did you think about when you were at convent school?'

To which, after putting her book to one side, she at last answered:

'About the Virgin, I suppose. We were taught – or, rather,

warned – to follow her example, to become as much like
her as possible.'

'Was this difficult for you? – I mean, did you find it a
trial?'

She frowned.

'I wouldn't say it was a trial, no. We believed. Completely.
I do still. But I remember I used to wonder sometimes which
of us as a result of all this would ever get around to finding
a husband and raising a family. Because we knew too, of
course, that – as young ladies – we were expected to marry
and to have children. And yet, at the same time, we were
expected to remain pure – like the Virgin – and to be modest,
and never to raise our eyes, least of all to look at a man. All
of which was, in a sense, very strange to me. But, as children
do, I accepted it. You know? – this was what they were
telling me, and this was what I should do.'

He pulled thoughtfully at his pipe.

'But it wasn't what you wanted. . .?'

'Oh yes, it was. I knew nothing else. I wanted nothing
else. I wasn't a rebel, like some of the girls. And these, in
retrospect, were certainly among the happiest days of my
life. "The World", as the nuns used to call it, was – for all
we knew – another planet. But the break, when it came,
was not I admit particularly painful. When I had at last to go
out into "The World" . . . it just seemed perfectly natural. I
found my niche quite without difficulty. I was, in any case,
very protected at home. There really wasn't a great deal of
difference.'

'But within a short time you were married and living, I
imagine, in an altogether different way. . . How did you
manage that?'

'Again, I didn't find this a difficult transition. He came
one day to visit my parents – we were at first very good
friends. But is seemed natural we should marry. Like me,
he was a Catholic. Like me, he was educated at boarding
school.'

'As was I, of course.'

'Yes. It was a natural progression.'

'What was he like?'

'Quiet. Boyish. Almost sweet. Very Polish.'

It didn't appear to bother him – or not, at least, in this instance – when she spoke of her husband. Perhaps because, having died, he represented no immediate threat.

'Mm. But you were sorry, I imagine, to have had no children?'

She was silent a moment. Then:

'When Marek died, I accepted that this was to be my lot. A young widow; childless. . .'

They looked at one another. Rather as though they were meeting for the first time. Then, suddenly, he knocked out his pipe.

'I'm tired. What about you?'

She didn't answer at once. Though he seldom went to bed before midnight, she wasn't exactly surprised. But:

'Yes,' she said. 'A little. Such an odd day: everything upside down.'

Was reluctant, nevertheless. It was something she could have done without.

She sat on the bed, combed her hair. It was dreadfully hot. And the nightingale was singing. The window was open, but the curtain barely stirred.

He'd come suddenly into her room. Removed his tie in front of the glass. She caught sight of his reflection: it was that of a young man grown suddenly old. His light brown hair flopped across his eyes still like that of a schoolboy; but his fine, sensitive features, in which his dark eyes seemed to burn, were drawn and anxious. It was the once handsome face of a man prey to fear and doubt. His lean yet resilient frame reflected the same tensions.

'Leonard, tell me – are you well?'

His shoulders, in their crisply laundered shirt, were at once defensive.

'Yes. Of course. Why?'

'You don't look well. I wondered if perhaps something was worrying you.'

The gaunt outline of his features, his reflection in the glass – both were equally without expression.

'On the contrary. Haven't I just told you? – really, I'd a most successful day.'

She was silent.

He turned. Looked at her. His look terrified her.

There was an emptiness, a helplessness in his expression she'd never seen before and would rather not have now. It was as though – briefly, unintentionally – he'd let slip the mask she'd so long believed to be his true face.

But the mask was so soon in place again it was as though the dreadful accident had never occurred. She was able to pretend she was mistaken; that, tired, she'd suffered a sort of trompe-l'oeil. Now, again, he was the man she knew.

He came across. Sat down next to her.

'I did, however, want to talk to you.'

'Yes?'

'Our marriage. . . We've no children. I wouldn't wish – should something happen to me – for you to be left alone again.'

'Leonard . . . please.'

'It's a fact we both have to face. I could meet with an accident – anything. Look what happened today: I was going fairly fast when, quite suddenly, the brakes went.'

She stared.

'My God, you – you might have been killed!'

He took her hand. Looked a moment into her eyes.

'I was lucky.' And, after a pause: 'Alexandra . . . have you ever really loved me?'

His question shocked her. For of course she hadn't. She respected him, admired his many good points, found him on occasion a good companion even, but that was all.

But couldn't bring herself to tell him this. Must lie to him instead.

'Yes, Leonard. Of course. I'd not have married you otherwise.'

But saw, in that same instant, what little choice she'd had. He'd literally willed her into marrying him. Shocked still by Marek's early death, she was in no shape to think for herself. And – as Leonard's personal secretary, forced into his company during almost the whole of her working day – had seen it as natural that he should at last propose to her and

that she should accept. But never until this moment had she
been so aware of how without love their marriage was. And,
meeting his gaze, was appalled to read in the depths of his
dark eyes a desperate will to believe.

In an agony of mind, she submitted to him. Partly dressed
still, she sank back against the pillow. Took him to her
breast.

He lay at last exhausted beside her. Turned his face
suddenly toward her, looked a moment into her eyes before
closing his own.

' "If 'twere now to die, 'twere most happy" – do you
remember?'

She forced a smile.

'Yes. The book you gave me for my birthday.'

He too smiled, but with closed eyes. In the low light of
the single lamp he'd the appearance of a corpse. Of the
saintly or noble sort one saw in marbled effigy; aristocratic
lords and knights, men of another time. Afraid suddenly
– of his silence, of this terrible semblance borrowed off
approaching sleep – she spoke again.

'Leonard, what was it like here when you were a child?
You used to come, you said, for the summer holidays: was
it the same?'

He didn't answer at once. When at last he did it was as
though his soul spoke through his lips. Some long silenced
inner voice, grown deathly cold. Hades, speaking from out
the blackened bowels of the earth.

'I cannot,' he said, 'forgive him. Nor ever will. I grew in
his shadow, like a sapling in the shadow of a great dark tree.
He destroyed me.'

She too felt this cold. Saw now the devouring self-hatred
which like an imprisoned thing pressed frantically against
those sealed lids. Himself imprisoned, he now imprisoned
her. Himself denied, he must deny.

My God! If she were to fall for his child – if his child were
as like to him as he to his father. . .

At breakfast he was again himself. Withdrawn, but at the
same time curiously intense. He feared perhaps that he'd

given too much away, that he'd shown only how vulnerable he was.

'What will you do today?'

'Well, this morning Mrs Hemery is going to show me a local recipe for what she claims to be the the world's most wonderful pudding.'

'Pudding. . .?'

'Yes. A meat pudding. It's not quite the weather for meat puddings perhaps; but we'll see.'

'And after?'

She frowned.

'After. . .?'

He looked up suddenly. She'd never seen dark eyes so without expression. They'd the quality, rather, of those peculiarly light blue eyes she so disliked, in which the pupil lodged like grit.

'Yes – after. This afternoon, I meant.'

She felt foolish. Like a schoolgirl reprimanded before the entire class.

'There are a few little jobs want doing in the garden – if it's not too hot. If it's too hot I shall read. Or do a little crochet work. I'm making a shawl for Mrs Hemery's daughter's baby – I think I told you. She chose and bought the thread – the pattern, too – and I said I'd make it up for her. Besides, I enjoy doing it. It means that – if it's too hot, or if it's raining – I've something to fall back on other than a book.'

'I don't, however, want this woman to become too familiar. It's best, always, to keep a certain distance between oneself and these people. She's known in the village as a harmless gossip: but, of course, gossips are only harmless so long as they've nothing of any real consequence to gossip about.'

'I promise you Leonard, our conversation is of the lightest sort. I'm hardly likely to take someone like Mrs Hemery into my confidence – had I any sort of confidences to impart even.'

'I'd like you to realise, nevertheless, I'll not tolerate her in any capacity other than that of a servant. This is all she is.

And I don't want her to think she has any special access to
you over or above my head.'

'No: well, I'm sure she realises this already. She's too
simple a soul ever to imagine she has some sort of special
access to me. She – '

Abruptly, he folded his napkin.

'Well, I'll see what I can do at the other end.' He rose,
kissed her lightly on the cheek. 'Goodbye my dear. Look
after yourself. All being well, I'll see you at the usual time.'

His 'usual time' was of course provisional. In fact, plastic.
He might be home at four, at seven, or at ten even. Or at
any time in between.

'Yes. God bless; and drive carefully.'

An empty admonition. When, in all the time she'd known
him, had he ever been less than careful?

She was in the kitchen with Mrs Hemery, washing up the
things.

Loved the friendliness of this room: and especially on an
afternoon like this – so dark and thundery she'd had to put
the light on.

It was a largish, delicately coloured room. High ceilinged,
and with an old-fashioned range and enormous, spotless,
white-wood table. It gave directly onto a small conservatory
whose air – heavy with the scent of green, of geraniums and
of rich, moist soil – she loved.

'When was it, did you say m'am, that Mr Quigley would
be over to dinner. . .?'

'Oh – it'll be a little while now. It was to have been
Thursday: but I understand he'd some trouble at the farm,
and had to put it off.'

'What a shame! Only I was going to say, if you want me
to do an hour or two extra – just let me know.'

'Yes, I will. Thank you.'

'I've not heard about no trouble up there, mind,' she said
as she replaced the lid of a pot and put it back on the shelf.
'I reckon the only real trouble poor Mr Quigley has is with
that lad of his.'

Her heart jumped. The woman's words went through her

like an electric shock. She knew at once to whom she referred: was surprised she was able to reply at all, let alone with any sort of composure.

'Oh? – who's that?'

'Young Michael Hook, m'am. You wouldn't think to look at him, but I reckon as he's the devil's own. 'Course, you know he was in the Navy? – well, he was. Took himself out of that though. Run off. And then, when they finally caught up with him, he was released from service on the recommendation of a psychiatrist. Poppycock! Little devil wants his backside warmed. Been in trouble ever since. Mind you – I'm not saying as the lad's afraid of work, and this is why Mr Quigley holds on to him. But come Saturday night and he's down the local – then that's it! But you must have caught some word of all this. . .'

'Nothing whatever, no. But I don't, of course, see anyone. I don't really know anyone here. Or not well enough to discuss anything of that sort. I don't think I've even seen this boy.'

'Not up Mr Quigley's m'am? You couldn't miss him if you did. Got the face of an angel, he has. Pretty eyes, and pretty lips – just like a girl. But he rides that blessed motorcycle of his like a fiend – he'll kill himself for sure one day. It was him, they reckon, as got old Jezzard's daughter into trouble: some to do there was about that! But she went off after to London, and the whole thing simmered down a bit. That's it, you see. His is the sort as always gets away with it. One of these days he'll catch it though. We never had no trouble here before he came. . .'

'But what has he done? – I mean, if he's broken the law, then surely he'd have been punished?'

'In these parts, ma'm, the law is about as well represented as it is on the moon. You can call 'em out – like on a Saturday night, when there's trouble down the pub – but it's like when you want a doctor these days: they either can't, or won't come. See, we've a reputation here for quiet folk as minds their own business. But he isn't, of course, a local lad: come from London, he did. And you know what some of them are like up there! 'Sides, he's a thief – and that's for sure. Mr Quigley himself knows that.'

She carefully wiped a plate and put it away.

'Has he been able to prove it?'

'I don't know as he'd want to prove it m'am. He's not the man his father was, I'll admit that, but he's been very good to that boy. I remember though – there was an unearthly row between them at the start. This was not so long after young Hook went to him. Knocked him to the ground, he did – Mr Quigley, that is. Knocked him to the ground and called him a thief and a liar. Just what was needed, I'd say. Brought him to order for a bit. And there's a lot more respect between them now, that's for sure. We've had a housebreak or two mind you – a thing unheard of before. Old Mrs Chapman – been widowed for years – was took off into a nursing home and her place hadn't stood empty only a night or two before someone got in and went away with those few articles as had any real value. The police were told soon as it was discovered. But you know what it is these days: they just don't seem able to catch them. Her cousin asked could they keep a watch on the place, but they told her frank: it just wasn't worth their while. Now what do you do about that? Makes one feel one's not safe behind one's own front door. Mind you, if it was him – if it was young Hook – then I've my doubts as to whether he'd try anything where there's people in the place. He's more likely to break in where some poor dear's just been carried out and never likely to come back. That's more his style, I'd say.'

'But, good heavens, I'd have thought something could have been done about it.'

'Well, there you are. It's like I said: there's some as gets away with murder.'

Though not perhaps intentionally, these last words were spoken in such a way that her previous unease sharpened suddenly to alarm.

'Murder. . .?'

'Now this, m'am, is only hearsay. And I hesitate to speak of something as may not have so much as a grain of truth in it. But there's some as says when young Hook was in the Navy and gone ashore in some foreign place he knifed a man to death in the street – they'd argued over what he asked for a tattoo he done on him supposedly. But how anyone could claim to know whether this is true or false is quite beyond me. There's none here as could prove something as happened hundreds of miles away when none of them was there at the time. Unless! – unless he's let something slip down the local – you don't know, and I doubt as he would either, the way he gets sometimes. What I say is – if there was any truth in it, it would have caught up with him somehow. I mean, they'd have court martialled him or something like that wouldn't they?'

'Yes: I'm sure you're right.'

'They'd not go letting him loose on a doctor's recommendation. . . Still, there is something about him – his appearance, I mean – as would lend credence to a tale of this sort. Nice looking he might be: but I've not seen him in a clean shirt yet – not on a Sunday even. And there's something about him altogether just never seems clean. . .'

She couldn't think what to say for a moment. She remembered the smell of his skin: musky, personal. But a delight. Alive. Real. Then, in what seemed to her a poor attempt to convince the woman of her lack of interest:

'Well, fancy all this going on around me and not knowing a thing about it. I might as well be in a nunnery.'

Mrs Hemery looked quickly at her. She at once regretted this last remark – innocently spoken though it was. To counteract any effect it may have had on the woman's imagination she quickly added:

'Not that it would bother me if I was. I've my garden; and this, really, is all that matters to me. Other people's affairs, I confess, fail to arouse in me quite the same enthusiasm.'

'Have I spoken wrong m'am? I didn't mean – '

'No, not at all. It's probably just that, as an outsider – a Londoner – I don't feel quite the same involvement. But it's perfectly natural I think, if one has lived all one's life in a particular place, to interest oneself in these things.' She smiled suddenly. 'It certainly sounds a lot more fascinating than some of the things one sees on television these days. . .'

'Jamieson, damn it!, wants me to represent him at the final
signing in Bonn this weekend.'

She'd seen, immediately he arrived, that something was
wrong. Now, suddenly, he came out with it. Glaring at her
the while as though it were her fault. Some sort of conspiracy
to remove him temporarily from her sight.

She said nothing at first. For fear of saying the wrong
thing.

'Well?'

'I don't know. . . What do you feel about it?'

'What I feel doesn't of course come into it. He expects me
to go, and that's that. What I want to know is what you
feel.'

'Well, in a sense, very happy for you. It's quite an honour
– isn't it? Jamieson must think highly of you to give you an
assignment like this.'

His ego of course derived a certain gratification from these
remarks. But he didn't intend to show his pleasure.
Suspicious as usual of some further motive on her part, he
only stared.

'But what about you? Aren't you going to feel terribly
alone here? – a little nervous perhaps? I'll be away a couple
of nights you know.'

'Would you prefer if I went back to London? I could
always – '

'No! – I would not. Here even, I can't be sure you won't
at once find someone to deputise for me.' Then, having
made an effort to control himself: 'No. For my part, I'd
rather you remained here. There's not of course the same
sort of social life as in town. . .'

'Leonard, for goodness' sake. I no more miss London than
you do. Why must I keep repeating this?'

'Because I'm not sure that you're telling me the truth.
You're young still. Beautiful. It seems natural that you
would miss the excitement, the stimulation of life in town.'

She got up suddenly. Came across to him and looked a
moment into his eyes. He seemed embarrassed briefly. A

little ashamed even. But cloaked this immediately behind a façade of determined implacability.

'But I don't. It wouldn't matter to me if I never saw the place again.'

He hesitated.

'And your friends? – your friends are all there still. Don't you miss them?'

'Yes, Leonard. Sometimes I miss them. But my happiness doesn't depend on this – on my friends, the theatre, concerts, dinner parties. I am equally, in fact more happy here. And that, I swear to you, is the absolute truth.'

He looked hard at her.

'But you weren't at first. I could see that you weren't.' And, in the dry-ice, purposely distanced tone of a medical practitioner: 'What made you change your mind?'

She looked calmly at him.

'If you thought I was unhappy, you were wrong. It seemed of course a little strange at first, but that was all. You must remember that I'm used to an enclosed atmosphere. To amusing myself, and to a set routine. Others might find this tedious: but it depends, I think, on one's inner life. On one's capacity to amuse oneself. On one's awareness of what are ultimately the more important things in life.'

He continued a moment to stare at her. Then, quietly, he kissed each of her eyes in turn. She felt no guilt. For she'd meant everything she said – every word of it was true. That she'd happened in coming here to have met someone who added infinitely to her pleasure was incidental. She'd no sense of having lied to him.

'Now: please do as Jamieson wants. As I want. So we can both be proud of you.'

She woke suddenly. Lay a while and watched the afternoon light on the ceiling.

She was reminded, she didn't know why, of early morning processions during the month of May. Of hymns to the Virgin clear on the morning air. Of a day's work accomplished before lessons were begun even. Of French polishing the parquet flooring with dusters on both feet.

Her days had attained, there, a sort of perfection. A perfect innocence. Like the summer flowers she pressed between the pages of her prayer book.

That there was no lasting satisfaction to be had from the pleasures of the flesh – this was what they were taught, though how the good nuns had come to this conclusion was a matter for speculation. . .

She'd left a note for him as arranged.

He'd come, as promised. (She dared not have him here at night. The risk for both would be too great.) Had tapped at the French windows.

Once inside, he embraced her wildly. (But oh God, suppose Leonard hadn't gone after all? Suppose, at the last moment, he'd decided against it? Suppose he returned now? The shock, she was sure, would kill him. . .)

But then, within the smallish precincts of her bedroom, with the curtains drawn against the light and the windows wide to the warm air with its deep, its Madagascan scents, she'd relaxed at last. Had opened herself to him as naturally as a flower to the marauding bee.

It had been her intention to speak with him first. To see if she couldn't get the truth from him. Now – too late, she knew – there crept again into her mind the tales told her by Mrs Hemery. Where they gave rise to a sudden flight of tiny, terrified birds; each a symbol of some separate alarm. . .

She sat slowly up and looked at him. Asleep still, he lay back against the pillow. One hand rested lightly, innocently in his groin. He'd the appearance of a child stupified by wine, prematurely debauched. And at the same time beautiful. More beautiful, in the early flush of his masculinity, than any child.

But there was a wickedness too. She easily envisaged him. . . Blonde young sailor gone ashore to play the fruit machines in some strip-lit arcade, to drink all night in some small, ill-lit bar packed full with thieves and slant-eyed whores, the juke box blaring. And the sudden flash of a knife in a dark back street. . . All of which clung to him still like a sort of unholy incense – she knew exactly what Mrs Hemery meant. He'd no real place in this cool, rectangular room with its whitened walls, its dark, old furni-

ture, its heavy beams, its nearly monkish simplicity, its
deeply feminine, reflective mood. The antithesis of all this,
she was yet unable to resist him. But knew, too, that Mrs
Hemery had spoken the truth. That she was right about
him. To have him deny this, however, would have destroyed
her.

It was as though he sensed her thoughts, for he was
instantly awake. His eyes were blue as Dutch delft.

But was afraid to ask what she was thinking. Afraid of
what she might say. His tension was as unbearable to her as
it must have been to him. She smiled, but dared not speak.
For fear he should lie to her, and that all trust between them
would then cease to exist.

He sat up suddenly. Kissed her full on the mouth, then
reached for his cigarettes. He put one between his lips, struck
a light. His lips were like a flower, full and voluptuous. But
she saw, with something like consternation, that his oddly
beautiful hands shook slightly. And noticed, too, that he
wore at least one ring on each. Strange, powerful symbols.
Of what, she didn't know.

He twisted suddenly round so she should see the tattoo
between his shoulder blades. The smoke from his cigarette
shuddered upward in the half light. She felt she wanted to
scream at him: effectively to dam the words which flowed
now from his lips.

'Geezer out East done 'at. 'E 'adn't took me money even
'fore 'e fell dead of a 'eart attack. Couldn't do nuffink for
'im – it was too late for that. 'Sides, me ship was due out
in 'alf an hour – 'ad to run like the devil I did.' He glanced
back over his shoulder. Grinned. ''S about all I 'member. I
was pissed, see – oops, sorry. What I meant was I'd 'ad a
drop too much. It's all a bit 'azy now.'

She dreaded his real memories. Dared not accuse him of
them. Watched him a moment – with his strange, his terrible
innocence. That there was an element of truth here, she
didn't doubt. If he hadn't been drunk it might never have
happened.

Forced herself at last to look. To touch this extraordinary
design.

'Pretty, innit?'

'No,' she said. 'No, it's dreadful.' And: 'What can it mean
. . . if not death?'

He turned again to face her. His eyes were wide, like those
of a startled child.

'Death. . .?'

'It's some sort of demon. Whose third eye – open here –
brings only destruction.' She took his face suddenly in both
her hands. 'Oh Mickey, darling, can't you get rid of it?
Can't you – '

He stared.

Took her hands down at last, forced a smile.

''Course not. 'Sides, I ain't superstitious. All that's old
wives' tales.'

'I thought all sailors were superstitious. . .?'

Anger showed briefly in the grey-blue depths of his eyes.
Like the slow, uneasy response to a coming storm in the
calm depths of the ocean. Anger – not only against herself
– but against God's justice. Against the fate he knew must
someday overtake him.

'You tryin' to scare me?'

She took his hand to her lips and spoke softly against it.

'Darling, no.'

Naked, his skin opalescent in the pale light, washed over
with the scented breeze which sent the curtains slowly out
like the reluctant sails of some great ship, he looked helplessly at her. The cigarette burning on his lip: one eye part
closed against the smoke. His fear was palpable, gave her
strength of a sort.

Gently, she removed the cigarette from his mouth. Put it
out. Drew him to her and, like he was a sick child, wrapped
her arms around him.

'You've no need, darling, to be afraid. I'll always be here
to take care of you.'

Fortunately, he saw nothing of her sudden terrible awareness of these two tragic figures – husband and lover – who
revolved together helplessly in her powerful orbit and for
whom she could do nothing. Of her desperation as, with
closed eyes, she turned her face toward the obscured heaven
and her stars.

Her lips shaped the words automatically.

'Holy Mary, mother of God. . .'

And now this other child. . .

'Help me, will you? I can't get the dam' thing to sit straight.'

At the door of her room, as she dressed for dinner. Unable to fix his black bow tie, he is forced to depend on her. Has the appearance – here, in the evening light – of a condemned man in his cell. For whom, God help her, she feels only pity.

'Stand still a moment. . .'

'You haven't answered my question.'

'Question?'

'Yes. Didn't you hear me? – I called out to you.'

'I was in the bath perhaps. I've only just come out. What was it?'

'I said – what did you do while I was away?'

'What did I do? – oh, the usual things. Except that there was no one to cook for.'

'Did anyone come?'

That he knew he'd no right to the information he sought to extract only increased his irritability.

She fixed the tie, set his collar neatly into place.

'What – here? Good heavens no. The milkman, the postman. . . But no one else. Why? – is something wrong?'

'No, no.' And then: 'You're looking forward to this I expect?'

'Not particularly, no.'

'Nor I.'

'You invited him Leonard. I didn't.'

He glared suddenly.

'That's what's so blasted awful about neighbours. You can't just ignore them. Not in a place like this.' And: 'I thought you liked Quigley?'

Mentally, she grit her teeth. Outwardly composed, she turned again to the glass.

'I've met him – what?, twice I think. I'm not really in a

position to say whether I like or dislike him, but he does strike me as just a little boorish.'

'That's the country bumpkin for you. Many women of course are fascinated by this type of man – I can't think why.'

She sat down before the glass. Reached for her cosmetics.

'No,' she said. 'Nor can I.'

Could feel his eyes on her as, carefully, she set about enhancing her own.

'Still keeping that diary?' he asked at last.

'Diary. . .?'

'The letters to "Q".'

'Oh, yes.' And: 'You know, as a child I loved writing letters. They ran into pages – each a novelette almost. I wonder now if the recipients weren't bored to death by them. They were – '

'And "Q" – is he bored?'

She said nothing for a moment. Merely looked into the glass. Then, when she was less angry:

'Leonard, if you don't want Quigley here tonight then please ring him and tell him so. It'll be no disappointment to me, I assure you.'

He stood awkwardly a moment.

'How can I put him off now? – he's probably left already.'

'Then why didn't you put him off before, if that's what you want.'

'I didn't say it was what I wanted. All I said was I wasn't looking forward to it.' And, with a conviction which startled her: 'I'm tired, my dear. So terribly tired. Rushing over there and back wasn't exactly a picnic.'

She turned suddenly.

'No, Leonard. I'm sure it wasn't. But we could easily have put this off: given you a day or two to get over it.'

He came across, placed both his hands on her shoulders. His touch was light, yet terribly intense.

'Were you glad to see me?'

She felt suddenly panicky. Had to make a tremendous effort to control herself – to remain as apparently composed as before.

'Darling, yes. Of course I was. I missed you dreadfully.'

How desperately he wanted to swallow, to ingest those tired words. Yet, in spite of everything, she meant them. It still wasn't too late. Her friendship for him remained miraculously intact. If at times he exasperated her she'd no wish to retaliate, to take advantage of his weakness. Perhaps because she'd never cared deeply enough for him to be hurt by him.

'Thank you,' he said at last.

But remained, as always, unconvinced. His tone, coldly formal, went through her like a keen blade. Inwardly, she shivered. As though subjected to a sudden icy blast.

'But whatever for. . .? There are times, Leonard, when I don't understand you at all.'

'No,' he said, falling back on a typically cryptic defence. 'I wouldn't expect you to.'

And returned abruptly to his room.

As did she, after a moment, to her preparations.

When there was a sudden shout of annoyance, a sound of drawers being ripped out and slammed back in.

'Is something the matter?'

And, when she'd no reply, got up and went to see.

'My links – they've gone!'

Her heart first missed a beat. Then accelerated wildly.

'Links . . ?'

'My cuff links. The gold ones with the monogram. I can't find them anywhere. They were here, in this top drawer. I never put them anywhere else.'

'Then they can't have gone far. You'll no doubt come across them sooner or later.'

'The sooner the better. Or I'll have to ask that woman if she knows anything about it.'

'Mrs Hemery? – now please Leonard, be careful. That would be wrong. She's as honest, I'm sure, as the day.'

'Who else comes here? – according to you, no one.'

'Look, don't worry about it now. You're sure to find them when you've time to look properly.'

'Let's hope you're right.'

She went again to her room. Sank down before the glass. Michael. . .

She'd gone down first. Had left him to dress. After which,

she remembered, he'd gone to the bathroom. He'd been alone up here ten minutes at least. Time enough in which to –

God, no. Please, no.

She passed slowly round the table and put light to each candle in turn. The meal was over: it was getting dark.

'The nasturtiums,' she said, 'were all taken suddenly by the fly. I can't understand it. Overnight, almost.'

'Soft soap,' Quigley said. 'That's all you want. Too late now perhaps. But keep it in mind for next time.'

The aroma of his cigar cut effectively across the soft night air. Carved deep grooves of hot acridity upon it. He toyed a moment with the offensive thing. Rolled its glowing tip slowly round the ash tray.

'That will stop the fly, do you think?'

'Stop 'em altogether. Spray with soft soap and they won't trouble you again.' And: 'Speaking of trouble – I've a lot with that lad of mine. He came back last night drunk and abusive: I had to give him a black eye.'

This to Leonard. Who, impatient:

'What – that tripe Hook? He wants more than a black eye. I'd take a whip to him if he were mine.'

She returned to her seat. Shocked, she was nevertheless able to maintain at least an appearance of normality.

'Who is this. . .?'

'Lad I took on not so long ago. Bit of a rough diamond, though you wouldn't think to look at him. Handsome kid, but a bit wild with it. He's only young, of course. He could improve yet. This isn't the first time I've had to warn him though: I'd trouble with him right at the start. What worries me is if he goes on like this he's going to have the police after him. I know what would happen then: he'd run for his mother's skirts – or mine. He's like an irresponsible child. Gets himself in a mess then goes all to pieces. Always got plenty of money – that's what I don't like. And it's not what I pay him. He spends more on a Saturday night than he gets from me in a week.'

Leonard looked disbelievingly at him. There was a hint of contempt in the tight line of his lips.

'Why don't you give him the sack? In times like these, you can afford to be choosy.'

'This is true, of course. But I'm reluctant all the same. My father never gave a man the sack if he could help it, and I try to be as fair myself. Also, I can't fault his work. He works like a Trojan – and willingly. You don't have to keep on at him. He might steal an hour or two here and there but he'll make it up some other way. I've no doubt I could replace him quickly – but I'd never get another to work like he does.'

Quigley's wife, who'd sat so far without commenting, spoke at last.

'For myself, I wish you'd do as Mr Harding suggests.' And, to her: 'I don't like this boy at all. I've seen him stagger out that barn of a morning and stick his head in a bucket to bring himself round. But this latest incident was certainly the worst. I'd been out to close the coop – we've a few chickens which we allow to roam naturally. It wasn't all that late: in fact, it wasn't quite dark. When, suddenly, into the yard he comes. On that terrible machine of his – and full of drink. How he made it back I can't imagine since, once he was off, he'd difficulty keeping his feet. Well, you can guess how I felt. 'Hook,' I said. 'where have you been? How dare you come back here like this?' Well, then he started. Shouting and swearing he was – really, you never heard anything like it. Of course, he couldn't speak properly – and this seemed to make him more angry. I can't repeat what he called me: it was too dreadful. I was appalled. I just didn't know what to do. Fortunately, Harry was in the barn. He'd heard the rumpus, came running out and – I'm glad to say – gave him what he deserved. But then you see he just burst into tears and cried like a baby. This, really, was what was so unpleasant about the whole thing: he doesn't look old enough for this sort of behaviour.'

She felt that she blushed. Yet, strangely, no one seemed aware of this. Not Leonard even. Or, if he was, attributed it perhaps to embarrassment at what was said. (Which in part it was. She'd no difficulty in believing what she heard:

but didn't want to believe it. Any more than she wanted to believe he'd taken the cuff links.) She was reassured only when she caught sight of herself in the glass. Still as the surface of the glass itself: her face a pale disc above the candle flame, luminous against the dark beyond.

'The lad's not right,' Quigley said. 'There's something somewhere not right, but I can't put my finger on it. For all the encouragement I've given him – and I've been, I think, pretty fair to him on the whole – he's still got to go out and make a fool of himself. It's rather as if for every step he takes forward he's got to take two back. He gets so far, then he has to self-destruct. Mind you, it was tough for him as a kid: he was one of a largish family, and the father walked out on them. Still, if he doesn't pull his socks up I'll have to do something. People here are beginning to talk and – I've told him: I told him again this morning. But it's almost as though he's asking for it – asking for me to give him the sack. Even though he's happy with me, and enjoys his work. I don't know: I can't understand him at all.'

She'd left a note for him to call at three – she must speak with him a minute.

Waited now at the gate for him.

Beyond, the afternoon light – though it penetrated in places as far as the ground – looked somehow unreal. Perhaps because she was cut off from it here, she didn't know.

Or it achieved, rather, another dimension. As in a dream. The meaning of which – though she understood it instinctively – escaped her conscious mind.

He came suddenly. From nowhere it seemed. Looked through the gate at her. His hair stood all on end like the stalks left by the harvester. With his flat expression, his no doubt deliberate omission of any sort of greeting, he too seemed unreal. A Pan figure. A sullen satyr woken from sleep.

She stared.

'Where,' she asked, 'are the cuff links?'

His eyes were the same bottomless, empty blue as the sea. He looked a moment directly into her own before:

'Cuff links. . .?'

His left eye was badly cut, the flesh over the lid bruised and swollen. Always lazy, the eye now opened with difficulty. His face was pale but calm. His expression that of a child who is wrongly accused.

Still she persisted.

'The monogrammed links Leonard had in his drawer – they've gone. There's been no one in the place except Mrs Hemery and myself – and I know I can trust her. There's a real danger that, if Leonard should question her, he will realise that she is innocent and start looking elsewhere. Or he may simply call the police.'

His gaze shifted vaguely from one thing to another. He shook his head.

'Dunno. . .'

She'd expected of course that he would lie. Wished now she hadn't asked. He'd probably convinced himself of his innocence long ago.

It was a blow, however. That, in spite of what he obviously felt for her, he could lie to her nevertheless. Exasperated by his foolish expression, by his uncooperative attitude, she took hold of the bars and shook them as she would like to have shaken him.

'Michael: are you sure?'

He blinked. Frowned.

'Sure what?'

'That you know nothing about it. He can't find them, and he's determined now to take poor Mrs Hemery to task. Can't you see what could happen – what could come of this? He'll not rest till he finds them – which he won't, because they're not there. They've definitely gone. The trail then, without doubt, will lead to you and me.' And, when he only stared: 'Look – if you took them, leave them in the letter-drop and I promise I won't say a word about it. I'll just pretend I found them on the floor or something. Do you understand?'

He picked with his finger at the cement between the bricks. He seemed both confused and annoyed. As though he couldn't make up his mind whether he'd taken them or not; as though her persistent probing was both deeply

upsetting, and deeply resented. Certainly he believed she'd
no right to inquire – which, if he was indeed guilty, she
found alarming. She'd a horror he might suddenly turn
violent, might have an explosive tantrum. The story told
her by Quigley's wife was still vivid in her mind. And
Quigley's comment – 'the lad's not right' – now came to
her more positively than at the time even.

This, she knew, was the moment in which to take a
firm stand. To be really tough with him. But felt, instead,
helpless. Wanted, rather, to shield him – from what, she
didn't know. From himself perhaps. Secure, as Quigley said,
in a good job and with good people he yet seemed bent on
rejecting every chance life offered him.

'Michael . . . what is it? What's the matter?'

He looked again into her eyes. His expression cleared
suddenly.

'Nuffink. Why?'

To have him speak normally to her was a tremendous
relief.

'No: I – I just wondered.' And: 'Your face – what have
you done to it?'

He touched the bruise lightly with his forefinger.

'Jumped a ditch on me bike an' a branch come back at
me. It's nuffink really.' He reached suddenly into his pocket,
brought out his 'key' and eased it into the lock. 'C'mon. I'm
gonna show you what it's like on the other side.'

Alarmed, she stepped quickly back.

'No Michael. I daren't.'

He lifted the latch, drew the gate toward him. It opened
with difficulty: the hinges were rusty and yielded only
reluctantly.

'Ah, c'mon.'

She took hold of it from her side and dragged it firmly
to.

'I've told you: I can't stay. I expect Leonard to turn up at
any moment – he was in that sort of mood this morning.'
Then: 'How did you get in? – over the wall?'

'Yeah. Same as always.'

'Was that easy? It looks rather high.'

'Yeah. But down there – right at the bottom – there's a stone seat acts as a step if I wanna get in or out.'

'Yes. I see.'

'Sure you don't wanna come. . .?'

'Darling – I can't.' She reached through the gate for his hand, pressed it gently. 'Off you go, please. It would be terrible if Leonard were to find you here.'

He kissed each of her fingers in turn, bit them suddenly like a playful cat.

'Let me know then. I wanna do like we done last time . . . fuck all afternoon.'

'Don't use that expression. . .'

But he'd gone already, as abruptly as he'd come.

He stood a moment and looked at what was left of the nasturtiums. The evening light had drained the garden of colour already, offset the carnage to a certain extent. But it was true what she'd said: the devastation was amazing. An entire area bereft both of its vivid blooms and decorative green. Too late now to replace them. Or he could put out a few geraniums perhaps. . .

Musing, turning these thoughts over in his mind, he became suddenly and dramatically aware that something was wrong. Something else besides. It was almost as though some unseen presence had crept up to him and whispered insidiously into his ear. His brain reeled momentarily.

He turned.

Looked slowly all around.

His eye lit almost immediately on the postern gate. He knew, without having ascertained even, that someone had been there.

A terrible tightness across his chest. His lungs laboured: it was as though the air had turned suddenly solid, unbreathable. His hands shook. He had to slip them into his pockets to inhibit them.

He went, like one caught up in a nightmare, toward the gate. Summer is passing, one part of his brain mechanically assured him. The nasturtiums have gone. There will be an early winter. We have all the signs. August already: cooler nights, shorter days are on the way. Before we know where we are. . .

And a breath of something: of terrible, burning frosts. That glacial breath which took and held entire summer's remaining flowers and – with the coming of the day, of the yellow, slanted sun – slipped reluctantly away leaving them wet and rotten upon the stem.

And Persephone gone underground to weep for them. . .

The gate! Good God, the gate was open! No sign of any key, but the latch – rusted, and awkward to manipulate – was up still. And, when he put his hand to it, the gate swung slowly wide. Barely able to draw breath, he closed it quickly. Glanced about him as though afraid someone had seen – as though he was himself the trespasser.

Now wait. Think.

Unnecessary.

It was her lover, he knew, who had passed this way. Here was his entrance, his exit. As for other lovers before him. His father. . . One hot August afternoon. This girl – a cousin of his, from the village. Lured into the garden. Where, crushed in his clumsy, his violent embrace, she at last yielded. Her clothing . . . everywhere. And he himself the shocked, the silent witness. Here, in this same place.

Here, they had tasted their first kiss. Here, she had bent to him like a full flower worried by a bee – had enslaved him as she had enslaved countless others. Her beauty a deadly nectar on which they first grew drunk, then drowned.

But wait.

He was not to act rashly.

He was determined this time to prove what he'd long suspected. He'd not pitch himself frenziedly against the steel walls of her terrible calm but would more subtly penetrate her defences.

What, then, would be her reaction when he presented her with his proof?

Oh, God. . . Oh, God, no. . .

Why must this have happened to him?

'Jamieson,' he said, 'has called a quick conference for Wed-

nesday evening. Which means it'll go on for an hour or two
at least – longer perhaps. He's ordered a working supper, so
you won't have to worry about that. Expect me when you
see me, that's all I can say. I estimate it'll be somewhere
around ten.'

'Yes,' she said. 'All right.'

He searched for some sign, some tell-tale signal. A light,
perhaps, in her eye. But saw nothing. She was too long used
to showing him a blank façade. Too long accustomed to his
persistent probing.

There were just two possibilities.

Either he was wrong. Or she was as good an actress as he
believed her to be.

'Darling "Q",

(Do you remember I told you I'd find a secret name for
you? – well this, I have decided, shall be it!)

Leonard will be away all day Wednesday – the day after
tomorrow. He has a late conference, and won't be back until
about ten. Come as early as you can however! Think of the
long, happy hours we shall have together. Darling, I love
your funny face. I think of it all the time. Fear nothing. My
two arms shall soon enfold you. So long as we are together,
nothing in the world shall touch you.

Goodbye my angel. Remember – Wednesday afternoon.
Take care meantime on that wretched motorcycle. If
anything happened to you I'd die.

All these little crosses are kisses from me. For every part
of your darling person.

P.S. Don't trouble to wash your pretty face. I like it as it
is. God bless for now.

Ever your own loving

Alexandra.'

When, later, she deposited this in the letter-drop she found
– tucked into the cavity – a folded square of kitchen paper.
Inside were Leonard's monogrammed cuff links.

Deeply relieved, deeply appreciative of this gesture, she

made – as promised – no mention of it when she saw him. Or only indirectly.

Her happiness, she told him when he avariciously embraced her, was now complete.

And left it at that.

He opened the gate. Gave her his hand. She followed him into the garden.

It was a wonderful, still August afternoon. The light had achieved already a slight slant, so that the Japanese anemones – tall on their strong stems – were lit through like those old fashioned, opaque glass lamps atop their slender stands. Virginal. Pale as porcelain. Like nothing synthetic she could call to mind, nothing manufactured. But cosmic. Miraculous. And the air, as she'd imagined, sweetly overlaid with the scent of roses.

They walked together slowly along the path. The occasional note of a startled bird was the only sound which came to her ears, magically amplified on the still air. They went, like a bridal pair, hand in hand, the anemones tall on either side. The narrow way was in places so overgrown, so deeply bedded in the mulch of countless seasonal falls, as to be barely recognisable. He, however, knew it by heart. Showed her exactly where to put her foot.

'I've always wanted,' she said, 'to come here. To smell those roses. If it could always be like this. . .'

He stopped suddenly.

'Yeah?'

She kissed his forehead. His closed eyes.

'Yes.'

He thrust his head suddenly in between her breasts. She took it gently in both her hands, laughed.

'Come along. Come and sit down.'

'I wish,' he said, 'I'd met you before. Things might have been different. . .'

'Darling, never mind. Think of me like this. Think of me as someone you've known for a very long time – your mother perhaps.'

They sat at last on the old stone seat under the roses. He put his feet up, dropped his head back into her lap. A loosened shower of flushed, creamy, scented petals came down all around like confetti – like snow.

One appeared suddenly upon his lips. Startled, she stared. It was like some invisible yet powerfully malignant presence had cruelly and resentfully gagged him.

She took it quickly away. He was smiling. Reassured, she too smiled. Somewhere, a thrush began to sing. The bench, her dress, his features – all were warmed by the afternoon sun. It was the only relatively exposed spot in the entire place. And with the sun now at its zenith, the wall at their backs even – soon to be deep in shadow – received some share of it. She couldn't think why Leonard should so dislike the place. With its trees, its shrubs, its secret intersecting ways, its incipient sense of mystery and overt fecundity, it seemed made for lovers. The ideal rendezvous.

She gently worked his T-shirt free of the front of his trousers and stroked his bare belly. Smooth browed, with suddenly unsmiling lips and closed eyes, his face was that of a drowned young sailor seen through clear tropical water, his hair adrift on the current like yellow weed. . .

She was desperately afraid for him. Like some sort of premonition.

His hair like a bundle of straw in her lap. Young Teuton. Young Teutonic sailor, one silver earring in his ear. Rose petals on his chest.

She passed her fingers lightly over the cut above his eye.

'It's getting better I think.'

And was reminded briefly of the origin of this wound. And that he had lied about it. But smiled nevertheless.

'Do you like it here?'

'Mm.'

'I think it's beautiful. I've always wanted to see it properly.' And, when he didn't answer: 'You're going to sleep!'

His eyes opened suddenly wide. As though he'd woken from an unpleasant dream.

'I'm not.'

'What were you doing then?'

'I was looking at you.'

'You weren't. You had your eyes closed.'

'But I saw you. And. . .'

'And?'

He stared.

'You – you were different. No. I dunno. I musta bin asleep.'

Uneasy, she watched his face a minute.

He laughed suddenly.

'You're so beautiful. I can't believe you could – I can't believe this is 'appenin' to me.'

She stroked his face. Smoothed his coarse hair back from his forehead.

'And I, darling, can't believe that this is happening to me.'

But – though nothing had actually changed – it was as if the scene had somehow darkened. As if the sun, though it still shone brightly, shone black. The birds even were silent. As if they too sensed something. It was like that stillness before the storm when, apprehensive, every tree stands stock still. It was as if, for the space of a few seconds, she heard the planet's heartbeat.

She looked quickly back along the path. Couldn't see the whole of it – overgrown as it was – but saw, framed by leafy boughs, its end. A live vignette. A peep as it were into a nightmare world.

And – my god! Leonard!

At the gate. Looking through. But come, oh God, from where? Or was this some dreadful dream she'd wandered into? But no, it couldn't possibly be. It...

It was as if he were having some sort of fit. His features so hideously distorted as to be barely recognisable. In a state it seemed of near collapse, his cry was that of a wounded lunatic. Terrible to hear. She couldn't believe this was actually happening. Her brain momentarily refused to accept the evidence of her senses.

'Michael, darling, wake up! Wake up!'

Got quickly to her feet. Was dimly aware of her lover's sudden consternation when it dawned on him that something was wrong.

She started down the path. Stopped. She couldn't bear it. It was too dreadful. He would, she was sure, attack her physically were she to put herself within reach at this moment.

'Ah! – yes! Oh my God, yes!'

Over and over. Part rage. Part pain. It was terrible. The cry of a tormented beast. She'd never forget it. Never.

Saw, too, his livid complexion. And the truth hit her at last. God – no! He was dying. He'd had a heart attack and was dying.

She turned.

'Michael – quickly! Help me! He's not well. He – '

The boy was on his feet already. But, with a stab of despair, of terrible cold disappointment, she realised that – frightened out of his wits – he'd no intention of helping her. His one thought was to get away while he could. He climbed quickly onto the bench and, in seconds, amid a shower of broken roses, had leapt up onto the wall and disappeared over the other side.

'Michael! Michael, come back!'

Her despairing scream died among the still shocked trees. Settled like snow, like the scattered petals of the roses.

She stared after him.

Turned again at last toward the gate.

Went slowly now along the path: stood a moment and looked. He was on the ground behind the gate, face downward in the grass.

She drew the gate slowly open, dropped down beside him and took him awkwardly into her arms. He was dead. She was too late. Poor Leonard. Poor, poor Leonard.

Gently, she smoothed the hair back from his forehead. As, just minutes ago, she had smoothed her lover's hair.

Somewhere overhead, among the incandescent green of the leaves, the thrush began again to sing.

FLIGHT OF THE OWL

Lawson looked at himself in the glass one morning and was shaken when he saw that he was no longer young.

Handsome in a somewhat severe, very English way, his once arresting gaze was now the cautious glance of one continually under pressure.

His moustache had greyed without his being really aware of it. Likewise his hair. Giving him an appearance which might, he supposed, have been described as distinguished. But which afforded him at this instant no real satisfaction. He'd have liked instead to see the muscular young athlete of his college days.

Age, however – always insidious – revealed itself to him as does the spectre in a nightmare: suddenly, shockingly. The firm muscle had given way to flab. The glowing complexion to the wan pallor of the businessman long starved of light and air.

He could perhaps have accustomed himself more easily to this unwelcome image had not his first reaction been one of desperate protest.

'But I've had no life. No moment of my own – no moment that was ever entirely mine!'

He'd his once handsome (though certainly never beautiful) wife, Myrna. His large, rather melancholy house. (Situated in what he called 'urban suburbia' – not quite in the country, though not quite out of it, and just a short drive from the railway station.) His responsible if heavily pressurized position. Promise of a financially comfortable retirement. . .

'Anthony! Tony darling!, are you there?'

'Just a moment.' Hastily drew the knot of his tie. 'I'm coming.'

Coming. Always coming.

Though never, it seemed, arriving.

Or not, at any rate, in quite the way – or at quite the place – he'd have liked.

Myrna.

She sat, as usual, against the pillows. Not so much plump as powerfully built. But she too was gone already to seed. The thick flesh turned flaccid, fallen from the bone. The blunt hands spotted with brown.

She'd a breakfast tray in her lap. As usual, she'd hardly given it a glance.

'You don't want it?'

'No. . . No, darling. I've tried. But, really, I can't.' Her eyelids came down like automatic blinds, fluttered. 'Your poor Myrna feels so terrible. . .'

A repeat performance. The longest running play in history. Same thing, over and over.

He tried a cheerful approach. It either worked: or it didn't.

'In what way exactly?'

She looked flatly at him.

'I don't know . . . I – here! It's here.'

'Here' was an ill-defined area.

'Ah, yes. But you should try to eat something.' And, brightly: 'This is your trouble, you know. Something in your stomach would help.'

She glared suddenly.

'I tell you darling: I can't. I feel so – so ill. . .'

'Mm. . .'

Her unscrupulous misuse of this one word appalled him. No doctor had yet been able to diagnose her 'illness', to give it a name. Which did not of course mean there wasn't something wrong – he'd no more faith in doctors than she. But – like a repeatedly deferred sentence – it had weighed on him now too long. A permanent threat.

Similarly, her abuse of the word 'darling'. Had she, he wondered, any real idea what it meant? Who, if anyone, had she ever loved? It was a spear, rather. Thrown with deadly precision. Or, at best, a blasphemy.

His reaction to all this was so complex as not to endure examination. He understood – perhaps better than anyone – what it was that aggravated her 'illness'. A powerful, dominant personality, she should in fact have been born a man.

Instead of which her energy was so blunted as to make it necessary for her to seek some external cause for her frustration. And so she took refuge behind a façade of sickness. Had, then, a legitimate excuse for her inability to act.

What he could not forgive was her having seduced him into marriage under false pretences. A marriage she hadn't really wanted.

Unable then to fulfil herself as a woman, she fulfilled herself as an invalid. He, however, was permitted no such frivolity. Either in this or any other direction. She inquired into all his activities. Demanded a full account of his day.

'Would you like me to send for the doctor?'

'Doctor? I've no use for that man. He's a fraud. No, no. You get away if you must. I'll be all right. I'll sleep perhaps. . .'

That he 'must', went of course without saying. Or she could never have afforded to indulge herself so shamelessly.

'Are you sure now?'

'Yes, yes. You go.'

But couldn't allow him to depart without a sense of having abandoned her.

'You have, I'm sure, more important things to worry about than me.'

He put the tray to one side. Bent quickly forward and kissed her on the cheek.

'The woman will be here shortly. Till then, rest quietly. A little sleep will do you good.'

She rolled her eyes at him.

'Your poor Myrna wishes sometimes that she could sleep for ever.'

Feeling like a cad, he left her to it. Left the house with a guilty sense of having escaped. Felt, with a sudden rush of foreboding, the fresh wind with its smattering of raindrops across his cheek.

It was early in the year. The birds were making ready to mate. The catkins on the old willow at the end of the lane hung in clusters.

At the foot of this tree a clear streamlet ran quickly past.

A few brave daffodils tossed up their trumpets alongside. There was a subtle change in the winter browns, greys, and self-effacing greens he so loved. The promised vibrancy of spring, with its riotous optimism, disturbed him. It was the season when dream and reality somehow merged. So that night, with its tumbled, its phantom events, and day with its new, peculiar light, its heightened accents, were somehow inseparable. Each, rather, seemed a continuation of the other. While winter, with its subtler tints, its gentle melancholy, eased him.

There were a few drops in the air still as he paused before turning out into the tortuously serpentine secondary road. He put the wipers on, looked quickly to left and right.

He'd gone only as far as the familiar red callbox over on the verge between two old trees and a high hedge of pollarded willows (and so incongruously placed it was like some ship put down from another planet: alien, alert) when a dark shape swooped suddenly down in front of him.

An owl. In broad daylight. After a small brown sparrow which had alighted momentarily in the road and flew now for the safety of the trees.

Too late. For she had him already in her feathered fists. But, rising abruptly with her burden, caught sight of the oncoming vehicle. Let it fall that she might gain height more rapidly.

He pulled quickly into the verge. Got out and walked across. He saw it already: lying, like a rolled leaf, on one side.

He knelt. Took it gently into his hands. The small beak gaped, spotted with blood. The open eye was glazed over with a bluish bloom like that on a grape.

It was of course dead.

He'd been sure of this before he got out even. Felt crushed momentarily. His heart ached for this wasteful death, which affected him as deeply as the heightened colours all around. The blazing emerald of the grass at the verge; the apple-green haze over the greyish bones of the hedge as each swelling bud came closer to breaking triumphantly open; the rain washed scarlet of the callbox; the chocolate flecks on the ochre breast of a startled thrush picking up pieces alongside.

He got slowly up. Carried the warm, lifeless bundle to the verge and set it gently down in the wet grass. His throat was tight. The world, it seemed, stood momentarily still. Mourned with him.

He returned to the car, settled abjectly into the driving seat. Distressed both by the tiny creature's fate and by what he felt to be its symbolic value as an omen, he fastened the belt.

The engine faltered, then came reluctantly to life. He let it die, tried a second time. It seemed all right. It'd get him as far as the station perhaps, if no further.

He'd gone a couple of miles when, suddenly, the engine stopped. He pushed the car clear and waited to see if anyone came along. If not, he'd have to walk back to the callbox.

He was lucky. A robust young farmer stopped his Land-rover and took him in tow. Drove him into Tiddenden – a largish village some fifteen miles from his home.

He passed through the place every day on his way to town. Was familiar already with its wide mainstreet, either side of which was a narrow walkway – one could hardly call it a pavement – edged with green, a few old weatherboard dwellings, and one or two handsome cottages built part of brick and part of timber.

There were, too, several low-fronted shops posted virtually from top to toe with brightly coloured bills advertising anything from ice lollies to detergent powders. There was a public house, a garage, a fish and chip shop, a hairdressers, and – further down – a rather shabby, long outdated teashop.

'Friend of mine – Freddie Hawkins – has the garage here. He'll soon put you right. Or, if it's to be a longer job, he'll probably lend you a vehicle. There's a slow train up from Mersham: you'd catch that easily.'

'Yes. Thanks. That's my station anyway.'

Hawkins was indeed able to offer him a car. A quick diagnosis on his own had showed a fault in the fuel pump, but he reckoned to have it fixed pretty quickly.

'Have it ready for you tonight sir, that's certain. I'll see there's someone here when you call.'

'Good. Thank you. Have you a 'phone here? – I'd like to get through to my office.'

'Over the way, sir.'

'Ah! – thank you.'

Across from Service Reception was a smaller room – Hawkins' private office perhaps. The door was open, and he went straight in.

The 'phone was on the opposite wall. He'd taken the receiver off and was about to dial when, with a sense of shock, he realised he wasn't – as he'd thought – alone. There was a girl in the office. Eighteen years old at most – just a child.

But it was the way she sat – on the floor next the radiator, her back against the wall – which struck him instantly as somehow outrageous. Not to say odd. And the way she looked at him: her blank, insolent, overtly hostile stare.

She had on a pair of miniature headphones, from which there issued a faint mechanical jingle. The lead from these disappeared into a side pocket of the shabby, silver-finish jacket she wore – along with a pair of skin tight jeans, similarly shabby and stained with grease.

The fluorescent light wasn't exactly flattering. She looked sick. And terrifyingly attractive.

For in spite of her toughness – or roughness was perhaps a better description – she'd a touching vulnerability. There was something missing. Something wrong. She'd a shock of bright yellow hair – never, apparently, combed – and was eating an apple.

There was no window here. The unfaced walls were washed over with white, and there was a simple desk with steel-frame chairs. Against this utility background she put him in mind of an unruly offender pulled in off the streets for questioning. The harsh light accentuated this impression.

Her eyes were a soft slate blue, black lashed.

He took the receiver to his ear. Distracted, he dialled a wrong number. Was obliged to try again.

'Bridges? – look, it's Lawson here. I'll be a few minutes late I'm afraid. What? No, no. I had a breakdown...'

But hardly registered what was said. For the girl got up suddenly, put aside the chair which stood in her way and – munching still – walked like a robot out of the room.

On the back of her jacket, in crudely daubed characters, was the legend: 'Fuck Off'. It was as effective as if she'd said it.

He replaced the receiver. Stared. Pulled himself together at last and went back to the Service Reception. There was no sign of her, however. Only Hawkins.

'Look – I must pay you for that call.'

Hawkins brushed this aside.

'Forget it sir.'

Again he stared.

'The – the young lady,' he stammered. 'I didn't disturb her I hope?'

Hawkins' round, bright face clouded.

'No, no.' And: 'She's a nice kid. Daft about cars. But she's in with a funny lot – these punks, or whatever they call themselves. You wouldn't believe this place on a Sunday when they come in on their bikes.' He shook his head. 'Well sir – if you'll just follow me I'll show you the vehicle. Mercedes estate: she's up for sale actually – had a complete face lift. Nice ride, too.'

He followed him outside.

But felt suddenly that he'd fallen asleep and was dreaming.

His day, though otherwise uneventful, seemed to him equally unreal.

In the evening, he called back as arranged. It was just getting dark. It had rained earlier, and there was a lot of heavy cloud still.

He left the Mercedes outside. The forecourt, beyond which an area of withered grass fought a losing battle with the constant passage of vehicles, was dismally wet.

He walked in. Hawkins wasn't there. The shop – a spacious shed, clean and bright – ran off at right angles to the reception. The lights were on still. But there didn't seem to be anyone about. There was a smell of oil, and rubber. Some half dozen vehicles crouched under the lights, each in its respective bay. Not quite alive, nor yet entirely without life. It seemed to him reminiscent of a hospital ward – which, in a sense he supposed, it was.

He slipped his hands gingerly into his pockets.

'Anyone at home. . .?'

And, when he got no reply, walked across to the office. Looked in at the open door.

'Ah! – good evening.'

She turned. Stared.

But lost his tongue suddenly. Couldn't think what to say next.

She wore an old black sweater, ragged at the cuffs, and the same grubby jeans she'd had on earlier. She'd an unlit cigarette between her lips.

Mesmerized, he watched as she struck a match and took a light from it. Until, at last:

'You'll remember I – '

'It's not ready.'

'Not ready? But I – '

'Mr 'Awkins was gonna finish it 'isself, but 'e was called out. 'E said to keep the Merc an' look in again tomorrow.'

He sensed some mischief here, but shrank from arguing with her. Was not, he felt, sufficiently in command of himself.

'I see.'

Her hair blazed under the fluorescent lamp – was, he realised, coloured. (Her natural brown was visible underneath.) She wore it shoulder length, but short on top. Her voice was small, light. And totally flat.

Nor was she very tall. Was stocky, rather, like a boy. Her small breasts were barely apparent, her complexion pale. There were shadows under her eyes – too many late nights no doubt.

'Yes. Well, if that's all right with him. Tomorrow is Saturday though: I shan't need a car. Only to get home tonight.'

'Yeah. Well. . .'

'I – I'll call in anyway. There'll be someone here, will there?'

'Yeah. All day.'

'Good. Thank you.'

But stood a moment. Felt he wanted to say something more. What, he didn't know.

She took the cigarette to her lips. The action was mechanical, indifferent. He lost his nerve. Turned quickly and left.

When he got outside it was raining. His heart beat like a sledgehammer.

Alone in the office, she was laughing hysterically.

He pecked his wife on the cheek.

'Hello dear. How did it go?'

'I've had a dreadful day. I. . .'

But left what she was going to say unfinished. Always rather vague, rather inconclusive, she seemed unable to hold a conversation. Or only if she wanted to argue.

She was up and about and fully dressed, however. Fairly well, he could see. But much engrossed in herself.

He sat down at the table. Spread his napkin.

'Did you take a walk?' he asked.

'Darling, I – A walk?, good heavens no. In my condition?'

'I wondered, that's all.'

Her features suddenly puckered.

'Tony, dear. I don't think you realise. I've had a terrible time. Really, I've never felt so ill. . .'

His knife and fork poised, he looked up suddenly. An extraordinary recklessness took hold of him, whirled him along like a leaf in a gale. It was like he stood momentarily outside of himself, was amazed at his own temerity.

'Not, I think, since last time.'

She stared. A deep flush, the colour of old madeira, crept up under her normally wan complexion. Her look was death.

'So that's your attitude!' And: 'You talk to your wife like that? – after all she has done for you? I should be ashamed.'

She got up. Left the room in a rage.

Miserably guilty, he stared at his plate. Never had he experienced so many, or so contradictory a batch of emotions at the same time.

★

He paused a moment before her door. Steeled himself for what was to come.

Quietly, he entered the room. Crossed to the bed where she sat against the pilows, her eyes closed, her hands clasped as in prayer. She put him in mind of a medieval tomb effigy – feature of many a childhood nightmare; the room itself of a chapel of remembrance.

He leaned across, kissed her cheek.

'Goodnight darling.'

Her eyelashes fluttered. She was like one who wakes from a coma. From death.

She looked bitterly at him.

'Is there something I can get you. . .?'

But could barely bring herself to answer him.

'I want,' she said, 'to rest.'

Her words were final, poisonous.

Painfully, he withdrew. Put out her light. Went to the window and opened the curtains a little so she shouldn't be afraid if she woke suddenly and it was dark.

Passing the bed again he could feel her hard, unforgiving eyes on him.

He went out, closed the door. Every muscle in his body ached with tension. There was no chance of any rest for him. He had offended the gods, and must lie awake with his fear.

Alone in his room, he stripped off his jacket and dropped it on the bed.

There was a quiet, a warm severity in the tones and contours of this room. Discreetly masculine, it was sparsely furnished with antique pieces. A bed, a chest and glass, two tallboys, and a small desk. The walls were finished in a warm snuff colour. The single, large window looked out onto the rather withdrawn garden with its dark shrubs and far screen of conifers.

Everywhere were photographic souvenirs of his family (his sister was a nun, and sent pictures from all over the world), his schooldays, his period of military service, his wedding. (No children unfortunately.) Along with cups, tankards and salvers won as a sportsman.

He crossed to the glass. Began loosening his tie. The warm glow from the lamp in the corner took the edge off his appearance somewhat. The decline wasn't so immediately striking as in the cold light of day.

He viewed himself as he might a stranger. With the same objectivity. Unfortunately, there wasn't much improvement on the earlier image. Though, physically, he was in fairly good shape still, accumulated tensions – both at home and at work – had taken their toll. His shoulders, however (as a youngster he'd played rugby and rowed with equal enthusiasm), did justice still to the expensive shirt. And his eyes retained a hint of their old, deep awareness.

He was getting tired, however. And looked it. And his belly was starting to show.

He whipped the tie off, rolled it carefully and put it aside. Released the button at his neck.

When his eye fell suddenly on the twenty year old, silver-framed photo of himself as a bridegroom. And she as a bride. Laughing into the lens in that self-consciously vain way she had. Together outside the lovely little Transitional country church where – as a budding young executive – he'd taken her for his wife. And she – with an avaricious flash of her eyes – him for her husband. She'd gained her prize: now he must take the consequences.

Their honeymoon was a miserable failure.

Born of terrifyingly strict parents, she'd not only a near total ignorance but a horror of the sexual act. Disappointed, though he understood the effect this must have had on her, he wooed her still with a gentle caution.

To no avail. His nudity she found ridiculous. And told him so. What fascination he'd had for her prior to their union disappeared it seemed as soon as he removed his clothes. Marriage was for her a duty only. Something she'd felt to be expected of her. And so she took refuge ultimately in real or imagined ill health as an excuse for her inadequacy. For which he felt obliged always to make allowances. In case he was wrong.

She wished to God, she'd once screamed at him, she'd been born a man.

He believed her.

Forgave her at last – though not easily. But he tried very hard, and eventually came to terms with what he now accepted as his own selfishness. He wasn't, he knew, the first man to whom this sort of thing had happened. Made up his mind to be patient with her. To try to understand.

His patience had stood the strain for twenty odd years. Now, he began to wonder.

He took the photo up. Searched desperately for some link, some slender tie with that happy smile he wore; the thirty-two year old innocent embarking on what he'd thought to be the one truly momentous event of his life – of his as yet short career.

Instead, the conviction that he'd wasted what were potentially his best years hardened. Took on a terrifying solidity.

He experienced, briefly, a burst of bitter rage. Which culminated – not in any violent physical action – but, amazingly, in the nearest thing to an erection he'd had in moons.

He replaced the photo. Stared at it a moment. But saw instead – so complete in every detail it was as though she were here – the girl at the garage. Her two full lips, habitually open. Her jeans so tight the heavy, double-stitched seams explicitly described the perfect contour of her thighs. And what lay between.

His heart knocked furiously against his ribs. He could feel the blood surge in his loins, lift him higher.

He dreamed of her all night. Woke exhausted.

Dragged out of his dream by the persistent ringing of the alarm clock, he felt like a man who has narrowly escaped drowning. Or like one who wakes from a major operation. A sense of nightmare: of having actually merged with the nightmare. A sense of complete panic.

He threw the covers aside. Sat a moment on the edge of the bed.

It took him a while to realise what day it was even. Saturday. No tearing off to town and back, thank God.

But – his car.

He'd his car to collect. She'd be there perhaps.

The idea of which made him so nervous he wished he didn't have to go. To continue as before, along the old familiar way, enduring the same miserable existence he'd endured all these years, seemed – if not exactly attractive – at least preferable.

But knew that it was already too late. That, as from yesterday, his life had dramatically and irrevocably changed.

When he got downstairs, the woman – Mrs Biss, a comfortable soul who helped with the house and did the majority of the shopping – was already there. She was making breakfast.

'Just yourself this morning, Mister Lawson. The Missus has said she doesn't want to be disturbed – not at present.'

He sat down at the table.

'Had she a bad night?'

'She didn't say. Only that she wanted to rest.'

He buttered a piece of bread. Cracked his egg.

'Be good enough to tell her when she wakes that I've gone into Tiddenden to collect the car.'

'I'll do that sir. Now you get on and eat something first. You've plenty of time.'

He drove fast. Not because he was in a hurry to get there, but to calm his nerves. His thoughts, however, scuttled back and forth like the motley crowd at a railway station.

It was a raw, rather bleak day. A strong wind pressed the trees toward the earth. The primroses, soft yellow against the creased green of their nascent leaves, shuddered at its force. Winter, angry at the coming carnival, strove to reassert itself.

He could hear the wind rush up over the bonnet and roof. Streak invisibly past the windows. A spot of rain clung tremblingly, threateningly, to the windscreen. Beyond whose ephemeral life were the gentle browns, the soft lovats highlighted with emerald, the nervous brushwork of the still bare branches against the changing, ragged greys of the sky.

None of which dispelled his fear. When at last he got into Tiddenden he was nervous as a schoolboy still. His shirt stuck to him.

But she wasn't there.

His eye went quickly round the place, but there was no sign of her. He didn't know whether it was a disappointment or a relief.

A relief he decided when – in the reception office – he settled with Hawkins and thanked him for his help.

'You're welcome sir. Any time. Sorry you were disappointed last night, but – ah!, here she is. Sherry! – run Mr Lawson's car out will you.'

She stopped. Turned, and went again into the shop.

He stood a moment like one struck. His heart beat so fast he was afraid to speak.

Hawkins grinned. Shook his head.

'It was her fault actually. I was a mechanic short, so I put her on the job instead. Too late, I saw she'd made a right mess of it. I was coming back to fix it myself but was called out.'

He put away his cheque book, followed Hawkins into the shop.

'Not to worry. . .'

'Took her on as a trainee – her father's an old friend of mine, we went to school together. Here in the village, y'know. But I'm still not sure. She plays me up a bit sometimes.'

'Yes. I see.'

His Jag slipped out through the open doors at the rear of the building. Came to a halt.

'I think you'll find everything's all right now – but you can have a test run if you like. Cor! – it's coming down a bit now sir.'

The rain swept in clouds across the concrete like torn canvas before a gale. Bounced viciously off the roof of his car. The repelled thrust of a thousand angry blades.

He hurried across.

She threw open the door. Her eyes were an incredibly sharp, slate blue.

'You wanna test run?' And, before he'd time to open his mouth even: 'Won't be a minnit Mister 'Awkins!'

Hawkins hesitated. Then – assuming perhaps that it was

his suggestion, and reluctant in that case to interfere – waved them off.

She sat back. Slammed the door.

His heart pounding, he dashed round and got awkwardly in beside her.

In a sense, he felt toward her as he might toward a child of his own. Was inclined to humour rather than to remonstrate with her. But knew of course that there was more to it than that. He was desperately attracted to her. Her odd, her fascinating looks; her body, the way she moved, spoke – all these things. The intensity of his feelings took him by surprise. Rode roughshod over him.

But he was afraid of her too. Of the situation in which he now found himself.

The engine woke smoothly. She let in the clutch, glanced both ways before pulling out into the road. The wipers slipped abruptly back and forth, cut clear arcs across the glass.

'I shouldn't have let you do this. . .'

She said nothing at first. Then:

'Why?' Smiled suddenly. It was a very odd sort of smile: not so much happy as hungry. 'I thought for a minnit you was gonna say no.'

He watched, mesmerized, as she expertly swung the wheel. Her hands were smallish – as was she herself, but strong.

'Do you have a car?' he ventured at last. 'You seem to do this rather well.'

'Me dad says to wait till I'm eighteen.'

'How old are you now?'

She put her hair quickly back from her face. Her smile had gone. Her expression now was extraordinarily grave. Like that of a child. There was, he thought, something very strange about her. But couldn't quite put his finger on it. Her every facial nuance was peculiarly intense – as though, inwardly, she lived at a very high emotional level – yet at the same time quite detached. It was like being with someone who – though apparently awake – was in fact asleep. Some part of her, it seemed, would suddenly slip off somewhere.

Only to abruptly reappear.

'Me dad's a sod though. 'E won't do nuffink I want.'

Shocked both by her disrespect and by her choice of language he hesitated a moment. Then:

'But you're not old enough to drive. . .'

She flashed him what, at best, he could only have described as a filthy look. Yet, in spite of what she said, he felt sure she did exactly as she wanted. Could probably twist her father round her little finger. Hawkins too. She'd this special quality, this childish appeal older men found hard to resist. Nor was he an exception.

'No. But I can.'

There was a hint of defiance, of petulant self-assertion. And a stubborn finality. He'd get no further with her on that.

It went, in any case, immediately out of his mind. For, whether by accident or by design (he strongly suspected the latter), her hand, as she changed suddenly down, touched briefly against his thigh.

The careless familiarity with which this was accomplished went through him like an electric shock.

'D – do you enjoy working at the garage?'

'Yeah.'

But could read nothing from her expression. Her features seemed to cloud and clear as quickly and completely as an April day. It was like someone literally wiped the smile off her face. Her eyes, then, were as empty as a summer sky. She was shy perhaps? – took refuge in this sort of behaviour.

'How long have you been there?'

'I done Sat'days when I was still at school. But I left when I was sixteen.'

'Left what? – school?'

'Yeah.'

'And now you work full time?'

'Yeah.'

He was silent a moment.

'Where are we going?' he asked at last. But knew very well that he was – quite literally – being taken for a ride.

She didn't answer at once. They'd left the village behind already and were hurtling smoothly along a main road flanked on both sides by flat, open country. The landscape

was virtually featureless, looked about to peter out. The
fields were uniformly green, or brown. The road uniformly
smooth and grey. The markers uniformly white. The rain
uniformly wet. A vast sky. Very few vehicles. One sensed
the sea here. As though – miraculously, beyond the next
bend in the road or over the brow of the next hill – it would
suddenly reveal itself. Majestic. Slightly unreal.

Then:

''Ere!' she said.

And pulled abruptly into the verge – a wide, unfaced strip
of chalky soil cut across with vehicle tracks. These so deep
in places they'd filled with water and, like miniature lakes,
held a cold reflection of the leaden sky.

The rain, however, had almost ceased.

He looked out through the window. The desolate
panorama was touched with melancholy. It was a dream
landscape. Verging on nightmare.

They were atop a slow descending rise. Ahead, and at a
slightly lower level, the road curved lazily away in opposite
directions. To the left, a huge hoarding – endowed it seemed
with something of the mystery, the peculiar significance of
a primitive monument – indicated which of these two ways
to take. To the right was a huddled group of sombre trees.

Nothing moved for as far as the eye could see. Flat fields.
The odd shack or outbuilding. A forlornly browsing beast
or two.

He felt like he'd fallen asleep on a railway train and woken
to find himself in a siding.

'Where are we now? – there's nothing much here.'

She laughed suddenly.

'Look! – the mud! It's white.'

'Yes. It's a chalk soil.'

She looked at him a moment.

And he at her.

Her smile had vanished without trace. Her gaze was at
once compelling and elusive. The only sound was of the
wind. And the measured flop-flop of the wipers across the
screen.

'Aren't you going to kiss me?'

But like she was thinking of something else. Her eyes,

too, had shifted focus. She seemed to look through rather than at him.

Her lips. . . So full. So naturally red. So moist.

'I – I'm not sure. I – '

His common sense warned against it. But he hadn't the will to resist her. Nor would he have chosen to had he been able. He wanted her more than he'd wanted any one thing in all his life.

She was not, he sensed, sexually experienced – in spite of her confidence. His conviction of which only heightened his excitement. But it was she who was obliged at last to take the initiative in loosening his tie and top button.

She slipped her hand in under his collar. Tentatively stroked the back of his neck.

'I bet you dress like this in bed, don't you?'

'No. I. . .'

Kissed her at last. Experimentally; with closed lips. When she slipped her arms suddenly up around his neck and fastened her mouth aggressively to his own.

Her warmth, the smell of her, assailed his senses like a powerful drug, paralyzed him. As in his dream, he allowed her her way with him. Fumbled at the same time with her clothes, the metal tab of her zip. Took it awkwardly down and thrust his hand inside. She wore no pants: instead, he made direct contact with her warm, silky belly with its childish navel, its defensive little forest of hair. Into which he inserted an exploratory finger, parting the wet lips with gentle fervour.

She laughed.

'Not now. I gotta get back.'

He stared.

Was unable momentarily to come down from his mountain.

It wasn't till he came at last out of his near stupor that the situation – as it now stood, and with all its implications – was fully clear to him.

He loved her deeply, was irrevocably bound to her. Nothing could alter this now.

But. . . Myrna. How was he – an essentially honest man – to go back home and lie to her, either verbally or by his actions?

As, of course, he must. Or she'd make his life unendurable.

'Darling – sweetheart – I must see you as soon as possible.'

Experienced a sudden surge of confidence. He could, he felt sure, meet and deal with this situation. Myrna passed virtually the whole of her day in bed. Really, there should be very few problems.

'I know a place we can do it. . .'

He took her hand into his own. But saw suddenly the small brown bird struck down by the predator. Felt the blood drain from his face.

Deeply disturbed, though not sure why, he thrust the apparition from him. Certainly there was nothing in her expression which could have given rise to it. Her oddly irregular features (the more fascinating because of this) seemed still as a lake. Though, as always, deep shadows went down below the surface.

'Well?'

She stared.

'There's this old cottage. It's stood empty for years.'

'Doesn't it belong to anyone. . .?'

She shook her head. Then:

'There was this old bloke looked after the trees up Spinks' place. . . When 'e died, no one bothered.'

'How long ago was this?'

'I dunno. I was just a kid. Quite a while. . .' And, like the idea appealed to her in some strange way: 'There's stingy nettles up through the front room floor.'

'I see.' He smiled. 'Sounds as good a place as any. Is it near here?'

'Yeah. Not far.'

He watched her a moment. Fascinated.

'You're Sherry, aren't you?'

'Yeah.'

'What's your other name – your surname?'

'Chaney.'

'I'm Anthony. Anthony Lawson.' Was at once aware how

ludicrously formal this must have seemed to her. 'But you must call me Tony, of course.'

She nodded.

'Yeah,' she said. 'All right.'

It was raining again. He heard it on the roof. And, against this, the odd quality of her voice: light, childish, rather flat, it charmed him. As did her uneducated speech, the way it seemed to come through her nose.

'Promise me it'll be soon – our next meeting. I can't wait for it. I want to talk with you, to hear all about you. Where do you live – at home?'

Again she nodded.

'Yeah.'

'Where's that?'

''Ere.'

'What – right here? In the middle of the main road?'

She smiled at last.

'No – Tiddenden.'

'What does your father do?'

Needed in some way to acquaint himself with her background, her people. Though, obviously, any mergence with either was out of the question.

''E keeps a shop.'

'Which one? – I know Tiddenden quite well. I pass through every day.'

'Butcher's.'

'Really? That's interesting.' He quickly scanned her features. Couldn't see enough of her. Was beginning now to appreciate how sketchy his earlier impressions had been. 'Look: I'll tell you what. I'll ring you at the garage. Will that be all right?'

'Yeah. Okay.'

'You're sure? They're not likely to be upset by that?'

She looked a moment at her hands.

'No.'

'Good. Now – into the passenger seat with you. I'll do the driving this time.'

She opened the door. Ducked forward. He reached out suddenly. Passed his open palm over her hard little backside.

She turned quickly.

''Ere!'

Grinned.

His heart beat like that of a trapped bird.

He dropped her off at Hawkins'. Told her he'd ring as soon as he was able. But, meantime, to 'keep it under her hat'.

She'd never heard the expression, he could tell. But was naturally shrewd.

'I won't,' she promised, 'say nuffink.'

He was shocked when he got back to find his wife up and about. And in a better humour than he'd have thought possible.

'What happened, darling, about the car?'

'The car? – oh, it's all right now. That chappie did an excellent job on it. It was the pump. Cost a bit, but that was to be expected.'

Was afraid, suddenly, she'd want to inspect the thing. That she'd some intuitive sense of what had happened. That her hidden eye had penetrated him through and found evidence of his deception. And that she hoped, by inspecting as it were the scene of his crime, to corroborate this evidence.

Incredibly, no.

Smiled instead. But there was an edge to her voice still.

'Darling! – we have worked so hard, Mrs Biss and I. I felt dreadful; but she managed to interest me in this really marvellous recipe. I couldn't resist giving her a hand. You can imagine – can't you? I was, as you know, half dead when you left. Really, I felt I was going to die. But . . . we got our heads together. And, between us, I think we did rather well considering. Your poor Myrna deserves a medal darling. I hope you like it. It's an old Hungarian recipe – no, not goulash. Something special.'

Her every other word was spoken, as always in italics. Her eyes were doing very bright things. But they looked inward rather than at what they saw. Watched only for the effect she was having – the impression she made.

His relief, however, was too great for him to react other than enthusiastically.

'I'm sure it'll be excellent.'

She reached out suddenly and stroked the back of his neck. Something she hadn't done for years. Bringing back to him the most violently delicious, most guilty memories of so short a time ago. But her nervously torn nails afflicted him. As far as she was concerned, it was already too late.

'You have a perfect wife, haven't you? What other husband could expect to come home and find that the poor invalid had interested herself in such things? Not many, I tell you.'

Her self-deception was remarkable.

'Yes,' he agreed. 'Perfect.'

Would have agreed to anything. Was only afraid she'd see through him suddenly. Would see his remarks for the flimsy garments they were. Depended, as always, on her hunger for flattery. The unashamed eagerness with which she lapped it up.

Her euphoria, however, was cut across suddenly by a flash of something dark. Like black lightning in a blue sky.

'Are you sorry now for what you said to me last night? I could hardly believe. . .'

He put his arm about her. Drew her to him. Felt that he embraced a nightmare.

'I'm sorry darling. Too much going on at work recently.'

Was only amazed his more recent exploits had escaped detection.

He was somewhere dark.

A country lane at night.

Had left the car. Had, he thought, seen something lying in the beam of his lights.

But – somewhere over his head it seemed – he now sensed a presence. Darker than the night even. Darker than the crowded trees which craned across the road, aching to lift their roots.

A presence to which he could put no name.

Then suddenly, in a smothering rush, something came down from out the sky. Silent. But with a crushing accuracy.

A great bird. About to envelop him in the protective

spread of her wings. But her concern was not that of the mother for her threatened young. Rather, it was that of the predator who fears the escape of her prey.

He woke in the dark of deepest night. Choking on a soundless scream.

The place was crowded, poorly lit, and too warm.

There was a smell of hot fat, of semi-synthetic foods, of cigarette smoke and condensation.

The formica table tops were not entirely clean – or, if they appeared to be, there was an odour to them. Legacy of the soiled rag with which they were wiped. In the centre of each was a bottle of ketchup (under whose cap was a slowly hardening ring of incredible red), another of Worcestershire sauce, salt and pepper, and a dirty ashtray.

In the background was a continuous clatter of washing up. Over which – and the steamy sigh of the tea machine – there rolled a boisterous tide of conversation.

She sat, with four or five friends, at a table near the centre. Like herself, each of these was a ruralised version of the fashionable city punk. The electric light yellowed their pale complexions, did marvellous things for the hollow-eyed, ghoulish look they cultivated. All wore heavy make-up – boys as well as girls. All were smoking cigarettes and eating or drinking at the same time. Their hair was cut and coloured like wheatstraw – all except one; a tall, thin boy who'd coloured his black. His rather sculptural features were powdered white as a vampire's. His eyelids scintillated – as did those of his girl friend – with a violet glitter shadow and black liner. All wore earrings: most wore at least two in each ear. The boy with black hair wore a nose stud too. For which reason perhaps he ranked high among them. Dark priest of the dirty tea cups. Of the heavy-duty dinner plates. Of the smoking ashtray with its sense-scalding reek of stale nicotine.

Across the street was the sea-front promenade with its misty lamps, its continuous flow of traffic. And the shingle beach – barely visible now in the fading light – with its broken necklace of fishing boats, its steep descent to the water's edge. And, somewhere beyond, felt rather than seen, the powerful presence of the sea.

It was a Monday night, just after six. (In another hour the place would have virtually emptied. The haze of cigarette smoke, which washed now like a sea mist over the homogeneous roar of conversation, would have drifted all away. The tea machine, exhausted, would drip dejectedly.) It rained still, as it had for days.

She pushed her part eaten meal of sausages and chips to one side. And – both elbows on the table – lit a cigarette.

'I done meself a favour over the weekend.'

'Yeah?'

'Yeah. There was this bloke come in Friday – middle-aged type, but not bad lookin'. 'E was on 'is way to London when the thing just stopped. Freddie said 'e'd 'ave it ready that night, an' it was me 'ad to do it cos Steve was off sick. But I'd seen this bloke look sorta funny at me, an' I thought – right!, I'm gonna botch this one.' She flicked the ash from her cigarette. 'So I did. An' when 'e come back it's not ready, see? But 'e's shittin' 'isself when 'e sees it's me, an' 'e staggers out like I'd 'it 'im over the 'ead or summink. I couldn't stop laughin'.'

'You cow!'

'Yeah, well, 'e come Sat'day, an' Freddie said to take 'is car out – an' I did. An' it was one big laugh cos I drove 'im out Ditchester way, an' I said did 'e wanna kiss me, see. So 'e did. An' now 'e wants to see me again.'

There was one great burst of laughter, like a brick through plate glass. But the boys were embarrassed; the girls jealous.

'Did 'e ask 'ow old you was?'

'No.' She began again to laugh. 'But it was that turned 'im on, see. 'E's one of them types.'

More laughter.

'You play your cards right, 'e'll give you summink to shut you up.'

'Keep you in goofies for life!'

'You wouldn't think to look at 'im, but 'e was really passionate. . .'

Another furiously amused shriek from the girls was drowned at last by the clatter of dishes at the counter.

'Daft, innit? I knew I could pull 'im easy mind – 'e'd that sorta look about 'im.'

'Is 'e married?'

'Yeah. I 'eard 'im say. 'E'd a wallet full an' all – I saw it.'

'You'll 'ave to twist 'is arm then.'

'No I won't. I've got 'im like that.'

Put her thumb down hard on the table.

'I'm beginnin' to feel sorry for this bloke!'

'An' me.'

'You wanna be sure first 'e's not as thick as 'e looks. . .'

'I gotta go, luv. I'm meetin' Daryl down 'is dad's place.'

A sudden scraping of chairs. The walls, the floating faces, somehow unreal.

Found herself alone at last with Rick Scrivener. Who, all in black, hung now across the table. Stared.

A sudden tension.

She felt like the whole of her body was screaming. Dreaded having to ask.

'Did ya get it?'

He unzipped a side pocket. Reached in and extracted a folded envelope. Slipped it across to her.

She looked.

''Ow many?'

'Six.'

'Six?'

'That's all I could get. I'll 'ave some more tomorrow.' And: 'A quid to you.'

She passed him the money.

'Fuckin' thief!'

'You want 'em. You pay.'

She opened the envelope. Shook the capsules out into the palm of her hand, where they seemed to glow briefly – to glare, rather – before she tipped them quickly in again.

'All right?'

'Yeah. Thanks. . .'

She was working under a Metro in grubby overalls several sizes too big for her. The Metro was on a hoist. A mechanic, Steve Shipton, was showing her which tools to use.

Then, suddenly, it was like everything started to swing.
The lights. . . Everything crazy. And she zonked out.

Shipton had her in his arms. Carried her through into the
office.

Where, huddled in a chair:

'No. I'm all right. Honest. I'll be all right in a minnit.'

They gave her a glass of water.

She sipped. It was like the glass smacked her in the teeth.
There was blood on her lip, but she couldn't feel anything.

She folded. Hit the floor.

'Now, come on luv, what was it all about?'

She looked blankly at him across the desk.

'Nuffink. Honest.'

'You bin like this a coupla times before. You oughta pop
along and see your doctor.'

'No. It's all right. See, when I was a kid I 'ad this fall.
An' I get like a bit giddy now an' then.'

Hawkins watched her a minute. Under the hard
fluorescent light she looked like she'd seen a ghost, and her
eyes were bleary.

She sniffed, looked past him.

'Do your parents know about it?'

She stared.

'Yeah. 'Course. I come off me bike. It was dad picked me
up.'

He rolled a ball point pen between his fingers. She looked
at it like it mesmerized her. If it wasn't for the fact he
couldn't smell anything, he'd have sworn she'd had a few.
She seemed groggy, confused.

'How d'you feel now?'

'Yeah.'

Automatic like. Then, when it suddenly got through to
her:

'All right.'

She stared. Sniffed.

'Yeah,' she said again. 'All right.'

'D'you wanna go home?'

'No. I'm okay now.'

'You sure? You look a bit dozy.'

She nodded.

'Yeah. I'll be all right.'

'Well, sit here for a bit if you want.' And: 'Were you late home last night?'

She jumped at this.

'That's prob'ly what it was. I didn't get to bed till nearly two.'

He looked shrewdly at her.

'Not takin' nothin' are you luv?'

Her eyes slipped past him again.

'Whatcha mean. . .?'

'Oh, all right.' He tucked the pen into a top pocket, got up. 'I wouldn't wanna find myself in a position where I'd feel obliged to talk to your dad, that's all.'

He wasn't able to telephone her as soon as he'd have liked.

An opportunity arose, however, toward the end of the week.

His sister-in-law, who lived in London, sent a letter to say she'd be alone over the weekend – Gerald had to go up north on business. Sorry it was such short notice, but could Myrna not come to stay with her for a couple of days? She did so hate to be on her own, but didn't want to leave the house. One never knew these days.

He put it to her as tactfully as he could.

'It'd be a change for you darling. Do you good. But, of course, it's entirely up to you.'

'I should think so. It would be another story altogether if I wanted her to come down here.' And: 'I don't know. I. . .' Looked a moment into the distance. 'Such a long journey. I don't know if I could stand it.' Her sister being of course absent, she glared at him instead. 'Why she can't come here, I don't know.'

'My dear, she told you: she doesn't want to leave the house.'

'No. But I must leave mine. She's so selfish. Always was. How she could expect me, in my condition, to go all that way – '

'Darling, she can't force you to. Explain to her. . . I'd be here, of course. At night anyway. And Mrs Biss will be here for the greater part of the day.'

'All the same, I should worry.'

'Look: either you go or you don't. It's as simple as that. But, whichever way you decide, you'll have to ring her. A letter would be too late.'

'But I can't travel by train – alone. It would be unthinkable. I'd have to have someone with me.'

'Myrna, my dear, if you wanted I could drive you up in the car. It's a journey I'd have to take anyway. We could leave a little earlier, and I could drop you off at your sister's before I went to the office. No effort at all.'

'You know very well how nervous I am in the car. . .'

'Then don't go.'

She looked very hard at him. Her eyes, slightly narrowed, had a steely quality. Both in the sharpness and the hardness of their expression.

'I shall have to think about it.'

'All right. Then, when you've made up your mind, let me know and I'll do whatever you want.'

She couldn't, of course, leave the subject alone. Brought it up again over dinner.

'I'll go,' she said. 'If that's what you want. It will give you a rest.'

'Darling, it's not what I want – it's what you want. Either way it makes no difference to me. I'd like to see you have a change, but if you'd rather remain at home I'd understand perfectly.'

'No – no. I'll go. I haven't seen her for a long time.' And, typically: 'Besides, one never knows. It could be the last time. . .'

'Perhaps,' he suggested, as carefully as he was able, 'she doesn't feel too good herself. Her health, as you know, isn't what it was.'

'Now, Tony, please! You know Elizabeth! She has the strength of a cart horse. She'll last a good deal longer than me, that's certain.'

'Mm.'

And left it at that.

She went on the Friday.

Returning later that day, he pulled in suddenly when he caught sight of the callbox.

He picked up the receiver, dialled the garage. Looked quickly out through the glass.

The high hedges, the closely grouped trees loomed over the narrow road. It was darker than usual. What was left of the daylight diminished even as he looked. As though, high overhead, a huge hand put it out. A spot or two of rain appeared on the glass: the tarmacadam seemed to shine already in anticipation.

'Hawkins'. . .'

His heart pumped like he'd just run a Marathon.

A youngish man. Not, thank heaven, Hawkins himself.

'Ah! – Miss Chaney: I'd like to speak to her a moment. Is she there?'

He spoke abruptly. Imperatively even. His nervousness infuriated him.

'Er – just one moment please.'

And, shortly after:

'Yeah?'

'Sherry?'

'Yeah.'

'Tony here. . .'

The sound of her voice excited him violently. His heart beat so fast he could hardly speak. Nor, at first, could he think what to say to her.

'I – I'd like to see you. Tomorrow. C-can you manage that? Or would you – '

'Yeah, okay.'

He'd a mental picture of her at the other end, holding on to the telephone. Her wild, untidy hair. Her habitually sleepy, inward-looking expression. Her small, barely perceptible breasts. (With their pinkish, their still secret centres.) Her tight jeans which left virtually nothing to the imagination. Her partly open lips – wet, like a child's. Fleshy, ripe.

'I – I'd rather not pick you up there. Could we – could you perhaps – '

'It's all right: I'm off tomorrow.'

'Is there some place you could wait?'

'D'you know the bus stop. . .?'

'What? Er, which one?'

'Across from the garage, an' a bit further along. There's a shelter. You can't miss it.'

'Ah, yes. I know. Good. After lunch then – is that all right?'

'Okay.'

'At about two.'

'Yeah.'

He hesitated. He'd have liked to tell her he couldn't wait to see her again. But didn't trust himself.

'Goodbye then.'

'Cheers.'

He replaced the receiver. Found that he was smiling. Glanced quickly round, afraid someone may have seen. But there wasn't, of course, a soul in sight. Only the car.

And a flurry of raindrops.

He remembered suddenly that here, somewhere, were the remains of the small bird he'd laid to rest among the primroses.

An age ago, it seemed.

But the primroses were still there.

The following day was beautiful. Incredibly sharp and clean – everything. Like someone had tipped a bucket of water over it.

The broad mainstreet, as he swung abruptly in, had however an air of unreality. Like a too sharp photograph. The tarmacadam was a smooth, hard, parade-ground grey picked smartly out with white. Old bricks showed fiery red under the warm eye of the sun. The lichens which grew there, or on the rooftop tiles, an amazing emerald green. It had, all of it, the look of a holiday postcard. Here and there, freshly painted weather-boarding completed the illusion. Gave, too, a sense of the sea.

The trees were smothered with pencil-sharp points of green, vibrant against a classic blue and white sky. The sort of sky more normally seen in May: big fat clouds against a clear, forget-me-not blue.

She was, as promised, at the bus stop.

He pulled quickly across and into the kerb. She dodged round the back of the car, opened the door and dropped in beside him.

He smiled. Affable. Avuncular.

But was instantly, violently desirous of her. Felt the blood fill out his loins.

'Right. Where are we going?'

Her face wore its familiar flat expression. He couldn't tell whether she was pleased to see him or not.

'Keep drivin', an' I'll tell you.'

He could not, regrettably, risk taking her home. Much as he'd have liked to. There'd have been an immediate scandal. But she was, he felt sure, shrewd enough to handle this on her own. If only because, for obvious reasons, she wouldn't want her parents to hear of it. She could no more afford to be found out than he.

He'd driven perhaps four or five miles, with her offering the odd direction in a flat monotone, before she indicated at last a narrow lane that dropped gently down among the trees into a rather magic, wooded dell.

Over on the right was a handful of cottages with small, tidy front gardens. Then a copse. And then a tumbledown boarded dwelling which stood alone not far from the brook at the bottom.

Here, on the left, were only trees.

He cut the engine. The silence was immediate. Disturbing.

The sun, like a pole-vaulter, had topped its zenith. Penetrated at an angle deep into the wooded well. Picked out and set alight the green of tender leaves not yet unfurled but – like the wings of a butterfly which, freed from the chrysalis, sits a moment trembling – crumpled still, limp.

The woods appeared empty. But no sooner was the engine silenced when there came to his ear several sorts of bird song which echoed about the dell like children's voices in the nave of an empty cathedral. Here was a whole hidden army of creatures who watched but were unseen.

He smiled.

'Well?'

She looked past him to where the cottage – splashed across

with sunlight, front door agape so that the light passed
through from back to front along the narrow passage way
– collapsed insidiously into the ground.

'There.'

He, too, looked.

'Is it safe?'

'Yeah. 'Course.'

'Sure there's no one there?'

'Yeah. It's been empty ages.'

He opened the door, got out.

'Why haven't they sold it?'

'What – Spinks? You gotta be joking. 'E'd rather see it
fall down. All this 'ere's 'is land.'

She shut the door her side. Came round, and stood a
moment beside him. She was not so tall as he: he wanted to
slip his arm around her, draw her to him, but was afraid
someone would see.

'What about those other places?'

'What – further up? It's 'is employees live there. 'E won't
'ave no strangers.'

'Can't say I blame him.' And: 'Come along then – we'll
have a look.'

It was, actually, in fairly good condition still. There was
a smell of damp, of rotting wood. But the sun streamed in
at the back and lent the place an atmosphere of warmth, of
cheer even.

He stood a moment in the passage, looked around.
Beyond, an overgrown garden showed through the open
door as a riot of lucent green. Here, a steep stair with leaning
balustrade ascended in what appeared by comparison semi-
darkness.

He spoke softly. As though afraid someone would hear.
Couldn't shake off a sense of his own intrusion.

'Do you know the place? – I mean, have you been here
before?'

'Coupla times, yeah. Me an' a friend come 'ere once when
we was still at school.' She giggled suddenly. 'We went
upstairs. We'd a coupla bottles of wine, an' we got really
pissed.'

He looked quickly at her. Didn't know what to say. He

was shocked. Wondered what her father would have felt had she told him.

'How old were you then?' he asked at last.

'Dunno. I musta bin about fourteen. We drank the lot an' threw the bottles down into the garden – I remember that. An' I remember I puked all over the place. Come on up, an' I'll show you.'

He glanced up the narrow stair. Except for the banister, it looked safe enough. In the close, musty atmosphere he could smell her skin, her warmth. Her eyes, in the greenish light, were frankly sexual. And yet, at the same time, totally without guile. A quality he'd often enough seen in animals, but seldom in people. Certainly never in a woman.

But, of course, she wasn't a woman. She was just a child. And would, he suspected, remain one for the whole of her life. She'd a quality of eternal adolescence, of a sexually equivocal Peter Pan. It was a quality which had nothing to do with age. And which aroused in him a feeling so strongly paternal as to make him ashamed of his desire.

'All right.'

She went ahead of him. At the top was a short passage. There was no light other than that which came through the open bedroom door. The smell of damp seemed concentrated here, and the boards were wet still from the previous rainfall. There was a hole in the roof perhaps? He couldn't see much without a torch.

He followed her into the bedroom – now completely empty.

It was a smallish, square room with one fair sized window which looked out on the back garden. The tangled weeds, the long neglected roses had a dingier, less romantic look from here. The light, of course, wasn't the same. Rather, it wasn't seen at the same angle. A small greenhouse simmered in the sun: empty save for an upturned pot or two. Some of the glass was broken, lay alongside in grimy shards among the nettles.

The room itself was in astonishingly good basic order. The wallpaper had peeled in a couple of places but retained its warm, tea-rose shade and was comparatively clean still. Over on the right was the empty grate. The chimney breast

– flanked by two shallow recesses – stood out from the wall, and there was a decorative, old-fashioned mantel.

In the nearer recess was an old iron bedstead. It was the only remaining piece of furniture. There was no carpet even: only the stained surrounds, and the bare centre boards. In the grate were a couple of abandoned lager cans and the odd cigarette butt. Suggesting the presence at some time of tramps or layabouts. The room was fairly light, there being of course no curtains. But, after the bright, warm scene outside, seemed somehow gloomy.

He turned. Looked at her.

Was afraid suddenly. Though he wasn't sure why.

She laughed. But it may have been a nervous reaction.

'Better get your things off . . .'

She went to the window and opened it. It came up easily: a warm breeze slipped in over the sill.

He removed his jacket. Put it carefully down on the bed. There was a mattress only: torn open in places like punctured flesh and stained by the rusting springs.

She sensed his embarrassment perhaps. Came across. Loosened his tie. Her expression was grave, like that of a child priest who prepares for holy, though not necessarily sacred, rites.

She opened his shirt, approaching each button in the same way.

He took her suddenly into his arms. Lifted her and put her gently down on the mattress. She laughed again. He climbed awkwardly onto the bed with her, his shirt flapping. His body pressed lightly upon her own.

'You don't,' he said, his eyes teasing her, warm with desire, 'care about me at all.'

What he meant by this, he had at that moment no idea. Whether it was something he actually felt, or whether it was intended only as some sort of self-stimulus, he didn't know.

Her smile vanished.

She reached up; touched him lightly. Touched his chest. His face. Her eyes were a vivid slate blue, dark centred.

She slipped her arms around his neck. He could feel her warmth through his clothes. The blood rang in his ears.

'I do though . . .'

He looked a moment into her eyes. Bent his head at last, pressed his lips into her throat. Felt her spine arch. Heard her breath accelerate. She was like a young animal, devoid of all inhibition. They kissed quickly, haphazardly. With a sort of desperation. Like it was all too big for them. Like they didn't know what to take first.

She sat suddenly up against him. Her features damp, distorted. No longer herself, but like one woken out of a deep sleep. Her spirit abroad somewhere still, her flesh abandoned.

Her fingers found his fly. Took it quickly down.

He kissed each of her warm eyelids.

'Darling . . .'

She dropped back on the bed. Drew him down between her open thighs.

When he woke he felt cold. A chill seemed to have entered the room.

He opened his eyes. Looked across at the window. The sun had gone. Heavy clouds obscured the blue.

Half asleep still, she lay in his arms. He semi-reclined in the corner next the wall, with his rolled up jacket as a support for his back. Allowed her to dominate him completely, quite happy to subject himself to her.

Until:

'Come on little owl – you'll sleep your brains away.'

She sat up at last. Began at once, in that peculiarly private way women have, to put her things to rights.

He, too, raised himself. Slipped his hand in under her arm and cupped her small breast.

She turned. Her face was pale, with a spot of red high on each cheek.

He lightly kissed the back of her neck.

'Sweetest thing . . .'

She reached for her T-shirt, began turning it back the right way again.

'What time is it?'

He looked at his watch.

'It's just after six. What are you going to do?'

She pulled the T-shirt on over her head.

'I gotta get back.'

'So soon?'

'Yeah.'

He thought quickly.

Took up his jacket at last, shook it out and reached into the pocket.

She stared. Waited.

He brought out his wallet, flicked it open and extracted a ten pound note.

'Please don't be offended. It's not because you've given me pleasure, but because I want you to buy yourself something – I'm sure you don't get much at that place.'

She took the note. Folded it carefully and put it away. Looked at him suddenly. There was, he felt, something to be read from her expression. But whatever it was, it eluded him completely.

'Thanks,' she said. And: 'D'you wanna come again?'

'What – here? Yes, of course. Can you manage that?'

'What about tomorrow? – I can come in the evening.'

'Yes. That would be marvellous. Can I pick you up . . .?'

'I can't give you an exact time. You'd better wait 'ere.'

'Yes, all right. I'll do that. I'll come at about six.'

'Okay.'

She slept on his shoulder all the way back to Tiddenden. In a sense – though deliriously happy – he was also a little disappointed. There were so many things he'd have liked to talk about. So many discoveries yet to be made.

He pulled in opposite the bus stop. The scene here had totally changed. All the colour had gone. A lowered sky – under which, ahead, the light entered at an angle and was seen again in the already wet surface of the street – oppressed the place, so that everything appeared almost in silhouette.

'This do . . .?'

'Yeah. Fine.'

As she made to get out, he put his hand over hers a moment.

'I love you. It'll seem like an age before we're together again.'

She smiled. But said nothing.

'Take care, won't you? I'll wait there till you come.'

'Yeah. Cheers.'

She tumbled out, threw the door to and walked quickly away. Suddenly uneasy, he watched her go. She walked like an automaton. As though she'd no will of her own but answered some signal she was programmed to obey.

He waited till she was out of sight then turned the car round and drove slowly away.

He put the lamp down on the floor. Afraid that – should they have to light it – it'd be seen on the mantel.

Was reminded suddenly of when he was a child. Of when he'd camped out one night with a friend in the ruins of an old abbey. It was to have been a ghost watch. They'd stuck it for perhaps an hour, then went home.

He'd brought the car rug up too. Shook it out and threw it down, double folded, on the bed.

The weather was bad still. Overcast, and with a fine rain. Everything seemed less friendly than before. Rather spooky. The four corners of the room were sunk already in shadow, concealed themselves from him. Empty. Or perhaps not. Outside, the greenhouse crouched among the nettles. Glowered at him with gaping, saw-edged eyes.

He stood a moment, looking down.

But heard her suddenly. Driving what must have been a borrowed car. He'd this crazy idea she might be with someone – her father perhaps, or a gang of violent youths.

Waited till she'd climbed the stair, then went to the door and took her straight into his arms.

She was alone, of course.

Encouraged by her example, he kissed her wildly. Collapsed with her on the bed where, ravenously, they tore at each other's clothes. Fell on each other like wolves.

Never in all his life had he dared act in so unrestrained a manner, dared be so happy.

He lay between her open legs. Sensed but couldn't see her pubic hair, the pinkish skin beneath, the deeply folded flesh from which – tantalisingly, warm and crumpled like the centre arrangement of some extraordinary flower – the inner lips emerged.

Was again desirous. But checked himself, spoke instead.

'Darling. . . Are you awake?'

'Mm . . .?'

Raised himself at last. Kissed the soft area of skin between her groin and belly.

'What's matter . . .?'

'Nothing. I just wanted to talk to you.'

He took her into his arms. Sank back and drew the rug up over them. She was silent a moment. Her head on his shoulder, her arm across his chest. Then:

'I was dreaming.'

He smiled.

'I still am.' And: 'What was it about – your dream?'

'Dunno. What's time?'

He felt for his watch, couldn't see a thing. Found it at last and brought it up close to his face.

'Good heavens – it's past ten.'

'It's so dark . . .'

'It was nearly dark when we came. What about your parents – won't they worry?'

'No. I said I'd be late.'

'Do you go out every night?'

'Nearly ev'ry night, yeah.'

'What do you do?'

'What? – when I go out? Dunno. Just muck around. There's not much doin' in Tiddenden. We – me an' my mates – we might go down the pub. Or there's the fish an' chip shop. Or we just pile into someone's car an' go down the coast or summink. We done that last night. I was really pissed, see, an' I fancied a swim. But when we got there it was a bit rough, an' Daryl 'Obbs – 'e's one of my mates – 'e 'ad to come in after me. It was a laugh really . . .'

'A laugh?'

'Yeah. I musta bin paralytic.'

The soft, yet raw quality of her voice delighted him. But he was disturbed by these casual revelations – by the echoes they set off in his mind. He'd a sense of darkness from her broken narative, of something impending.

'Do your parents know about these escapades?'

'Yeah. Sort of.'

'What do you mean, sort of?'

'Well, I tell 'em a bit . . .'

'But not all? – hm. I'd worry myself stiff over you if you were mine.'

She smiled.

'I am yours.'

He thrilled to this. Yet, at the same time, his heart seemed suddenly to sink. Not so much because her remark implied a shift of responsibility – from her to him – but because he sensed a certain hopelessness in any sort of concern on his part. Or anyone else's if it came to that. Her parents must have given her up long ago.

'Your father's a butcher you say . . .?'

'Yeah. Next but one to the post office.'

'What about your mother?'

'Oh, she's all right. We don't get on too bad really.'

'Does she go to work?'

'Up till she 'ad my li'le brother. But not since.'

'How old is he?'

''E's seven now.'

'Are there any others in your family?'

'Yeah. I've got an older brother. 'E's nineteen. 'E works with dad.'

'Wouldn't he like to work at the garage?'

''E done Sat'days with Mr 'Awkins when 'e was at school – sort of odd jobs like. That's 'ow I come to work there. But me dad wanted 'im to learn the trade, see, so 'e could take over the business when 'e retires.'

'Do you get on well with him?'

'Me brother? – yeah. But 'e's got 'is friends an' I've got mine. We don't go out together or nuffink – not very often.'

'Why's that?'

'Well, we don't like the same things. That's all it is really.'

'What sort of things does he like?'

''E plays cricket, an' football. An' 'e likes photography.'

'Has he got a girlfriend?'

'Oh, yeah. But that's about as far as it goes. 'E looks after 'is money, see. 'E don't believe in throwin' it away.'

'And what about you?'

'What . . .?'

'What sort of things do you like?'

'I dunno really.' He sensed a deliberate evasiveness. 'Only thing I really like is cars. But that's a bit vague . . .'

'I don't think so. Did you always want to work with cars?'

'Yeah. But I wasn't much good at maths, see. So, when I left school, Mr 'Awkins took me on as a trainee. Which means I get, like, one day at college; an' the rest of the week I'm at the garage.'

'Mm . . .'

Both were silent a while. Then, suddenly:

'D'you mind if I ask you summink?'

'No. Of course not.'

''Ow old are you?'

'About as old as your father I expect. Fifty-three.'

She thought a moment.

'Yeah. Me dad's forty-five. You don't look that old though . . .'

He laughed suddenly.

'What's matter?'

'No – nothing. But age is really only a relative thing, you know. My boss – in fact he owns the company – makes me feel like a schoolboy sometimes. He's into his seventies now, but you wouldn't think so. And my father can give him ten years on top of that.'

This didn't reach her at all. And, of course, it hurt. For, as she saw it, at fifty-three he'd one foot in the grave already.

'Is your father still alive . . .?'

'Very much so, yes.'

'Christ!' And: 'You're married I s'pose?'

'Yes.'

''Ow old is your wife?'

'She's fifty-one.'

'Is she beautiful?'

'Striking, rather.'

Again she was silent. Until, at last:

'Do you love her?'

He didn't know how to answer this. A sense of loyalty – or of superstition perhaps, which made him as careful of

what he said in her absence as in her presence – prevented
him from issuing an outright 'no'. Nor would this have been
entirely true. For he had loved her at one time – or thought
he had. Felt, still, a degree of compassion for her. There
were moments of warmth even. But, my God, this child –
with her chillingly shrewd little mind – was right. Till now,
he'd never known what love was. But was reluctant to speak
of this – of the relationship in all its complexity – to a girl
thirty-six years his junior. These were things best kept to
himself. Nor could she be expected at her age to concern
herself with them.

He compromised.

'We are, in many ways, very close still.'

'Where is she now? – I mean, d'you live far from 'ere?'

'Actually, she's away. She went to stay with her sister for
one or two days. She returns tomorrow.'

'Yeah? Does that mean you won't wanna see me?'

He turned his head. Brushed his lips against her hair.

'Darling, no. I'll see you again as soon as I can.'

'We could go to the sea . . .'

'Anything you like. All I want is for you to be happy.'

She sat up suddenly. He couldn't see her; or only very
dimly. But had an odd sense of her being able to see him
quite clearly. On a psychic level perhaps rather than a
physical one.

'Do you love me?'

Again his judgement warned him. As it had when he'd
been about to kiss her.

Again he ignored it. But was deeply aware of the foolishness of an outright admission of his love for her.

He felt, in the dark, for her face. Lightly touched her
cheek.

'Yes. I do.'

Then, after a pause:

'And you? – do you love me?'

She arched herself suddenly like a startled cat. Crawled
across him and got off the bed.

'Where's that lamp? It's bleedin' dark in 'ere.'

There was an edge to her tone, a hardness backed up by
her choice of language, which made him at once uneasy. As

did her deliberate avoidance of his question. He'd rather she'd lied to him than said nothing at all.

He sat up. Reached quickly over the side of the bed.

'Hold on a minute. I had it here somewhere. Ah!'

He picked it up. Put it on. She stood a moment, her back to him, trapped in its beam.

He'd an odd feeling he'd been talking all this time to someone else – gone now, with the darkness. And that this was a stranger, an intruder. Someone he didn't know at all.

The light crudely illuminated her still androgynous body with its subtle hints at approaching womanhood. He saw the cloven path of her spine; her firm, boyish backside. Which, as she glanced suddenly over her shoulder, she seemed somehow to flash at him.

There were areas of her body which he'd recognised all along as having a particular significance for her. And which she used either to tantalise or to shame him. While with other areas – her breasts for instance, her most feminine attribute – she was apparently less generous, or effective. In fact, she gave little.

There was an arrogance in the posture which shocked him. He remembered the slogan she wore on the back of her jacket: got the same message – on a rather more personal level – now. There was a strongly sexual tone to it – to the implied message – which made it more crudely powerful. And a hint, too, of challenge. He sensed both an insult and an invitation. Was both disturbed and excited.

She'd a pale down along her lower spine like the fluff on a boy's cheek. And a small tattoo above the divide between her buttocks which he wasn't at this distance able to decipher but which caught and held his eye.

She reached for her T-shirt, pulled it on. Her tone was openly contemptuous.

'You lookin' at my arse?'

He felt like a schoolboy caught reading a pornographic publication. Was momentarily confused.

'I – I was just . . .'

But was sufficiently excited still to find – as he thought – a convincing excuse for her behaviour. This was, after all, an entirely new experience for her – one she'd yet to learn how to handle.

While convinced, however, of her sexual inexperience, he was only too well aware that it was she who controlled the situation – that it was he, rather, who was green. Her handling – both of the situation and of himself – was frighteningly professional.

Which awareness did not, of course, prevent him from falling into her trap.

He got quickly off the bed. Came up behind her and placed both his hands on her buttocks.

She turned like a snake. Put her own closed fists defensively between them, thrust him away from her. Her expression, in the stark light, ran the gamut of several sorts of emotion. None of which was at this stage entirely clear to him.

"Ang on a minnit!"

Unsure of her, of what she meant, he smiled.

'What is it . . .?'

Her lashes dropped suddenly. She spoke in a small, flat voice.

'Fifty quid – an' you can 'ave it.'

He felt a chill go through him. Laughed out loud. If only because he couldn't think what else to do.

'You little minx! – you're not actually blackmailing me?'

She glared.

'Blackmail?! I thought you loved me?'

He looked a moment into her eyes. The fixed intensity of their expression alarmed him.

He went again to the bed. Took up his jacket, removed his wallet and plucked out two twenties and a ten. He was as nervous, as unsure of himself as a man half his age.

'There!'

She took the notes, folded them carefully. Picked up her jeans and slipped them into the back pocket.

'Do for now I s'pose.'

'I – I don't really know what you're trying to say.'

She put an unlit cigarette between her lips. Her expression was masked. Unassailable.

'Okay. I want a little pocket money. But on a reg'lar basis, see?'

He was again deeply shocked.

'You can have whatever you want, you know that.'

She stared a moment.

Then, suddenly, she flashed him one of her bright, her oddly abstract smiles. It was like she smiled for some hidden camera inside her head. A sort of secret connivance with another, perhaps cleverer self.

She lit the cigarette. Tossed the match into the grate and threw her arms around his neck.

'Fifty. Every week.' And: 'Is that all right?'

It was this momentary loss of confidence which provided him with the perfect excuse for his own weakness, while allowing him again to deceive himself.

'Extortionist!'

She laughed. Swung suddenly round and thrust her buttocks at him.

'You can 'ave it now!'

He blushed madly.

Took refuge behind a whole heap of hopelessly fragile excuses – which he regretted before they'd broken even on the slavered shore of his lips.

Knew, of course, that he was the loser.

Knew, too, that something was wrong. That something had forced her into this.

Certainly she hadn't liked asking him for money. Of that he was sure. Any more than she actually enjoyed making love with him. (Alone together, without their clothes, he'd the impression that his nudity – her own too perhaps – embarrassed rather than excited her.) She was too deeply independent to have embarked on an affair had she not wanted something out of it.

And it was this that worried him.

For what, he wondered, could she possibly want with fifty pounds a week on top of whatever it was she earned at the garage? (He'd offered to put the money into a bank or

savings account for her. But she'd refused.) What sort of
drain on her finances would warrant such an amount?

Clothes?

She didn't seem to care much about her appearance. All
he'd seen her in so far was an old pair of jeans and a sweater.

Make-up?

She put plenty round her eyes. And it probably cost her
more than she'd care to say to keep her hair looking like
she'd been dragged through a bush backwards.

But could surely have managed all this on her weekly
salary?

He thought first, with fast-maturing jealousy, of a boy
friend. Someone nearer her own age. Young, good looking
– out of work perhaps, and sponging on her for extras. But
forgot this idea almost as soon as it occurred to him. It just
didn't fit in with what he knew of her already. He couldn't
imagine her taking up with him in order to satisfy a lover's
pecuniary demands. One person only counted sufficiently
with her in this respect: herself.

Further analysis of the situation proved at present useless.
He was like one lost in a maze: nor, at this stage, was he
particularly keen on finding a way out of it. He was happy
merely to remain her slave.

Their affair blazed on through April into May. He saw her
as often as he could without arousing suspicion. Dared, even,
congratulate himself at last on the success of his deceit. The
technical aplomb with which he conducted this, his first and
only indiscretion.

Each meeting with her was like a reunion. But was
marred, too, by the circumstances under which it took place.
Inevitably, it was a hurried affair. Inevitably, too, they met
at the empty cottage. For the simple reason there was no
place else they could go. A far from ideal backdrop to their
love-making, it depressed him deeply.

He'd have liked instead to show her off. To take her out
of an evening – to London, for instance. To show her things
she'd never seen. But this was of course impossible. And so,
rather than lose her through his own foolishness, he was

perforce confined to the squalid little upstairs room haunted
by heaven knew what ghosts.

She looked at him suddenly.

The blue of her eyes was part swallowed in the poor light
by the eclipsed suns of their expanded diaphragms.

'The old man died 'ere.'

He watched her a moment. Then:

'What – in this room?'

'Yeah. On that old bed. They didn't find 'im till days
la'er.'

He didn't know whether to believe her or not. She was
aiming for an effect perhaps? – or was indulging some secret
fear. But there was something in the way she said it which
made it seem like a threat. Though in what sense, he wasn't
sure.

Her face shone suddenly all across with a bright, metallic
smile.

'I 'member when we come 'ere – me an' my friend. She
kept on 'ow creepy it was, an' s'pose we was to see a ghost
. . .' She laughed. 'But I was so pissed I didn't really care.
It was great.'

Another time, his eye was caught suddenly by the appallingly assaulted flesh of her arm. Livid lumps; like some
creature had sunk its filthy fangs into her and drawn her
blood.

Terrified, he seized hold of her wrist.

'Here – what's all this?'

She snatched her arm away.

'Insect bit me . . .'

He stared.

'Darling, for goodness' sake see a doctor. If that turns
septic, you'll know it.'

Again she laughed.

'For Chrissake! – you sound like my mother.'

★

Foremost among those shades which haunted his imagination was that of herself, a drunken child, giggling and turning sick within these same four walls which now looked blankly down on their stolen hours together.

Had a brief and, for him, terrifying insight one afternoon into what it must have been like.

They'd made love, and were asleep together on the bed. The day was spectacularly warm and sunny: a prelude to summer.

He'd lain a while awake, wonderfully happy. Was forced at last to wake her too, but could get no response from her. He shook her violently, afraid – though God knows why, unless it was the Lord's vengeance – that she had died. Her flesh was warm, her limbs supple. But she was otherwise like one dead.

He shook her again. And she woke. But was unable to pull herself together.

'Angel – please. We can't stay much longer. I must go.'

He sat her up, but had to support her to keep her from falling back on the mattress. It was like she was a puppet, and some malicious influence just snipped the strings.

'Come along darling. I have to get back, remember?'

'I wanna wee . . .'

He felt suddenly desperate.

'You can't go here.' But then: 'All right – I shan't look.'

She tumbled off the bed like one deeply intoxicated. Her face was white as chalk. He'd have believed her drunk, but smelt nothing.

He dressed himself slowly. While, unavoidably, he heard her helplessly urinate somewhere behind him.

Had been obliged at last to put her things on for her.

She lay against him like an exhausted child.

He'd no idea to this day what it was all about. She'd been – or had seemed – perfectly all right at first. Had fallen, he remembered, suddenly and heavily asleep – but tended to do this after making love. Had difficulty, too, with her speech; and it took her a minute at least to process what he said to her. At first terribly afraid, he then thought it must be some sort of mystery illness – a 'bug' perhaps.

Had rung her later, as promised.

She was evasive. Said she was fine.

For some reason, he hadn't liked to insist. Nor had he referred to it since.

Sometimes, she'd bring along her cassette player and head-phones. And, after they'd made love, would lie incommuni-cado for the rest of their time together. He'd attempted once, when he wanted to say something particularly important to her, to remove them. She was angry. Told him to 'Shut up. It's Bowie'.

Or, if she did speak, might veer off suddenly into a wild, staring, incoherence. Would talk nonsense of an incredible kind. Delighted, it seemed, in confusing – or even fright-ening – him. It was like someone threw a switch inside her brain. Altering her mood dramatically and destructively. He'd no idea whether she really believed these wild romanc-ings – she'd begin, for instance, with 'Guess what? I walked into J.C. this morning. I don't know if I was sorry for 'Im or not: but I did ask what the Christ 'E was doin' in a place like Tiddenden' – or whether they were calculated either to shock or disturb him. Which, of course, they did. He was careful, however, not to rise to her bait. But, as with an over-imaginative child, to ignore it rather.

Or she'd turn vicious and taunt him. Drive him half mad with what she knew were impossible requests.

Why did he never come down the 'caf'? Or wouldn't he be seen dead in a place like that? Why was he always so afraid? Did he think her father would get to hear of it and expose him for what he was – a bum fuckin' cradle snatcher? Have him put in the stocks on the village green? Or he was ashamed of her perhaps? She wasn't ladylike enough for him – was that it? No? Then why didn't he send his ogre of a wife packing and take her to his place where she could at least keep dry while they fucked and not have the rain come in and wet her backside when she was on top? What had he ever got from that old cow? – nothing, she bet. Not that he was much of a lover: if she hadn't had a go at him first he'd never have got started with her either. Oh, and she could use a little extra this week: another ten quid would see her over. What? That was her business. If he couldn't do what she wanted without keep asking questions then they must split. Call the whole thing off. It didn't matter that much to her anyway.

Other times she'd cling to him – literally. With a desperation that alarmed him.

'I'm so scared . . .'

'Darling – of what?'

'I. . . I dunno. Everything.'

But could be happy too. Frighteningly so. Could also be reasonable and intelligent. They talked one day about books; and he was surprised to learn she'd read quite a lot at one time. So why, he asked, had she suddenly stopped reading? She was at once evasive. Her gaze passing through him – a peculiarity with which he was already familiar – and fixing, not so much on something else, as on nothing. But a 'nothing' which seemed to him terrifyingly tangible.

Or she'd slip naturally into her one enduring image – that of a child. His child perhaps. When he'd take her face into his hands and try to imagine what such a child would have looked like. But it was powerful, common blood which produced features like hers: the sort of looks which, though far from perfect, literally stunned one.

He'd kiss her gently on her full, her unconsciously flamboyant lips. Would allow her to lie quietly in his arms where she'd while the time away, her eyes looking it seemed past some – to him – invisible open door. Though into what sort of Wonderland he hardly dared imagine. This, though, was not a rôle she assumed: it was an expression rather of that fear which he sensed to lie at the bottom of all her many moods. At such times, he felt more like a father to her than a lover.

But she'd play on this too. Would act like a little girl in the sort of way only a grown woman could. The sexuality with which these performances were charged drove him mad with desire for her. It was she, then, who was master. And she knew it. Twisted him round her little finger.

As to her threat to 'call the whole thing off', he knew (as did she) that the money was too important to her for that. But – as she was again aware – he was obliged to take her seriously for fear he'd push her too far, force her to act according to her word.

They went once into the woods down in the dell. Where, among the flowering may and sweet cow's parsley, she threw herself suddenly up against the trunk of a tree and ordered him to 'fuck me up the backside'. And, when at first he made no move, verbally lashed him, scorned him for 'a wimp'.

He did as she asked. Shook with excitement. But the wood turned dark for him suddenly: and he'd a cruel awareness that it was he – not she – who was abused. Felt both guilty and ashamed.

She puzzled him a great deal. He'd lie awake at night, alone in his room, and try to discover what it was about her that so disturbed him. For she seemed to him sometimes like a machine from which some vital piece was missing. So that, while she remained capable of operating on an apparently normal level, her performance was so erratic, so oddly incomplete, as to cause alarm.

He probed delicately with regard to her background. She was apparently happy at home, though she didn't actually say so. Her parents couldn't possibly have suppressed her since she came and went as she pleased. Nor, on the other hand, did they seem the sort who didn't care what their children were up to so long as they were out of the way.

He went one night into her father's shop on the pretext of picking up something for Myrna on his way back home.

Her father and brother were both there. He saw her likeness in each. Her brother was as good looking as she in a more clean cut sort of way. His expression was more settled, more open. Both were like their father, though he was a more obviously rugged, 'country' type. She, especially, resembled him. He saw the same handsome irregularities in the father's features as in the daughter's. But, like the boy, his expression was more open. Unshadowed by complexities. His manner was affable yet respectful. He saw him instantly for what he was: a good, hard-working man with sound, old-fashioned principles. But susceptible perhaps – as, of course, he was himself – to her will.

He left the shop – with its sun-warmed, weatherboard façade – feeling like a scoundrel.

What, he asked when he saw her next, were her ambitions? Or hadn't she any?

Her reply blew through him like a winter wind.

'Yeah – I wanna die before I'm twenty. An' I wanna be in a glass coffin, so everyone can go: "Ahh . . . Innit a shame?".'

He dreamed about her almost every night. But they weren't all pleasant dreams – quite the contrary. Mostly he woke from them upset and anxious.

He dreamed for instance that – bowler-hatted, and city-suited – he was with her in an empty children's playground. And there was a merry-go-round. And she – wearing only a ragged T-shirt – sat astride one of the prancing wooden horses with its flaring red nostrils and rolling eyes. And every time she came round her own eyes flashed angrily at him and she reached out and slapped his face. And he stood, unflinching, and waited till she came round again.

Another time he dreamed he was with her in a picture gallery – the National Gallery perhaps. And again he was dressed for business; and she – as in life – in an old jacket and jeans. She wore, too, a long scarf round her neck; the ends of which were thrown back over her shoulders. And they were looking, in the cold afternoon light which came in from somewhere overhead, at a monumental picture of a female nude. And she turned suddenly, her eyes glittering strangely, and spat at him.

What disturbed him particularly about these dreams was their quality of offensiveness. In them, she displayed something never far from the surface in life. A quality of obscenity – though not necessarily in the sense that she was herself obscene. In the sense, rather, that something obscene was happening to her – as with one possessed.

When, in the dream, she spat at him or slapped his face he experienced the same emotional trauma he'd experienced when she urinated in his presence. What, he still wondered, had made this so necessary that she no longer felt bound by the social taboos attached to the act but, like one depraved, must execute it instantly?

It was, however, the sort of question he couldn't ask – had an opportunity arisen even. His sense of what was circumspect forbade it. He knew her intimately. Knew her body like he knew his own. (Knew, too, the small tattoo at the base of her spine, with its peculiar humour. Two words only: 'Fuel Injected'.) But retained too deep a respect for her individuality ever to probe into so personal a matter.

He doubted in fact if she remembered it.

Which in itself opened the way to darker passages of investigation from whose uncertain threshold he instinctively withdrew.

'Now darling, please. . . Your poor Myrna hasn't the energy for a complete tour of the place. I can't do it.'

What she termed 'a complete tour' was in fact a walk to the bottom of the garden.

'All I want is to show you these. Look: they're up again. And I didn't think they'd survive those heavy frosts.'

Had dragged herself after him up the path. Scintillating, flashing, in that irritating way she had. Unconscious of him, of what he said to her. Thinking only of the thousand eyes she imagined to be charting her dramatic progress.

'There: d'you see?'

'Aha . . .'

But glanced only briefly at the brave red spears thrusting up through the soaked soil. Her eyes – narrowed as against a threatened attack – flashed quickly round the garden.

'Aha . . .' she said again.

Though what she meant by this – whether it was intended to express her pleasure at what was pointed out to her, or whether it was directed against some espied enemy – he couldn't tell. But was gripped by a quick irritation, which closed inside him like a fist. So that within the space of a few seconds the patience which had endured for years – and under far heavier pressures – snapped at last. The accumulated frustrations broke like water from a dam. He'd never spoken so sharply to her in all the time they'd been together.

'Well – do you see them or don't you?'

Shocked, as by a physical assault, she stared. Her eyes, narrowed still, appalled him. So huge a wound was opened in her ego, she could not for a moment believe this was actually happening to her. But, like one struck down in violence on the field of battle, achieved a brief and terrible lucidity before falling – literally – apart.

'How dare you! How dare you speak to me like that? Me – a sick woman!'

Miserable, swept by a sense of shame, he looked helplessly at her. Felt like a child in short socks and knickers. The prospect of a scene with her terrified him. Culminating, as it undoubtedly would, in violence and nervous collapse. And, worse, in an enforced sense of his own guilt.

'All I wanted was to show you the flowers . . .'

'The flowers! The flowers! You drag me all the way up here to insult me!'

Head high, her whole person vibrating it seemed with a scorching sense of the injury done her, she turned abruptly away. But – unaware, as she often was, of everything round her; burning only with her wound – her foot turned suddenly under her and off the edge of the path into the soft soil alongside.

Heart in mouth, he darted forward. Caught hold of her arm.

'Darling! – be careful!'

Shocked at the prospect of a fall from which – though it hadn't actually happened – she was already convinced she could never have recovered, the colour drained from her face. Her eyelids fluttered, and she rocked on her feet. There was no physical injury: her imagination, however, toyed daringly with what might have become of her.

'My God. . . I could have been killed!'

'Come along – I'll help you inside.'

He got her back to the house and into a comfortable chair. Brought her a glass of water and two tablets. She fluttered and rocked for a minute or two. Till, suddenly, her eyes flew burningly open.

She looked accusingly at him. The power behind her stare belied the collapsed sack of her body, her limply dangling arms.

'Tony – what's wrong with you these days? You've changed so.'

Without ever realising it was she who – all those long years ago – had changed him. Or estranged him rather. Forcing him further and further away from her.

'I could have died – you know that, don't you?'

This voice with which he now spoke had nothing to do with his own, his inside voice. Was that of a stranger, rather. Someone unknown to him.

'Come darling: I'd never have let that happen.'

'But it was your fault! If you hadn't snapped at me like that – '

'Look: all I wanted was to show you the flowers. I thought you'd be pleased . . .'

But something had gone. Somewhere inside, the bond had broken. He floated free, like a ship which has slipped its moorings. Observed this little scene – which took place, it seemed, on some far shore – with an incredible, cool detachment.

'Ah!, yes. The flowers.'

The mysterious symbolism of which was lost on him. These too, he supposed, were in secret conspiracy against her.

(Suppose they were? Did he care?)

Her eyes filled suddenly with tears. Horrified, he could only stand and stare. Like some misbegotten, clumsy monster in a demoniac fairy tale. Slave to an appalling mistress. Unmoved witness to her plight.

She extended a limp, blunt paw.

'Tony . . .'

Sickened, but maintaining a neutral mask, he took it in his own.

'Tony, darling. . . You are my friend still, aren't you?'

His heart lurched. He grinned like a ghoul.

'What do you mean . . .?'

'You're different. Changed somehow. I – I don't know . . .'

Which, of course, was true. More true than – hopefully – she realised.

'Nonsense. I can't think what you mean.'

The whites of her eyes shone painfully, like those of a landed fish.

'I don't know. I – '

He bent quickly forward. Kissed her powerfully resentful brow.

'Come, come. Take your tablets. And I'll make you a nice hot cup of tea.'

She clung a moment to him. Wrung his hand.

He smiled. Loathed himself.

But loathed her too. More completely, more positively, than he'd loathed anything in all his life.

What before had been for him an existence seemed now like a prison sentence.

The walls of the bus shelter were scrawled over with crude graffiti, and only dimly-lit by the colour-devouring, fluorescent orange of the mainstreet lamps.

It was late. And it was raining.

She sat on the damp wooden seat at the back of the shelter under the daubed slogan: 'No Nukes'. To which someone had added: 'Soviet CND Traitors'.

The last bus had gone almost an hour ago. All she saw was the rain and a solitary car passing through. The shelter was flooded briefly with the penetrating sweep of its two bright beams, exposing her frightened face. It was difficult to imagine it was the same place as during the day. Or during the early morning rather, when there were queues here as long as your arm. Girls going off to work; kids on their way to school; pensioners off to the next town to do some shopping. There was a Marks' there. And a Woollies. All the multiples.

Here, there was nothing.

He stood suddenly before her. Made her jump.

He shook his head.

'Couldn't get none. Tomorrow, 'e said.'

'When . . .?'

'Tomorrow.'

'When tomorrow?'

'Tomorrow night.'

She looked blankly at him a moment. Then:

'You sure?'

'Yeah. Nembies. Five for a quid.'

'They was ten for a quid . . .'

'Not now they ain't. 'E' 'as to nick 'em, see. Not like when 'e was gettin' 'em on a script an' it was more or less legal. Price is bound to go up.'

Bunched and shivering, she sniffed.

'What – ev'ry time?'

With the collar of his jacket turned up against the rain, he seemed etched like a lean vampire on the orange tinted night sky.

'It's a risky business. I could get a coupla years for this . . .'

She daren't argue. In all this dump, he was her one sure contact.

'Yeah. All right.'

He grinned.

'See ya then. Stay cool.'

'Sure you'll 'ave 'em tomorrow . . .?'

'Yeah. I'll be at the caf.'

'Cheers.'

Watched as he faded off into the dark. She had to clench her teeth to keep them from chattering. Felt like she wanted to scream.

'Wednesday,' he said, 'we'll go to the sea. Would you like that?'

And – when, unexpectedly, she'd agreed – had gone home with this one thought in mind.

But dreamed that night that he woke suddenly, and was alone. Not here in his own room, but in the upstairs room at the cottage.

It was pitch dark. And he was cold. And could hear the rain beating on the broken roof: plop-plopping on the bare boards in the passage outside. And he'd an overpowering, a suffocating sense of someone – or something – in the room with him.

But could see nothing. It was too dark.

He'd tried to raise himself, but fell back. Stark terror pinned him down as effectively as a spear. His heart beat like a drum.

The window was down. A chill gust of air shook the ill-fitting frame, brought the rain in with it.

There was a sudden soft rush across the ceiling. A bird. Some sort of bird, swooping down. He heard its wingtips graze against the plaster-board: could smell the choking dryness of the dust which came slowly down . . .

But woke then in his own bed. With a stifled scream on his lips.

It was just getting light. But for a moment he hardly dared breathe even, let alone look. It wasn't till his senses had accustomed themselves to the fact that he was really awake that he was able at last to pull himself together.

He sat up. Looked at the clock. It took him a minute or two to realise what day it was.

He got out of bed and went to the glass. Was shocked by the haggard, dishevelled stranger he saw there. The dark images of his dream seemed superimposed still on his pale features. Haunted his dark eyes.

Went then to the window. Threw it wide and drew the mild, rather thundery air deep into his lungs. It was raining – as in his dream. But gently. The garden stood motionless in the early light. Unable to shake off this sense he had of something about to happen – something dark, monumental – the comfortingly familiar, emergent shapes of the evergreens helped focus his thoughts.

It was then that he made up his mind. He would ask Myrna for a divorce . . .

Was again optimistic when he picked her up the following evening and drove east toward the coast.

She was all right to begin with – quite herself. But grew suddenly apprehensive – nervous even. Kept touching her

face, her hair. When her trembling fingers would fly off
again in search of something else.

'Darling – are you all right?'

She didn't answer. Had quarrelled with her parents
perhaps? – but obviously didn't want to talk about it.

'Is there anything,' he persisted, 'I can do?'

She stared a moment out through the windscreen. Slowly
shook her head.

To his subsequent regret, he left it at that.

It had gone seven already when he drove at last into the
melancholy, faded little resort with its sinisterly dignified
Victorian apartment houses, its one-time movie theatre
converted now into a bingo hall, its dramatically angled
shingle beach. A town of steep, back-area inclines; from
where the sea seemed to rise straight out of the street.

He parked alongside the promenade.

They got out and walked across to the beach. She held
his hand, seemed more herself for a bit. Smiled even when
he found her a particularly pretty, coloured pebble which he
slipped into her pocket.

There were signs of a storm on the horizon. Or, at least,
of further rain. As the mainstreet, with its neglected façade –
its hopelessly unfashionable shops; its second-class boarding
houses with their once genteel, yellowing lace curtains (or
was it nylon perhaps?), their miserably dark wallpapers and
unhappy potted plants; its shabby tea shop ('See the caf? –
that's where I meet my mates.') – as all this fell slowly back
behind them, he became more conscious of its gathering
might.

Here, before the beach took an abrupt plunge toward the
hungry tide with its multiple curling tongues, the fishing
boats were strung haphazardly along its crown like a scat-
tering of empty nutshells.

She sat a moment on the side of one of these. Laughed
suddenly when it tipped a little under her weight. He could
smell the fumes off the street still: mingled with the scent of
wet wood, of tar, salt, and fish. Could hear the shingle shift
as the water drained from under it and returned again into
itself. Heard, too, the far flung, sepulchral screams of the
nervously prowling gulls.

He smiled. Wished he'd thought to bring his camera. (He'd no picture of her, he realised. Nothing to keep. But, superstitious, shuddered at the idea.) Her eyes, however, were fixed already on something else. And the smile was gone as suddenly as chalked symbols from a slate.

She got slowly up. Stared.

He turned. Followed her gaze.

Saw nothing except the old pier with its hundred references to, its powerful evocation of childhood days forever gone. Its furthest point barely visible against the surly mass of cloud which had merged already with the horizon and was eating its way inland.

The front façade, with its toll-gate and ticket office, was lit by a freak burst from the setting sun. The entire landscape assumed for a moment a near nightmare quality of appalling contrast. The tide was not yet fully in; the encrusted structure only part submerged. Its gaunt supports garlanded round with glistering lengths of seaweed and clusters of resolutely anti-social barnacles in their firmly sealed, metallic shells.

Both light and colour, however, drained rapidly away. The clouds closed like the two covers of a book, and all was seen again in monochrome. The oncoming storm seemed literally to sweep in along the length of the pier, which loomed now as a less than substantial silhouette against the growing darkness.

This –

– and the sea. Featureless save for a bobbing tide marker, its leaden waters grazed by the odd bird winging in at low level.

And of which, he now realised, she was alone aware.

Then, again, her expression seemed to light up – to burn. He put his arm around her, drew her to him. Heard the water rush in over the pebbles and – having shaken them like peas in a colander – hurry out again to prepare for a further assault. A lone gull wheeled against the grey. Shrieked mournfully. A sudden rush of cold air whipped his hair across his eyes.

She turned her face away. But held on a moment to his clothes as though afraid to let go. He bent toward her – was going to kiss away the tear which bulged at the corner of her eye. But she broke suddenly away from him. Began stumbling down the beach toward the sea.

He stood a moment, looking after her. Then – as his shocked senses warned of her intention – went quickly in pursuit of her.

His heart began to pound against his ribs. He shouted out to her, but she didn't look back even. Staggered on down the shingle, slipping and sliding as it gave under her feet. Fell on her knees once, like a child. But picked herself up again and stumbled on.

The first, full drops of rain flattened themselves on the smoothly rounded stones. On the taut skin across his cheek. She was at the water's edge already: walked out now into the foaming surf.

Or perhaps she was heading for the pier? – for the crumbling pavilion with its festering ornamental ironwork; its wooden decks – gaping in places, the timbers rotted all away – on which a single, part collapsed, canvas chair threw out its chest before the wind; its arrowed signs pointing the way to what might now seem the naive amusements of a forgotten era; its shut off rooms and halls, through whose broken panels the salt air alone had access. The whole wallowing like some great stranded hulk to which the sea laid subtly corruptive siege.

'Sherry! Darling – come back!'

She turned at last. But seemed not to recognise him. Was like a child who stands on the threshold of some forbidden fairyland.

'Sherry!'

But his voice was lost in the roar of an incoming wave as it first rose like a powerful horse then threw itself down upon the shore where it ran angrily forward, snapped at the shingle, before slipping again into the wallowing, sullen waters behind.

She looked away. But was not, as he'd persuaded himself, heading for the pier. Was walking, fully clothed, into the sea. Was going – my God! – to drown herself.

Flabbergasted, he stopped dead.

'Where are you going? – come back!'

Then, when she took no notice, plunged in after her.

Didn't think to remove his shoes even. The water was rough, flecked with white. She was up to her waist already. Made no attempt to swim, but trod precariously on like one who walks a tightrope. He caught quick flashes of her expression: fixed, staring, shot with fear. Not so much of what she actually saw as of some spectre hid from him. Some dread shape visible only to herself. Nor was she aware even of the sudden, hissing flash which rent open the far horizon and plunged boiling into the sea.

'Sherry!'

But felt as if his lungs were going to burst.

It was trying to rain still. But the cloud lost only an occasional, huge blob. He couldn't believe he wasn't dreaming – that this wasn't a continuation of his nightmare when, pinned down upon the hard mattress in that shabby upstairs room, he shrank before the approach of an unspeakable horror.

A terrific clap of thunder followed the lightning. Took his breath away. The water rushed past him in its furious bid for the shore, tugged at his legs. A poor swimmer, its strength alarmed him. With every fresh assault he felt that he would go down, never to breathe the air again.

But found himself now within reach of her. Caught hold of her arm.

She snapped suddenly back, like a fish on the end of a line. The violence of which movement took him by surprise. And – out of his depth, dizzy with the whirling of the water – he almost lost her. But knew that, if he let go, neither he nor she would ever be seen again.

Furious, though apparently unaware who he was, she did all she could to free herself of him. Wrenched his arm half out of its socket. Still he held on. Lost sight of her once when a large wave broke over them both, stunned him momentarily. But, when the water subsided, saw that her strength too was exhausted. Drew her firmly toward him, and staggered back with her to the shore.

No single soul had seen this little drama. Only the odd, circling gull, its trained eye turning first this way then that. Nor was there much to be seen from here of what lay beyond: only the steeply ascending shingle beach, the tarred planks on which the boats were hauled to the top, and – up on the crest – a precariously perched hull or two, and the occasional oddly surrealistic chimney pot, sole evidence of the houses across the street.

No sooner had he got her back when she vomited violently. And again. Her body wracked briefly with tremor.

'For God's sake! – what's the matter? Are you ill?'

She stared.

Then, all at once, began to laugh. It was raining hard. The rain ran off her white face like someone had emptied a bucket over her. Then, just as abruptly, her laughter dissolved into tears. A further, tumbling roll of thunder rattled overhead. The rain came straight down, like on a cinema set.

'Come along. We'll go to the cottage – get these wet things off.'

He helped her, sobbing still, back to the car. She tumbled in. Sprawled in her seat like a broken doll. No more laughter. No more tears. Nothing. Only, as she looked vacantly out through the windscreen, her wracked body; her soaking wet clothes and hair; her pale, dirty face.

He let in the clutch. Pulled abruptly away.

She crawled off into the corner by the window like some small insect seeking sanctuary under a stone. Drew her knees up to her chin, reminding him suddenly of when he'd first seen her at the garage.

He shook out the car rug, handed it to her.

'Off with those things, or you'll catch your death.'

She turned her face away.

'Leave me alone . . .'

Her voice was small, barely audible. She'd exhausted herself completely.

'Darling – please. You can't sit there in those wet things. I'll get a fire going if I can. Meantime, take those clothes off and wrap yourself in this. Then, when they're dry, you can put them on again.'

She reached for the rug, took it from him. He picked up the lamp, went across to the chimney place. A quick inspection showed it to be fairly clean – as far as he could see. He'd have, in any case, to risk it.

He went quickly down the uncarpeted stairs with their drunkenly angled banister. Had intended to see what he could find in the garden – it was light enough still outside. But remembered suddenly what she'd said to him once about nettles growing 'up through the front room floor'.

The door stood partly open. Leaned inward on one hinge. He looked into the long abandoned room. In the pale light it appeared at first fairly respectable still. It was completely empty – as were all the rooms here – except, in the far corner, for a single, straight-backed chair. No carpet; no curtains. But, oddly, picture hooks on the rail still over the mantel.

And, exactly as she'd described, the floorboards had rotted away in places and nettles thrust up through the gaping holes.

He went cautiously forward. The boards groaned ominously. He brought his foot down hard, and they cracked convincingly. With his bare hands, he tore up several planks, breaking them into smaller pieces. He eased his conscience by reminding himself that the place was falling apart anyway – nor was he the first vandal here. He brought a petrol soaked rag from the car, and carried his booty back upstairs.

It was now nearly dark. She'd taken her things off and crouched still, wrapped round with the car rug, in the corner. She turned her head when he entered, but said nothing. The room was cold, drear. An occasional dull thud of thunder could be heard still in the distance. But the rain, at least, had given over.

He smiled. Put the wood down before the grate. There was no fire basket, so he structured the wood crosswise in a high pile and thrust in the rag he'd brought from the car. The flame was reluctant at first: he blew till he felt he'd break a blood vessel. Finally, it caught. And for several minutes burned feverishly. Then the chimney began to smoke. Belched great, stinking clouds back into the room.

'There must be something up there – a bird's nest perhaps.'

He was right. Seconds later the thing came down, well

alight, and spilled out in all directions. He chased around, stamping the flames out with his foot.

None of which provoked the smallest reaction from her. She only stared, her face white in the flickering light of the fire. He realised suddenly how completely exhausted he was himself. Turned, his whole body aching, and looked at her.

The firelight brightened the place considerably. Made it seem more cheerful. She though, pale still and shaking, huddled in the corner like a frightened child.

He came across. Crouched down and put the hair back from her face. Deeply disturbed by her behaviour – not only on this occasion, but on past occasions too – it was, he felt, time she offered him an explanation.

'Sherry – darling – what is it? What's the matter?'

She stared momentarily. Then, as unconvinced as he by her lie:

'Nothing.'

'But there is. There's been something the matter for a long time. I've a right, I think, to know.'

She shook her head. Shook it again, violently. Her eyes, though they looked still into his own, seemed at the same time to slip through him. Eluded him completely.

He waited a moment. Then, gently:

'What were you up to? – you frightened me.'

She didn't answer.

He searched her face. Got up at last and went back to the fire. Threw on some more fuel and spread her things out as best he could. A flash or two of lightning contested still with the firelight, but the thunder was long in replying, could barely be heard now.

He glanced back over his shoulder.

'I was going,' he said, 'to speak to you. To tell you what I have in mind.' He paused. Licked his lips. 'I – I'm going to ask Myrna for a divorce. I thought we could – '

'You must be bloody mad!'

He stared.

'How do you mean . . .?'

She said nothing for a moment. Sniffed miserably. Then:

'All right – I'm on sleepers. I shoot the stuff. 'E didn't

'ave none when I saw 'im last, an' I'm so sick for it I could scream.'

It was like the room fell down around him. What strength he had left drained abruptly away. Down. Down. And out, it seemed, through the soaking wet soles of his shoes.

Knew at once that he'd suspected something of the sort all along. (But ignored a nagging suspicion that, in imparting one truth, she hid another. Deceived himself still.) God knows, he'd seen the signs. Had enough hints. In spite of which her words struck him now with the force of a physical blow. Left him momentarily speechless.

When, however, he did speak he inadvertently hit the nail right on the head.

'So you don't really want me at all?'

'Yeah, I do . . .'

But this, of course, was the truth she kept from him.

'By which you mean you want the money?'

'Okay, I want the money. If that don't suit, you know what you can do.'

The flat, matter-of-fact tone in which these few words were spoken was more shocking than any outburst. It was like when he'd dreamed she turned suddenly and spat at him.

But there was of course no point in arguing with her at present. Or in lecturing her on the risk she was taking. He was not, however, going to allow her to waste herself in this way.

'All right: we'll take it from there. If you don't stop messing around with this stuff I'll not give you another penny. It's up to you.'

'You wouldn't do that. You've too fuckin' much to lose. I need your money, yeah. But no way do I need an old fart like you.'

Her words hurt him deeply. He felt like he was hanging by his fingers from a precipice, made a desperate attempt both to restore the situation and to salvage something of his dignity.

'You've as much to lose as I Sherry, as you well know.'

She glared.

'Don't gimme none of that shit!'

But the wind was out of her sails already. She began snivelling like a little dog.

He went across. Helped her up.

'Angel, please: listen to me. I love you very much. And I need you. But you need me too, I think. We need each other.'

She choked back her tears.

'What am I gonna do . . .?'

'Now look: do as I say. See a doctor – see if he can't sort you out. You've got to get well again.'

She looked at him a moment. Her expression was peculiarly obscure.

'Yeah. All right.'

'Promise?'

She sniffed. Wiped her nose on the back of her hand.

'Yeah . . .'

'When?'

'Gimme a day or two. I don't want no one to know about it.'

'So long as you take my advice I shan't say a word to anyone, I swear.'

He felt for his handkerchief. Like the rest of his things it was soaking wet still.

'Here: let me wipe those tears away.'

He gently mopped her face. Kissed her closed eyes.

'Now – promise me?'

She nodded.

'Yeah.' And: 'What's time?'

He looked at his watch.

'It's getting on. Where are you going now?'

''Ome, I s'pose.'

'Get something on then, and I'll drive you back.'

He watched as she went across, pulled on her T-shirt. Thrust the wet ball of the handkerchief back into his pocket.

'Where did you get this stuff in the first place?'

She was on her guard at once.

'Friend of mine.'

'Some friend! – but what made you want to do such a thing?'

She dropped the rug from round her waist. Her small

backside flashed with a familiar arrogance in the light from the fire.

'Dunno.'

She grabbed her jeans. Got shakily into them.

'It was – I just . . . wanted to know. I wanted to know what it was like.'

'And?'

She didn't look at him.

'Yeah – it was all right. I liked it. It gimme a good feelin'. I didn't 'ave to worry.'

'But worry about what?'

She thought a moment.

'Dunno really.'

'Your parents must be comfortably off. I'm sure they've never refused you anything.'

'No.' And: 'But like I was always so scared . . .'

'Of what?'

She fastened her fly.

'School. . . Everything.' Turned suddenly. Shook out her hair. 'What about this fire?'

'Don't worry. I'll put it out.'

He came across. Kissed her gently on the lips.

'I'll give you a ring, shall I? Perhaps then, if you're feeling better, we could talk about what we're going to do.'

She dropped her eyes.

'Yeah. Okay.'

A soft flicker of lightning lit the bare walls briefly. But there was no thunder. Only, down in the dell, the hoo-hoo of a newly woken owl.

She sat at the table, a lighted cigarette in her hand. An untouched cup of tea cooled in front of her.

She smoked nervously, kept rolling off the ash. The ashtray was full besides with bubble gum wrappers, matchsticks, and a bus ticket or two.

The largish room, with its stink of stale food and cigarette smoke, was nearly empty. They were going round tipping out the ashtrays and wiping the tables over.

Every time she put the cigarette to her lips she looked at

the door. When at last her gaunt friend wandered in – his
leather jacket open, a studded leather belt down over his hips
– she made like she'd jump right out of her seat. Her heart
beat wildly. She had to keep both hands on the table to stop
them shaking.

He came straight to where she sat, pulled out a chair.

'Where you bin, you fuckin' – '

'Cool it will ya? Everyone'll 'ear.'

'You've let me down again I'll blast your bloody 'ead off.'

''S all right. I got 'em'.

''Ow many?'

He looked at her across the table. Kept it locked a moment
behind his lips. Then:

'Fifty.'

She flicked the ash off her cigarette. Stared. Then,
suddenly, her face seemed literally to break open in a wide,
tired smile. She started to laugh. Put her hand up in front
of her face.

'Oh, Christ! Yeah!'

'All right . . .?'

'Yeah, yeah.' She dragged her purse out of her pocket.
'Show me it, an' you can 'ave your money.'

He'd a rather aquiline nose, and his eyebrows – black, like
his hair – met across the bridge. The rhinestone stud punched
into his left nostril flashed hypnotically. His eyes, shaded off
with vivid mascara, were like two small pieces of coal.

He reached inside his jacket. Took out the familiar folded
envelope. Except that it was bulkier than she'd ever seen it
before.

'Wanna count 'em?'

She shook her head.

'You done me, you'll soon 'ear about it.'

He slid the packet across the table, and in under the rim
of her saucer.

'There y'are then. They're all there.'

'Cheers. I'm goin' sky 'igh on this li'le lot.'

She took a crisp new ten pound note out of her purse,
flicked it across. They were like two deeply committed
opponents at a deadly game of chess.

'Don't let me down again Rick, please . . .'

He pocketed the money.
'When d'you want 'em?'
'Soon as you can get 'em.'
He got up. Pushed the chair back in.
'Right. See ya then.'
'Yeah. Cheers.'

He'd driven, in the morning, to the railway station. And – now – all the way back. And still the damned thing was there.

Here beside him. On the seat. The local paper. Which he'd picked up yesterday and forgotten to give her.

It was a wonder she hadn't asked.

He turned into the drive. Pulled round the curve and rolled at last to a halt in front of the house.

The day was warm still. Clear, clean, and sunny – as it often was in early June. Here inside the car it was hot, even though he had the window down.

He unfastened the seat belt, put the window up. Was about to get out when again he remembered.

The blasted paper.

He reached for it. But, before he had hold of it even, his heart stood suddenly still – before accelerating wildly. The heavy type half way down the page – freed, it seemed, from the surrounding text – leapt at him.

'Teenage girl dead in drugs drama.'

He sat a moment, transfixed. But knew, without having seen it even, what the story was about. When at last he allowed the smaller type to slip unhindered past the gates of his mind it was as though he'd seen it before somewhere. As though he'd lived this moment a long millennium ago.

His eye skipped frantically down the lines.

'Friday night. . . Bus station. . . The outside toilets. . . Ambulance. . . Too late. . . Dead already of an overdose.

'I don't know,' a teenage friend said later, 'why she did it. But she was always on about someday she'd "bang a really big one". She was warned once about her job because she was on drugs. Last night there was a whole crowd of us. We were really happy. When we left the Star and Anchor she seemed all right. We walked down the bus station

together, and she said she was going to take a fix in the
toilet. I was worried because she'd had a few drinks. I waited
ages, but she didn't come back. So I called the police. I was
really scared.'

'Her father, who keeps a butcher's shop in Tiddenden –
just a few miles from the scene of the tragedy, told me:

"She was a good girl. Very quiet really. We can't believe
this thing has happened." '

There was, it said, to be an inquiry.

He put the paper down. Loosened the knot of his tie. He
felt suddenly cold, but broke at the same time into a sweat.

What was it she'd said to him? – that she wanted to die
before she was twenty and be in a glass coffin 'so everyone
can go "Ahh . . . Innit a shame".'

Instead of which they'd follow her anonymous wooden
box into total obscurity.

It was only now that he realised how hopelessly out of
touch he was with her, with her world. And she with his.
How at variance their two worlds were. And how, foolishly,
he'd blinded himself to this. As he had to the question of
her exact feelings for him. For, while he'd been right when
he reminded her of her need for him, she did not of course
love him. Never had. Herself the predator, she was in turn
preyed upon. But it was he who – if not in quite the way
she'd predicted – was the ultimate loser. She had at least her
death; to which she'd looked forward as other girls look
forward to their wedding.

All that was left to him was her memory. And the certain
sense that he'd never love again.

He was jerked suddenly back to reality when he heard her
voice – Myrna. Standing, furious, at the front door.

'Tony! – I've called you three times. What, for goodness'
sake, are you sitting there for?'

He opened the door. Got out.

'It's all right: I'm coming.'

Coming. Always coming.

'Where's my paper? I asked you for it yesterday.'

He reached across the seat.

'I have it here.'

But never, it seemed, arriving.

SMOKE

Martin's mother smiled suddenly at him across the tea table. She was seldom so attentive these days: but, instead of pleasing him, the smile set off alarm bells in his mind.

'We've someone coming to stay,' she said. And: 'Guess?'

Martin lowered his eyes. He didn't need to guess. He knew.

'Squadron Leader Penny,' he said.

Again she smiled.

'Darling, you're a mind reader!'

He looked sideways at his sister. She was alight with excitement. His mother, too, seemed to shine. But in a different, because more complex way.

But now, abruptly, her smile vanished.

'What's the matter darling? – I thought you'd be pleased. . .'

'Yes,' he said quickly. 'I am.'

But loathed – as children, ever upright, instinctively do – his own lie. Nor had he a friend in his sister. First, she was younger than he. And secondly, she was as bowled over by the newcomer as was her mother.

He retreated instead behind the façade of his untruth.

'I scored against St Augustine's in the end of term match,' he said. And, putting all his disappointment over the proposed visit into these next few words in the hope she'd be deceived: 'But we lost anyway.'

'Oh, darling; I'm sorry. Never mind, you did your best.'

But she was thinking, he knew, of something – or someone – else.

His mother. Bright and sharp as a penknife. Boyishly slim, and with small, fine bones. But with whom his relationship seemed poised of late on the brink of disaster.

Of which both were apparently aware, but neither spoke.

★

His story went back a little before this. Back, in fact, to the night his father died. Here, in this same seaside town. In this same gaunt old house. Just over a year ago.

Prior to the funeral, his father's body – banked about with roses – had lain upstairs in the big front bedroom now occupied by his sister and himself. His mother, shattered, wouldn't go near it.

And so, on a warm June afternoon, he went in with Cecily – his sister – and they took the sheet down from his face. Cecily, who was seven at the time, started to giggle. Probably because she was nervous. Martin – unable to believe that this was the man who just one or two nights before had closed, quite literally, this chapter of their lives – only stared.

'And that,' his father had said as he put the book aside, 'is the end of the story.'

And so it was.

The end.

His mother was for a time severely shaken. The apparent stability – or as near a stability as could be maintained in time of war – of their former existence came tumbling down around them.

His father had worked for the government. It was all very mysterious and exciting. He was an important man; and this of course was reflected in the day to day events of their early years. Equally important people came to stay, bringing expensive presents for their mother and leaving behind a memorable aroma of cigar smoke. They talked a lot about aeroplanes – a then relatively new, tremendously exciting field of discovery. His sister hadn't the least interest in aeroplanes. But – as did he – she loved all the comings and goings, the stimulating new personalities who made at the same time such a fuss of her.

But then, suddenly, and over what had seemed an unendurably long period, his father fell seriously ill. Eminent medical men – personal friends of his – came and went. Conversed briefly, in hushed tones, with their mother downstairs in the hall.

Then, again, he was better. Was making an unexpectedly good recovery.

Then, in the deep of night, his mother's horrified scream: 'Children! Children! Quickly – Daddy is dead!'

And he was. Dead in her arms. Like the crucified Christ taken down from the cross. His bloodless, emaciated frame naked save for the sheet she'd dragged from off the bed and drawn across his thighs.

Daddy-pop of the fiery, deep madeira eyes; of the amazing brain; of the mysterious, faintly salacious sense of humour and sweetheart since childhood of his petite, romantic, impressionable and susceptible wife – gone.

Cecily was just seven.

He, nearly ten.

His father's affairs were in a complete mess (and were not settled yet); his mother apparently unable to deal with them. As with both children, whom she packed off almost immediately to boarding school.

Everything, for a time, was bleak.

Martin didn't adapt easily to the sudden change; his sister even less so. His new school – with the Roman Catholic fathers – was authoritarian in the extreme, physically vast and gloomy, and the daily routine near monastic in its severity.

His father's death, he was soon aware, entailed, too, a shock decline in finances. The half dozen servants were whittled down to the dour but dependable housekeeper whose husband was serving abroad somewhere, and who'd a constant fear that – when she left the house at night to return home – German paratroopers would drop down on her out of the trees. She was also terribly houseproud. And, childless, was appalled at the amount of clearing up she had to do after them when they came home on holiday. His mother was now too withdrawn to interfere on their behalf and so Vera's word was law.

All those faces familiar to them when their father was alive seemed suddenly to have disappeared. Lost either to an increasingly ravenous war or – a more likely explanation, for most were too old for the services – to greener pastures.

There were a few new faces, however. Mostly male. And of whom Vera, for one, did not always approve. Martin, bewildered by these persons, found himself for the first time in (albeit silent) agreement with her. Few parties were given now. But, when they were, they were very different from those held under the admittedly rather conservative auspices of his father. There was little real conversation; a lot of laughter; the radiogram blared; and there were undignified goings on unheard of in his father's time.

But there was – during the school holidays – an occasional trip, with their mother, to London.

This, for her, usually meant some further threshing out of their father's affairs. So that both he and his sister were left more or less to their own devices.

Above all, there was the hotel.

Whose rear façade – all black with soot, but no less imposing for that: in fact, more so – overlooked the railway station.

Which in itself offered endless diversion. For here, under the far-off rafters with their blacked-out glass, were echoed the frantic comings and goings in the hotel foyer – though more tellingly. The atmosphere was so fraught that no knowledge of the travellers – of their joys or sufferings – was required. The poorly-lit platforms were like a sort of purgatory peopled with grey ghosts who came and went and were never seen again. At times they were partly obscured in furiously energetic clouds of steam which, momentarily, ate up whole sections of this vast crowd – or, alternately, spawned a further solemn host.

The station clock in particular was powerfully present. Under its four, cruelly impassive faces silent groups of servicemen gathered with all their kit, waiting for trains which would take them God knows where or into what nightmare worlds. Whistles shrilled; hearts were broken. The crowded trains, pulling hard, puffed slowly off into the distance and were lost at last in darkness.

Would he ever forget. . .?

His excitement as their own train approached was every
bit as feverish as that of his sister. When at last they pulled
into the station and trekked forward to the front he'd stand a
moment and look at the fabled monster which had personally
conveyed them over such a vast distance and stood leaking
now at every joint like a dog which has just come out of the
water. The massive wheels with their meticulously oiled
rods; the spotless paintwork with its painstakingly picked
out initials 'GWR'; the sudden, earsplitting rush of released
steam which flew up out of the boiler to lose itself at last
among the ornate ironwork way overhead – pure magic.
Their own, their busily breathing engine. Here, in the flesh.
Huge. Magnificent. Like some sort of mythical beast which
has chosen, in the depths of the forest, to suddenly reveal
itself. . .

And then the hotel. Pre-war, one of London's best. Part
stripped now of its splendour because of the bombing – the
station had already sustained a couple of direct hits – part
shut away. But still the impressive awning over the splendid
flight of steps at the front; still the gloved and uniformed
commisionaire at the top; still the magnificent revolving
doors which literally whirled one off the street and into the
hushed, thickly carpeted, luxurious foyer with its red plush,
its white marble, its palms, its gilt and dark mahogany.

And the smell.

A smell of fine wines, cigars, and perfumes – none of
which was easily come by at present. In a word, grown ups.
His mother, too, wore a full length Russian sable – with a
little trilby hat with a veil – in which he loved to bury his
nose.

His mother always made a considerable impression when
she arrived. People were drawn to her like pins to a magnet
– men especially. Small, striking, she was – in her thirties
even (which, of course, was terribly old) – a natural coquette.
(He preferred this somehow to 'flirt', whose implications
were rather less tasteful.) He sometimes felt, during these
trips, a little older – certainly wiser – than she. Was puzzled
by her susceptibility, by her apparent (perhaps willing)

naivety. She hadn't the vaguest idea about people. Made the most embarrassing mistakes.

But these visits were nevertheless tremendously exciting. Until. . .

One night.

It was very late. He and his sister had been in bed – they'd their own room: his mother always booked a suite, which she couldn't really afford, and there was always some belt tightening to be done later – for hours.

He was woken by a lot of suppressed laughter. Giggling even. It seemed at first very dark, because of the blackout. But there was in fact a sliver of yellow light down the opposite wall from the corridor outside.

He could smell his mother's perfume. And he could smell a man.

And, now that he was fully awake, could just discern them sitting together on his sister's bed. The man seemed very amused by it all.

'You see?' his mother teased. 'It is as I said.'

'And the other. . .?'

'Here – Martin, my little boy. He's the elder of the two.' She reached forward now, put on the bedside lamp.

He lay resentfully flat, his head deep in the pillow. Caught, he felt, at a disadvantage.

The man wore uniform – but so, of course, did almost everyone these days. He was a RAF officer, and there were three rings round his cuffs – two thick, and one thin. Which meant that he was a Squadron Leader. Hatless, he smiled in a very friendly sort of way.

'Hello,' he said.

His mother spoke still in a whisper.

'Martin – this is Squadron Leader Penny. He's a bomber pilot. He didn't believe I'd two small children asleep upstairs, so I brought him to see you.'

He resented, too, this rôle in which his mother automatically cast him – as a 'little boy'. He didn't like the Squadron Leader, any more than he liked her other new friends. He could, he felt, have told her a thing or two about him. But was obliged to act – as he was taught – like a gentleman.

(Why was it adults forced one to lie, and to act deceitfully, when all one's instincts told one otherwise?)

'How,' he said, 'do you do?'

There was a further explosion of laughter, at once stifled – on account, he assumed, of the late hour. But he saw the joke, of course. Here he was, flat on his back, but as conscious of his manners as if he stood – fully dressed, and to attention – on both his feet.

The Squadron Leader smelt of his skin – a deep, sweet, animal smell. Unmistakable, though largely bathed and shaved away. He smelt, too, of whisky. His eyes were alight with excitement: as though he hoped, now, for the fulfillment of some boldly extracted promise.

He'd fairish hair, strong but light coloured brows from under which his grey-blue eyes probed with an alert precision. He'd a ready smile, which drew deep furrows down his closely shaven cheeks, and a schoolboy enthusiasm both for life and – Martin suspected – for women.

This much was obvious.

There was, too, a schoolboy immaturity. Or carelessness was perhaps a better word. If there was, as Martin supposed there must be, any sense of responsibility then it was apparently reserved for that moment when, kitted out in full, he climbed up into the cockpit and flew out at dusk to hit back at the enemy. Off duty, the pace was a trifle forced. The gaiety a mite artificial. Betraying a ruthless determination to enjoy himself at all costs. But whether this was because he feared each leave could be his last, or whether it was a more deeply seated trait, Martin could not at this stage tell.

But he sensed the danger at once.

'Oh, darling,' his mother managed at last, her amusement a trap only for her companion's attention, 'you're a scream, really!'

He went back to boarding school with a sense of something dreadful about to happen. Something worse even than the complete change brought about by the death of his father.

For his mother, he knew, had lost her heart. And to someone so unlike his father it hardly seemed possible.

'I have a new friend,' she wrote him a few days later. (As if he didn't know!) 'Or, rather, we have. Squadron Leader Penny thought you were wonderful – both of you. He is sure, too, that you are very clever. . .'

Which was simply her way of making the whole thing up into a palatable ball.

The next time his mother went to London she went alone. And, when he saw her again, was so amplified she deafened him – though not of course literally. Figuratively, rather. In that there was this powerful excitement which came through vividly in her speech and gestures. Always flamboyant, she was now so exaggerated she took one's breath away.

Or she was so silent and withdrawn – and in so different a way from during her time of mourning – that none dared intrude. Though seldom sharp with him, Martin sensed at such times a resentment against his presence. Or even – which was worse perhaps – a total unawareness of what was going on outside her mind.

A handful of letters fell one morning on the mat, some bordered still with black – friends in far-off places who'd only just got the news. At first mesmerized, she then swooped like a hawk. Literally casting all others aside in favour of the one – scrawled boldly across in bright blue ink – she bore away with her.

She'd sit for hours before the bedroom glass, making what he could only have described as 'faces' at herself. Turning her head first one way, then another, and with her small mouth pursed in what she evidently felt to be a very pretty way but which struck him as rather silly. Cynical even. And so engrossed with what she saw she'd no idea who came or went.

It embarrassed him that he saw her in so unflattering a light. And, more especially, that she was so totally unaware of this. He marvelled at the innocence – or ignorance perhaps – with which she paraded this new aspect of herself.

And yet, for all her apparent foolishness, she seemed to sing. She shone. No, blazed. Fire bombs went off in her eyes. Yet she was secretive. Powerful. More self-assured than for a long time.

He stood, one afternoon, beside her at the glass. Till, after perhaps ten minutes – during which time he officiated, like an altar boy, with the pots and jars – he could bear it no longer.

'Aren't you coming down? – you were going to show me the nest. . .'

She didn't answer at once. Then, when he'd begun to think perhaps she hadn't heard him:

'Mm . . .? Oh, darling – not now. Mummy's busy.'

'But you said. . .'

She took up the hand glass with its art nouveau obverse, an early gift from his father. Twisted a recalcitrant strand of hair neatly into place.

'Why don't you see if you can find it? – that would be much more exciting. Then you can come and tell me about it.'

He was not so easily put off.

'But you were going to tell me about it. . .'

'Well – later perhaps.'

He stared.

'Why not now?'

She turned on him suddenly.

'Darling, for goodness' sake, run away and amuse yourself.'

He went.

Down into the garden, where he picked at the young leaves of the laburnum till the sun sent long shadows across the lawn and, finally, Vera came out in search of him and remonstrated with him for being late for tea.

And now, finally, this invasion into the privacy of their home.

'The Squadron Leader,' his mother was telling his sister, 'has been posted as an instructor. That means he'll be able to see a lot more of us – you'd like that, wouldn't you?'

'Yes! Yes!' his sister squealed. And: 'When is he coming? How long will he stay?'

'Sh!, don't get so excited,' his mother begged, though nearly as excited herself. 'He'll be here in the morning – in time for lunch, I hope. And he's coming in a motor car, too. You'll want to take a look at that Martin, I bet.'

'Mummy, mummy,' his sister shrilled, 'how long will he stay?'

'Only for the weekend. But he'll come again, I'm sure.'

'What – during the holiday? Before we go back to school?'

'Oh, yes. I should think so.'

Martin quickly swallowed the remainder of his tea.

'May I,' he asked, 'go upstairs now?'

'But darling, you haven't finished. . .'

'Yes I have. I don't want that piece of bread.'

'Why? – aren't you feeling well?'

Her sudden concern – if only a formality – confused him.

'I – I've got a bit of a headache,' he lied. 'And I want to put my things away. . .'

'Well, all right. But don't make a habit of this. You shouldn't, you know, leave the table till everyone else has finished – not at home even.'

Martin, remembering the number of occasions she'd done just that, bowed his head as he knew he ought.

'I'm sorry. . .'

'Go along. Off with you. We'll excuse you this once.'

And the normally tight-lipped housekeeper in a tizzy too over the impending arrival. Quite chatty in fact as she carried his worn leather suitcase upstairs for him.

'Gentleman coming to stay then! – that'll be nice. A little strange perhaps. . .'

It was then that Martin realised she, too, did not entirely approve. That she was, in an oblique sort of way, hinting at something.

'How do you mean?' And: 'On the bed please Vera. I'll unpack it.'

'I was instructed to unpack it for you, young man. And what about your ration and clothing books? – or have you given them to your mother?'

'Yes. I gave them to her downstairs. What did you mean – "strange"?'

She drew back the locks with her thumbs, and the catches flew open.

'Well, after all this time. . . Although I suppose it's not long really since your father died.'

He felt, suddenly, deeply shamed. Sensed a slight here – against either his mother or himself, he wasn't sure which.

He stood a moment as she put back the lid and looked into the open case.

'Do you mean,' he asked at last, 'that he shouldn't come. . .?'

'Well, of course, that's not for me to say.' She began removing the topmost garments, fussing over non-existent wrinkles as she put them out on the counterpane. 'And aren't I always telling you? – you ask too many questions for someone your age. What your mother chooses to do is none of my business – nor yours either. Now, come along: we must get these things away. And what's all this, I'd like to know?'

'That's my Dinky car. I swopped with Saunders, but he hadn't a box for it.'

'And what did you swop it for?'

'My ration at the tuck shop. He wanted it back after – the car, I mean. But I wouldn't let him have it.'

'Whatever will you get up to next? – I daren't think.'

The big front bedroom. The room in which his father died. Withdrawn somehow. Like it, too, prepared for the coming invasion. Put on a mask.

'I don't,' he said, partly because it was true, and partly to excuse himself – though why, he didn't know, 'like the Squadron Leader . . .'

'Now, please: you mustn't say things like that.'

'But it's true!'

'Now! – that's enough!'

The holiday.

Weeks away from boarding school, from Jesuit severity – all spoiled.

'Those whom God has joined, let no man put asunder . . .'

But his father, of course, was dead. Surely, then, it was different? Surely it shouldn't matter quite so much?

The Squadron Leader arrived at precisely the time he'd promised. In fact, a few minutes earlier.

Martin, when he heard the car, went at once to the window and looked out. His mother must have looked too. But – playing, no doubt, one of those silly games grown ups sometimes played – she didn't go to the door. It remained instead firmly closed, like a castle gate against the enemy.

He knew at once what she was up to. She'd keep him waiting purposely, so as to whet his appetite. Was putting him, too – here, on her home ground – in his place. Inviting, thereby, a spirited assault. Both on her property and person.

The car was a two-seater Frazer Nash. Grey, with red leather. Wide wings swooped down to the running boards, and there was a spare wheel on the back. Martin liked it a lot. But that didn't alter his feelings with regard to its owner.

A wonderful, warm day. With a soft breeze; clear blue sky; and that peculiarly sharp seaside light. The front garden – its high brick wall on one side half smothered with rambling roses: a partition fence on the other – deeply green and washed across with colour.

A wide, neatly kept gravel path went down to the gate. It was flanked on the left by hollyhocks, delphiniums and dahlias which rose tall over the asters, begonias, and Sweet Williams at their feet. On the right was the largish lawn, smooth as velvet.

He heard his mother's voice downstairs in the hall, warning Vera of the Squadron Leader's arrival. But still she didn't go out. Put a stop, only, to Cecily's excited shrieks.

The Squadron Leader, armed with a dozen deep red roses and a single light suitcase, was smiling as – setting the suitcase down a moment – he unlatched the gate and pushed his way in. The smile – wide, and deeply grooved – ground, as it were, to a halt when he realised there was no one to welcome him. His expression now (or as much of it as was visible under the angled peak of the cap) was a trifle anxious.

Martin ought, he supposed, to go down. He didn't want them to call him. Was at the door when his sister came flouncing up in a rage. Her presence was apparently not required.

She bounced across to the window, her footfall flat with anger and disappointment.

'We've got to wait!'

Of course. They'd already served their purpose.

The Squadron Leader – a little puzzled perhaps; adults were so stupid – was ringing now at the front door.

Vera went scuttling nervously up the hall to answer it.

When she finally came to tell them lunch was ready, she said that they were to eat with her.

On the way down, he saw that the lounge was closed. Heard the clear, light ring of glass against glass. Followed by his mother's similarly light, tinkling laughter.

The heavy double doors seemed literally to vibrate. Like those closed upon some vital conference.

They were not, in fact, allowed down until evening. His mother then sent word that they 'might come now and meet the Squadron Leader'.

'But we've met him already!' Martin indignantly declared.

'Never mind about that. Now, are your face and hands clean both of you? Oh!, Martin – look at that tie! Put it on properly please. And pull those socks up. You don't want to go down there with your socks around your ankles. And hurry now, will you. I've the blackout to see to yet.'

The drawing-room was open when they went down. The atmosphere there bright but formal. They were expected, obviously, to be on their best behaviour.

The Squadron Leader stood at the far end, his back to the fireplace. He was of course hatless, but – though very much at ease – otherwise correctly dressed. His left hand lurked under cover of the flippantly raised skirts of his tunic, toyed restlessly with the small change in his trouser pocket. The other was occupied with a cigarette.

The whole was intended to convey a totally open, likable sort of chap. But it seemed to Martin that behind this pleasant façade there resided a shrewd man of the world – though, of course, he could not have offered so succinct a description.

His mother sat nearby in one of the deep, chintz-covered armchairs. She also was determined to appear at ease. But the whole of her seemed somehow to dance outside herself, like a blinding shadow, and her eyes shone out like searchlights.

In the grate – with its cold, ornate copper screen – was a huge china urn, sculpted all around with vines and full of deeply blue delphiniums from the garden. The long, heavy curtains obscured both the lingering twilight beyond the now closed French windows and the blackout blinds.

The air smelt of flowers and of cigarette smoke. And, only faintly now, of the new mown grass outside. Where, far beyond the spacious confines of these four high walls, the air reverberated – like a tuning fork – to the flight of heavy aircraft. On, and on, and on. As if it would never again be still. As if the vibrations first swallowed themselves, then spat themselves out. To continue. . .

And – in the garden – a blackbird sang a lone, full-throated song.

'Darlings! – the Squadron Leader is here. He'd like to say hello.'

Martin approached circumspectly. His white shirt and grey knickerbockers as nearly spotless as his mother might have wished.

'Ah! – hello there!' And, as Cecily first tramped quickly forward then pirouetted upon a seizure of shyness: 'You remember me, I'm sure.'

Cecily, half her fist in her mouth and her blue eyes shining with excitement, was speechless in the presence of her hero. Her honey-blonde, Shirley Temple curls blazed like an aura under the electric lights.

He winked first at her mother. Then, crouching, the smoke from his cigarette embracing the line of his loosely dangling wrist before spiralling up in front of his half-closed, laughing eyes:

'My goodness! – you're even prettier than when I saw you last.'

She wriggled and flounced but remained at a distance still.

His grin widened. Swept out across his features like ripples on a pond. Martin could picture him in the officers' mess. A 'good type'. Popular both with his own and with the ground crews.

'Now come along darling,' her mother snapped. 'You're not that shy.'

There was a touch, too, of hardness in her eye as she recognised – probably for the first time – the woman, and therefore potential rival in her child. Not, it seemed, an altogether comfortable revelation. For, though certainly shy to a degree, his sister's behaviour now was that of a born coquette. Fascinated, she yet withheld herself from him.

Then, suddenly grave, she traipsed forward at last.

'I don't,' he said, equally serious now, 'remember your name – are you going to tell me?'

Unable at first to look at him, totally overawed, she stole instead a sidelong glance at her mother.

'Well, darling. . .? Oh, dear. This is an exhibition.'

And, when she spoke her name so softly that no one heard:

'Now! – that won't do. The Squadron Leader can't hear you.'

He grinned again.

'If you tell me yours, I'll tell you mine.'

She looked at last into his eyes. Which, at present, were on a par with her own. There was a hint, still, of humour in his expression. But she sensed his sincerity.

'Cecily,' she said, speaking more clearly now. And her heart was lost forever. Martin especially was aware what a lasting impression this moment had made on her.

'Ah! – of course. That's nice, isn't it? I'm Peter. Peter Penny.' And, after a quick, conspiratorial glance at her mother (there was, Martin supposed, some sort of private joke between them in connection with this): 'That's a funny name, isn't it?'

She stared. Shook her head.

'I like it.'

He looked up suddenly.

'And you're Martin – I remember that.'

Martin thought this must be largely due to the amusement he'd given him at their first meeting. But there was, too, a suggestion of something else. Some hidden symbolism. A preordained destiny.

'Yes,' he said.

'Martin,' his mother interrupted, 'is terribly clever. He's the bright one – like his father. Though what sort of direction this will take, I've no idea. He'd like to fly, wouldn't you darling? But his father had hopes for him as an aircraft designer. And he is, of course, terribly interested in your motor car – aren't you darling?'

Hands behind his back, he answered as was expected of him.

'Yes.'

The Squadron Leader stood at last. Cecily, now that his attention was centred on something else, seized the opportunity to eat up as much of him as her eyes could swallow.

'Perhaps I can take you for a spin sometime. But not this visit, I'm afraid. I shan't be here long enough.'

'Are you flying now?' Martin asked, aware that some sort of conversation was expected of him. 'Mummy said you'd been posted as an instructor.'

'That's right. I'm off ops for a bit. Change is as good as a rest they say.'

He was equally jolly, equally friendly, as with his sister – though not, of course, as indulgent. His thick, light coloured lashes dropped in a sleepy but rather calculating sort of way. Obscuring something of his eye's expression – especially when he smiled. So that his humour – or whatever else he might be feeling – though frank, was somehow mysterious.

'I'd like to see your aeroplane. . .'

'Keen, are you? I'll have to see what I can do.'

'Thank you. That would be very exciting.'

'I can't promise, however. Last raid of my last tour we took a chimney off the Group HQ – how's that for low level? But I'd a distinct impression the top brass weren't all that amused, so I'm not asking any favours at present.'

Martin stared momentarily. But wondered then whether the Squadron Leader was perhaps exaggerating.

'You're shooting a line, sir!'

The Squadron Leader looked at first astonished. Then broke – literally it seemed as far as his face was concerned – into laughter. Cracks and lines shot out in all directions across his handsome features like the rays of a rising sun. He guffawed like a schoolboy. Then, turning to their mother:

'No good telling him about Gremlins then!'

And, laughing still, drew deeply on his cigarette. His eyes, though alert and penetrating, seemed veiled again in mystery. An impression accentuated by the busy clouds of smoke which emerged abruptly from his mouth.

'Oh, Martin! I'm sure the Squadron Leader was – '

'No, Evelyn, please. He's a shrewd lad, this one. Well, Sonny: what will you do when you get older, hm? If you don't go designing aircraft, that is.'

'I haven't really decided yet. . .'

But didn't like the casual use of his mother's Christian name in his hearing. Its very naturalness implied an established intimacy.

'Your mother says you're keen to fly. . .'

'Yes, I – '

But the Squadron Leader had opened his eyes already. Pilots, he realised, weren't necessarily as they appeared in the familiar propaganda: clear eyes turned skyward, clean chin set hard in defiance of the common enemy. Pilots were also people. Nor were they always nice people. He could not now see himself settling down very well if they were all going to be like the Squadron Leader.

' – I was.'

'Well, I'll see if I can't pull a few strings for you. Bend the rules, you know? You'd like a close look at a Lanc, I'll bet.'

'Yes sir, I would.'

His sister, meanwhile, was vying again for the Squadron Leader's attention. Aeroplanes normally bored her to distraction. Now, with a sense of shock, Martin realised how much she'd learned from him and was turning to her own advantage.

'That's a bomber! A Lanc's a bomber! It can carry more bombs than any other aircraft.'

'Yes. There's not another like her.'

She thought a moment.

'Why "her". . .?'

He glanced again at their mother. Grinned.

'I don't know really. Perhaps because she's beautiful.'

'Are all aeroplanes "she"?'

'Yes, of course. Ships, too.'

'Why?'

She'd her head back, and was looking dizzily up into his eyes.

'I don't know really. . .'

But grinning, again, from ear to ear.

'Now children,' their mother interrupted, 'that'll do. It's getting on. Time you two were upstairs in bed. Martin — take her up, will you? And ask Vera to come in a moment before she leaves.'

'Yes, all right.'

Cecily threw her arms impulsively round the Squadron Leader's legs.

'Goodnight!' And, on the same impulse: 'I do like you! — you've got lovely blue eyes!'

He smiled. His eyes twinkled in a very grown up sort of way. An expression normally reserved for her mother. He was teasing her, of course. But she responded with a shriek of pleasure.

Martin saw his mother narrow her eyes slightly — as she always did when she didn't like something. Quickly, he grabbed his sister by both shoulders.

'Come on!' he hissed.

And propelled her in the direction of the door.

'See you both in the morning then.'

'Yes. Goodnight sir. Goodnight mummy.'

'Goodnight darlings. Not a sound now — promise?'

Cecily dropped off at once. Tired out by the day's events, and by its glorious last half hour.

Martin, too — though disturbed at first by the host of images which projected themselves upon the screen of his lowered lids — was soon asleep.

But then, abruptly, woke again.

Was woken rather. By the sound of the gramophone. They were down there still. At nearly three in the morning.

He got out of bed, crept across and opened the door. There was no light up here, but he made his way without accident to the top of the stairs. Peered through the banisters.

The hall below – also in darkness – seemed charged. As though the air down there was made up of iron black electric particles which virtually crackled in their intensity.

There was a light, however, in the drawing-room. One of the two doors stood partly open, permitting – were he able to descend without observation – a glimpse of the mysteries within.

It was as if he were dreaming. And – when he got down – as if he stood at last before the tabernacle in some great darkened church, the sacred chamber barely able to contain its brilliance.

Except that the feeling here wasn't like in a church. Which is to say, it wasn't holy. They'd the radiogram on – not loudly, but it seemed so in the silence. And they were dancing. . .

'Smoke gets in your eyes' – sultry, full-throated chanteuse with the carefully cultivated Mid-Atlantic accent so popular with her genre.

He was afraid at first they'd see him. But he needn't have worried. Each was so absorbed in the other, Adolf Hitler could have walked in and they'd have been none the wiser.

The Squadron Leader was minus his jacket and tie. His hair, boyishly dishevelled, fell across his eyes. Which, overtly lustful, gazed amusedly into those of his partner. He held her very close. They barely moved at all; it was as if their bodies had lost all awareness of the dance. His partner seemed hung on his embrace like a rag doll spiked on a paling. Her head back, the lids of her part-closed eyes fluttering like one in shock. The Squadron Leader smiled. Unlike her, he was totally in control. Not only, Martin suspected, of the situation but of himself. There was more than a hint of logic at work behind the lazy lashes, the deeply grooved, sardonic smile, the poised angle of the head.

They were going, he knew, to kiss. Like in the movies.

And they did. But differently.

And, more shocking than all he'd seen so far, his mother now slipped her fingers inside the Squadron Leader's collar and gently massaged his throbbing throat.

This, for Martin, was total betrayal. Unwitting – or, worse, willing – subjection to the seducer.

She looked, in fact, altogether stupid.

Something he'd not have thought possible yesterday – or at any other time till now. But realised, in the same instant, that his resentment went back in fact further than that. To the loss of his father. To the complete change, not only in their circumstances, but in his mother's behaviour toward him.

And the absence of a tie, the open collar, as obscene somehow as open flies – and all that this implied. Here they were, these two grown people, getting up – in secret – to what they (or his mother, at any rate) would certainly have condemned in anyone else. He could just imagine what she would have said had she caught the housekeeper in a similar situation.

He remembered Vera's disapproval. Her hint at impropriety. . .

But blamed his father, too. For having brought him up to believe that everyone adhered to the same rigid principles he himself enforced.

What did it all mean?

Who, if anyone, was innocent?

Was it perhaps, in some obscure way, his fault? Was he, like the disciples in the Garden, in some way lacking?

He crept back upstairs, shaking. Why, he didn't know.

But then was struck, as he slipped in under the bedclothes, by the unlikelihood – after what he'd just seen – of the Squadron Leader spending what remained of the night in his own room. . .

His heart beat furiously. Hot tears sprang up in his burning eyes.

He was out of bed early the following morning in the hope of avoiding any embarrassment over the bathroom.

Only to find the Squadron Leader already there.

The door was open and, naked except for his pyjama trousers, he was having a shave.

Martin stared a moment, his heart in his mouth. If it had seemed to him last night that he stood in a great dark church, here was the devil himself! But – which was really odd – just like an ordinary man.

The shaving in particular seemed to Martin as powerfully erotic an act as any the devil might be expected to indulge in. Not necessarily evil; but very magic.

If the Squadron Leader knew he was there, he gave no indication. A warm, early sun flooded the small room with light. All those things so long familiar seemed now unfamiliar, part of another world – the Squadron Leader's world. Even – and here Martin could not resist a snigger – the lavatory.

But the mirror especially. In which were reflected now those part humorous, part cynical features he was getting to know so well.

The Squadron Leader was not strictly handsome. Rather, he had presence. His actual features were far from regular; the eyes a little deep, tired. Whether this was due to the strain of war – which Martin would have preferred – or to the strain of hard living – which Martin thought more likely – remained to be seen. But he was of course rather older than was usual for a pilot in these times. His jaw was angular, the muscles tight. His lips – the lower one, rather – was full, sensuous. The upper was thinner, rather cruel. His eyes were carelessly warm, yet hard. A quality Martin found difficult to describe. But, he now decided, a bit like the light in here: warm, casually embracing, but so sharp nothing escaped detection. All, instead, was mercilessly revealed. The Squadron Leader himself even. But he stood up to it rather well, as Martin expected he would. His type got away with everything.

His physique was that of one still fairly fit after what must amount to some pretty heavy punishment. Rather like that of a boxer – except that, here, the damage was done on the inside. But he was young enough still to wear the combined assault of tobacco, drink, and women. Plus the stress of flying. His shoulders were straight and hard. A shadowed

groove down the centre of his back (which disappeared tantalisingly into the top of his trousers) revealed the presence of
deep muscle along the path of his spine. His shoulder blades
slid smoothly back and forth below the shallow mesh of
flesh and muscle which part disguised them.

And then the strong column of the neck; the thick, straw
coloured hair cut close at the sides and behind the two small
ears as neatly formed as a woman's. On top, the hair was
longer. Straight and floppy as a schoolboy's. And ending,
at the back, is an unruly knot the colour of the wire brush
his mother sometimes used on her shoes.

'Don't run away old chap. I shan't be long.' And, as an
afterthought: 'Is it urgent?'

Martin, who'd been about to slip away, blushed furiously.

'No sir. I – no, it isn't.' Angry at having been caught out,
his curiosity yet got the better of him. 'How did you know
I was here?'

The Squadron Leader whirled the shaving brush expertly
over his morning beard, which vanished under a billowing
lather.

'Ah!'

Martin pondered this cryptically short reply a moment.
Then, unable to come to a satisfactory conclusion – or to
one which didn't substantiate a purely superstitious reaction:

'Did you sleep well sir?'

Not a flicker.

'Like a top!' And: 'Look here – you don't have to call me
"sir". Call me Peter.'

'Vera said to call you sir.'

He lifted his chin, tickled the soap in under his jaw. The
movement of his hand, the way he used the brush, reminded
Martin of Mr Holmes the painter who came last year to do
up the summerhouse.

'Vera?'

'Yes. She's our housekeeper.'

'Oh, I see.'

Martin, because he felt there to be a lurking disrespect in
the Squadron Leader's reply, rushed at once to her defence.

'She's all right really. She looks after us when mummy
goes away – that's if we're not at boarding school.'

'Mm.'

Martin ran his finger along the jamb of the door.

'Mummy said to call you "sir", too.'

The Squadron Leader had a 'cut throat' razor which he slapped deftly across a leather strop. The muscles of his arms and chest worked in unison. His eyes, against the white of the shaving soap, were the colour of certain blue-grey stones to be found on the beach. But they twinkled in opposition to their hardness.

'Well, now you have it from the top so as to speak – no more "sir". You make me feel like a schoolmaster.' He grinned. 'I don't know about you, but I never did like schoolmasters.'

He tested the blade against his thumb.

'That'll do I think.'

He drew a long, precise stroke down the left side of his face; cut away both foam and whiskers.

Martin, fascinated in spite of himself, edged at last into the small room and eased himself onto the cane seat of the bathroom chair. The Squadron Leader's false camaraderie made him want to put him to the test – to say something that would really shake him. But his false sense of propriety forbade it.

'Oh, ours are all right. Some of them anyway.' And: 'Are you enjoying your stay here?'

'Wizard. I'd like to come again – if your mother will have me.'

'Have you been down to the sea?'

'Not yet, no. I'll pop down this afternoon perhaps. It's not so far, your mother says.'

He didn't answer at once. Then:

'My sister thinks you're smashing. She said so.'

He chuckled in a way which seemed to indicate this was a compliment he was used to. From ladies, anyway.

'Well, I don't know . . .' And, turning suddenly, the fingers of one hand impressed upon his face still: 'Perhaps because I promised her my sweet ration.'

Martin looked at his feet. Was momentarily at a loss.

'Have you,' he then asked, squinting up again into the Squadron Leader's already part-shaven face, 'ever met any

Germans – any real Germans? Vera is sure there are some here already. She's afraid to go out in the dark in case they jump on her. She says they drop them secretly from aeroplanes.'

The Squadron Leader picked carefully at the hair over his upper lip. It was so quiet here Martin could hear the whiskers click as they were cut down.

'I've not,' he said, 'actually spoken to any – not, that is, since war broke out. But I've been pretty close to a few up there.'

He made a quick half gesture toward the sky, his fingers returning at once to the more urgent task of smoothing a path for the blade.

'How close sir? – I mean . . .' Confused, he blushed again. But couldn't bring himself somehow to use his Christian name. 'Could you see their faces?'

'Not quite, no. Any bomber pilot who let a Jerry fighter get that close would be asking for trouble.'

'Wouldn't that be the job of the gunners – to keep them away?'

'Oh, yes. But the skipper has to stay awake too, y'know.'

Martin let this sink in a moment, remembering all he'd read about night fighters and the way they crept up on crippled bombers during the return journey. Then, abruptly:

'Have you ever been shot at – badly, I mean? I mean, has your aeroplane ever been badly damaged?'

'By flak, yes. Over the target area. You know what flak is, I expect. I made one very ropey landing after flak damage to my tail section and landing gear.'

'Was anyone hurt?'

'I'd two dead on board,' the Squadron Leader answered in what seemed at first an oddly matter-of-fact sort of way. 'The rear gunner, and my wireless operator. Both bought it over the target area. J-Jezebel, too. Then, on the return, we fell foul of a night fighter. But the mid upper got him before he could finish us off. All the same, it was touch and go. They'd the fire engines and the blood wagon out for us when I finally put her down. Those of us who were alive got out all right, but the old girl went up in flames. Sparks,

Set what was left of the fuel alight. And – Bob's your uncle! She was a write off after that.'

'Gosh! – it must have been awful!' And, tentatively: 'Were you scared?'

The Squadron Leader wiped his blade on a wodge of toilet paper. Set it down and viewed his newly smooth jaw in the glass. His features now were without even a hint of a smile. And it was then that Martin realised how deep an impression the incident had in fact made on him.

'You could,' he said, 'put it that way. It certainly made me think.'

Martin looked at him for what seemed an age before: 'What did you think about?'

The Squadron Leader put the plug in the basin, turned both taps on full.

'What I was doing – or what I wasn't doing, rather. What I ought to do before I got the chop. Trouble is, you forget. Too quickly, y'know? Same with this war. As soon as it's over, they'll forget. Like after the last one. Can't blame them, can you?'

Martin wasn't sure what he meant. But he'd an inkling. He was a naughty boy, and ought perhaps to do something about it before it was too late. But hell! – you only lived once.

In spite of which the Squadron Leader – in the last minute or two – had taken on an added dimension. Which complicated Martin's feelings toward him somewhat. He was no longer just a bounder. He was also a hero.

'No. I suppose not.'

The Squadron Leader splashed his face and neck with water, grabbed a towel.

'Still, I was lucky really.'

'Have you ever been to Germany? – other than on a raid, I mean.'

'When I was just a lad – for a holiday, y'know? But they're all too serious for me, those Jerries.'

'Have you been anywhere else . . .?'

He laughed.

'Not really. Just a short spell when my squadron was posted.'

'Where was that?'
'Egypt. Back in 'thirty-eight.'
'Gosh! I've always wanted to go there. Was it hot?'
The Squadron Leader grinned.
'It certainly was. Now! – I must get dressed.'

At breakfast they were again served separately. But they'd a minute or two with the Squadron Leader in the hall as he was about to drive their mother off somewhere.

He was smartly dressed, wore his cap at a dashing angle, and smiled the whole of the time. Cecily literally threw herself at him. Shrieked with excitement. She then got a wigging from her mother, which turned her red and petulant, and there were threats to send her straight back to bed. Throughout the whole of which incident the Squadron Leader remained impartial, smiling as before.

Martin, however, was almost as embarrassed by it as his sister. Felt, too, that his mother was unnecessarily severe. And that, in an oblique sort of way, Cecily was in fact being punished for something else. Something to do with her being a little girl rather than a little boy.

Then they were gone. And the house, it seemed, fell suddenly asleep. Cecily went off on her own somewhere, and Martin found himself with nothing to do.

He wandered at last into the garden. Into the warm sanctuary of the summerhouse, where he took possession of a deckchair and watched the breeze at work among the boughs of the ornamental cherry.

Here, for the present, was neither sight nor sound of war. But Martin, as his imagination dreamed among the endlessly shifting leaves, thrilled still to the Squadron Leader's heroic tale. To the images it invoked.

He taxied, in the gathering dusk, out onto the peri-track. And, the four mighty Merlins at full revs, lifted at last off the runway and grabbed for height.

A sickening lurch as the Lanc, her belly empty now, shot up like a lift. Below, an incredible show of pyrotechnics.

Crippled, she dipped away. But soon fell prey to a lurking night fighter.

The flash of her guns amidships. Another, bigger flash. And the fighter sank slowly away into the bottomless pit of night.

A shower of sparks on the home airfield. A billowing ball of flame. . .

To Cecily, he supposed, the Squadron Leader was like a sort of Father Christmas – as generous with himself as with the gifts he brought. But more dashing, by far. A source of endless fun. And whose maleness was in some strange way more powerful than that of a father or brother.

He wasn't sure exactly how his mother saw him. But knew that – like both her and his sister, though for a different reason – he was himself enthralled.

Except that, unlike them, his vision remained painfully clear.

The evening of that day, with its two extremes of emotional temperature, would long remain in his memory.

The half hour before dinner was spent with the Squadron Leader in the lounge. This was obviously at his suggestion, for Cecily – though the threat of punishment was apparently withdrawn – was still under something of a cloud.

Their mother, however, was not present. She was in the kitchen with Vera, assisting in the preparation of the evening meal. Which, in itself, struck Martin as unusual. It was as though, by her absence, she disowned all three of them.

The Squadron Leader played first on the piano. And Cecily – in her element, and altogether unaware of the atmosphere outside – pranced like a circus horse to a succession of rolling tunes last aired, no doubt, in the officers' mess. And of whose implications she was instinctively aware. She twirled, shrieked, and threw up her skirts until – half dead of excitement – she collapsed at last in a squealing heap on the sofa. Where the Squadron Leader teased and tickled her till she was altogether exhausted.

He turned himself next into a 'gee-gee'. Sat her up on his shoulders and galloped round the room snorting and whinnying in a magnificently convincing manner.

Then, for Martin's benefit, he became an aeroplane; simulating to perfection the sound of four engines turning over, catching, and roaring at last into life. He made a bombing run; went into action with the twin Brownings; blew up a night fighter, and puttered finally to a halt on the home airfield. Both children were amused by this; but Martin was particularly fascinated. For him, it was more than just a lot of funny noises; it was the closest he'd yet been to the real thing.

But the evening died on a sour note. The Squadron Leader was to leave early the following morning. And, when Martin and his sister went in to say goodbye, there was a decidedly charged atmosphere between the two adults.

The Squadron Leader stood again before the mantel-shelf with its Chinese vases and ormolu clock flanked on either side by bronze cherubs. Their mother was seated – not, as before, close by – but near the window. Motionless; her eyes dark wells in the evening light, her features set like a mask. Martin then realised, with a sense of shock, that they had quarrelled. Or, at least, that there had been a serious disagreement. Though what it was all about, he couldn't imagine.

The Squadron Leader, though, was as friendly as before. Whatever had transpired since they saw him last didn't appear to have affected him too deeply.

Either that, or he was a very good actor.

He kissed Cecily, and shook Martin's hand. Firmly, as though he were a grown man.

Their mother looked on without a word. Her expression was that of one in a trance.

Like when their father died. Only different.

'I suppose, now, I shan't see you again. Is that it?'

Martin, his heart in his mouth, listened at the top of the stairs. What his mother meant by this, he didn't know. Other than that it confirmed his own fears as to the Squadron Leader's sincerity. But the tone of her voice appalled him. Bitter, defensive, and at the same time potentially explosive, it made him afraid of what might follow. Something terrible must have happened. Something really big, to jolt her like that.

The Squadron Leader, however, remained apparently calm.

'Look – I told you. I only saw her a couple of times. I hardly know her.'

A pause. Until, at last:

'Then give the letter to me. I'll burn it.'

'Yes. Of course. If that's what you wish. But really, you're taking it far too seriously. . .'

'Give it to me!'

From where he stood even, Martin could feel the commanding power of her stare.

The Squadron Leader, undaunted in battle, fell before her attack. There was a further pause. During which, with what seemed a certain reluctance, he at last parted with whatever it was they were arguing over.

'Now: promise me it will never happen again.'

'I don't', he said, 'understand you at all. All this is based on assumption.'

'She would understand. Of that I'm pretty sure.' And, abruptly: 'Who is she?'

'I told you – I don't know. Someone I met at a party. In fact, I'd forgotten all about her. But you know what women are. . .'

'You forgot, yes. But she didn't.'

The Squadron Leader spoke at last with some asperity.

'Well that, I'm afraid, is quite beyond my control.'

An odd sort of silence.

'Darling, I – swear to me you'll never see her again.' And, on a broken note: 'I beg you. . .'

He answered gravely.

'I will never,' he said, 'see her again. She's of no interest to me whatever.'

A further silence.

She was, at last, convinced. Or nearly so.

She said something in a lowered tone which Martin didn't quite catch. Something about her 'poor heart'. And:

'Never, never leave me.'

There was a longer, deeper silence.
Martin thought it was time he went.

But had made up his mind already that, when the house was
quiet, he would slip down and see if there was anything left
of the offending letter.

It was another hour or so before his mother – followed,
shortly after, by the Squadron Leader – came up to bed.
Martin had difficulty in keeping awake. Was on the verge
of sleep when he heard them.

Now, again, his eyes were wide open. He sat quietly up
and hugged his knees; waited till they were settled. It wasn't
long before the house at last fell silent, and the water finally
stopped rushing.

The case clock on the wall downstairs struck a half hour
after midnight.

He peered across at his sister. She was fast asleep; half
turned into the pillow. The night light was nearly out. Fluttered grotesquely across the wall like pale, desperate fingers.

He put back the bedclothes, slipped across to the door.
His heart beat so fast he was sure everyone could hear it.
His sister, however, didn't move. And, when at last he
opened the door, there was neither sight nor sound of
anyone.

It was also very dark.

He had to steel himself for the long descent. Every nightmare he'd ever had leapt up before his mind's eye, astonishingly vivid. Seemed to blaze against the darkness.

There wasn't a light anywhere, indoors or out. Or, if
there was, he saw nothing through the heavy curtains and
blackout blinds. But he daren't put on the landing light.
Nor, for the present, did he dare switch on his torch.

After what seemed an age, he at last reached the bottom.
Released his breath and listened a moment. Not a sound. All
he could hear was the slow, reassuringly regular tick of the
clock.

He put on his torch. Familiar objects stole now out of the
darkness like friends from out the past. Paused, part-formed

by what now seemed to Martin a very small light. Familiar,
yet – as with old friends – somehow changed.

He grit his teeth. Crept across the hall, the narrow beam
wavering before him. It hovered now over the mahogany
panels of the drawing-room doors with their ornamental
knobs and lockplates.

Cautiously, he turned the knob on the right and one heavy
half swung silently open. Surprised, the room – the objects
in it, rather – turned their eyes upon him. Again, the familiar
was somehow slightly changed. It was a bit like entering a
room full of people all talking loudly but who then fell
suddenly silent, turned to stare. Curious. Part resentful.

The air was close, and smelled of flowers.

He went straight to the fireplace. Crouching, he peered
past the ornamental urn into the dark recess of the grate –
blacked by Vera to a shining perfection. The beam of his
torch probed the cold depths of the fire basket. His heart
jumped. There they were! – the charred fragments of the
letter!

Some of the pieces were not quite burned through, and
the ink was still visible on them. With bated breath, he
looked on them as Carter must have looked upon the treasure
of Tutankhamen.

But listened rather than looked. Listened with all his ears.
Could hear the clock in the hall still, but nothing else. Ought
he perhaps to have closed the door after him?

But reached instead tentatively into the grate – having first
taken stock of the pattern formed by the pieces so he could
replace them more or less as he'd found them.

From what was left, it was evident that this was a love
letter. The hand was full and rounded, like a child's. The
characters carefully formed in the manner of an artless,
certainly honest, but probably rather slow thinker. He'd a
mental picture of a fashionably dressed, red lipped, naively
romantic woman who – like his mother – had fallen victim
to the Squadron Leader's charms.

'Ring me, please, when you – '

And:

'I must . . . you again. I pray for you every – '

And:

'I don't forget that – '

And:

'. . . my darling. Those same stars I see from my window watch – '

And that was all.

He carefully replaced the fragments. Was, he realised, biting so hard on his lip it hurt.

He got up. Crept back to the door, slipped out, and closed it silently behind him.

He looked quickly across at the stair. No one. Nothing. As soon as he'd gained a footing there, he put out the torch.

He reached the top without mishap. And was crossing the landing to where a second, smaller flight led up to his own bedroom, when suddenly the landing light went on.

He froze. Stared. It was as if he were trapped in the full glare of a searchlight.

Equally astonished it seemed, the Squadron Leader, too, stared.

Again, he wore only his pyjama trousers. Had come – not from his own room – but from the large room at the back of the house. The one into which Martin's mother had moved after his father's death. And retained now as her own.

Neither spoke. For each was guilty. Each was afraid.

The Squadron Leader recovered first.

'Goodnight old man. . .'

'Goodnight sir.'

But saw only the pale face conjured up by the charred fragments of the letter. The sad, withdrawn gaze of a woman compromised.

Life, during the days which followed, ground it seemed to a halt. And, while the threat of a storm appeared to have diminished – like a brief but violent gust of wind – there was a sense, too, of anti-climax. Of suspension.

Cecily, of course, mourned the Squadron Leader's absence – and hence, if only indirectly, that of her mother. Who was more often away from home than before even.

She seemed again furiously happy. Whether she had in

fact forgotten her quarrel, or whether there was instead a
degree of self-deception at work here, Martin couldn't be
sure. Any more than he could have put a name to any of
these peculiarly adult, terrifyingly esoteric goings on.

When she returned from these trips it was in a nearly
visible aura of night clubs, theatres, and the precarious
romance of the blackout. All of which illusion was broken
by the reality of an occasional air raid. Or, worse perhaps,
by the Squadron Leader's return to duty and their enforced
separation. Plus, Martin guessed, a certain uneasiness on her
part as to what he might get up to in the meantime.

And it was as if something of all this rubbed off on her –
like gold dust from the wafer thin pages of his leather bound
missal at school.

And her eyes so bright and flashing she frightened him.
Like one in the grip of a fierce fever.

Cecily alternately moped and pestered Vera for news of
her mother's return so that – when at last this came about –
she might then pester her mother for news of the Squadron
Leader. But for Martin there was only boredom. And a sense
of rejection. Of neglect.

His mother, when she was at home, no longer asked for
news of his activities. Her mind was always miles away.
Quite literally. Prey both to her passion and a nagging sense
of doubt. It was as if every time she returned, she left it
behind. Along with all the feeling of which she was capable.
And brought back only her fraught, her prancing nerves,
and a devouring restlessness.

Vera may have sensed his discomfort.

Did her best, in her grumbling way, to divert them both.
She took them down to the sea as often as she was able –
something for which, normally, she was always 'too busy'.

There – in her hat and coat, and with her handbag on her
arm (she always 'dressed' for the beach, as in winter) – she
squinted into the lens of Martin's box camera while nagging
him to 'hurry up and get it over with; she did so dislike
having her photo taken'. (Something to do with a story her

mother had told her about losing one's soul. Like if one looked in a mirror, or had one's portrait painted.)

She was not, of course, attractive. They both agreed on that – Cecily rather more fiercely. Her eyes were black and hard as beetle's wings; her lips like tightly tucked in sheets. But she'd a basic dependability, a steady if irritable temperament, which ultimately endeared her to the children. And could be relied on, even if reluctant, to participate in whatever they might suggest. Provided, of course, that it wasn't in any way 'improper'.

Cecily, however, insisted on engaging the attention of total strangers – uniformed ones especially – and Vera, poker faced, threatened to put a stop to the 'excursions', as she called them, if she didn't behave 'more like a little lady'.

Her fear of strangers seemed based, not on the usual reasons ladies gave for repudiating their advances, but on the 'far from remote' possibility of their being Germans in disguise. And so the gulls wheeled persistently overhead while they sat together in a formidably tight little circle surrounded by the enemy in British uniform. The Germans, she reminded them, were only 'over there'. What was to prevent them popping across whenever they felt like it? – oh, yes!, it could be done, believe you me.

Martin did try pointing out that the Channel was fairly wide at this point, but it made no difference. One could never, she said, be too careful.

Stranger things had of course happened. And it grew into a rather exciting sort of game – while they drank lukewarm tea from the thermos flask and the wind took Vera's hat on a flight or two along the front (very dangerous: for the Enemy might seize on this as an opportunity to introduce himself) – to pick out those who looked most likely to have been sent by Hitler to put their sneaky talents to the test in this small, unobtrusive, totally dull little seaside town.

For that, Vera assured them, was how the Invasion would come about. Not by force, but by stealth.

'The enemy,' she reminded them, 'is always listening.'

Once, her hat blew over the barbed wire where you couldn't walk. And she had to go home without it.

★

'Suppose,' Martin suggested, 'the Squadron Leader is a spy? I mean, he does behave in an odd sort of way sometimes.'

But Vera did not – as he'd half hoped – jump at the idea.

She told him off instead for 'walking with your dirty shoes all over my clean floor'.

And then, without thinking:

'He may be a philanderer – but he wouldn't, I'm sure, stoop to anything like that.'

'What,' Martin asked, 'is a philanderer?'

She slipped a pot of clean water in through the bars of the birdcage, drew down the glass panel which kept it – and the canary – in place. She could, Martin knew, have bitten her tongue.

'Never you mind!' she snapped. And then, suddenly nervous: 'And don't go repeating what I say to your mother please!'

'Is it something bad?' he persisted.

'Lord!, you children!'

But there was evidently a deep buried desire to unburden herself to someone. It was natural perhaps, having spent more time in his company over the previous week or two than in all the years she'd been here, that she should turn to him.

She looked at him a moment. Martin presented as reliable an appearance as he was able to muster. She obviously decided she could trust him.

'You're growing up a bit now. But you mightn't, perhaps, understand . . . I'm not criticising, you see. It's just that, during this unsettling period – having just lost your father and that – your mother, quite innocently of course, could fall prey to persons whose intentions are not entirely honourable.'

'How do you mean?'

She took in her lower lip, held it fast a moment. Then:

'The Squadron Leader, I'm sure, is a very fine man. But your father, I feel, would not altogether have approved of him.' And: 'I took his jacket – there was a spot of something on the sleeve. Your mother asked me to see that it was removed. His wallet was inside still – though I didn't know that at the time. Like her no doubt, I never gave it a thought.

But, when I sat down and took the jacket across my knees, there it was on the floor!' Again she paused. From her expression, Martin realised how shaken she'd been by the experience. Ever upright, the sight of the fallen wallet must have horrified her. 'I didn't see inside, mind. It fell face down. But it was open. And, when I picked it up . . . There was a photo. Of a lady.' She shook her head. 'Well, I don't know. But it seems very wrong somehow.'

Martin, haunted still by his personal vision of the sad author of that fateful missive, stared.

Vera, of course, mistook his silence.

'But I don't expect you to understand. These things are not for children. And it's not my place to comment on them. It seems a pity, that's all. That your mother should be so taken advantage of, I mean.' And, wagging her finger at him: 'And no repeating what I've said please. Your mother would be very cross were she to hear about it. And your sister is certainly too young to understand.'

Martin was so grateful for her collusion he wouldn't have dreamed of betraying her confidence. But he couldn't help wondering, as far as his mother was concerned, whether she'd got it quite right . . .

'I promise,' he vowed, 'I shan't say a word.'

Then, one night, his mother returned late. She was deeply excited. Her 'London' aura fairly blazed about her, like a sort of silent fanfare. Proclamation of a victory won through sheer determination.

She came at once to his room. Alighted like some small jewelled predator on the side of his bed.

She'd her glossy sable coat on still. Every hair of which seemed stiff with excitement as, smiling, she put the hair gently back from his forehead. She smelt of perfume, of cigarette smoke, and of her carriage compartment – that is, of engine soot. Just a whiff, but unmistakable.

He was angry, because he knew very well why she'd come. But there was, too, a deep appeal to his sense of the romantic. Of long journeys taken at great peril. Of that strange magnetism between man and woman – that 'love which knows no fear'. And of the terrible melancholy this love apparently engendered.

'Would you like to hear a secret?'

As when she'd asked him to guess who was coming for the weekend, Martin knew at once what she was going to say.

But this, of course, did not occur to her. She was going, she told him, to marry again.

So, really, it didn't matter that they were lovers already . . .

'Would you like that darling? – would you like a new daddy?'

Martin – furious at an interest renewed after long neglect, and with such intensity – didn't at first know what to say. Not that it mattered what he – or anyone else – said or thought. Her mind was long made up. What she had learned with the discovery of The Letter had served only – despite her bitter disappointment – to strengthen her determination.

Now, at last, she had what she wanted. But was barely recognisable as the woman who was married to his father. Or perhaps, as an act of bravado, she somehow disguised herself – or an aspect of herself – and behaved now as she thought was expected of her. But Martin felt, as he looked into her electric eyes, that she was an undeniably beautiful but rather frightening stranger.

'Yes,' he said, deliberately brief. 'All right.'

But 'new daddies' were more like an unpleasant medicine: they took some swallowing. Did she really imagine this man could step without fuss into his father's shoes – and so soon?

Perhaps not. For her eyes were at the same time terribly shrewd. All this was a formality only. Having, as she thought, secured her lover, she wasn't going to let anyone mess things up for her now.

'Now darling, please. No nonsense. The Squadron Leader is very fond of you both. We'll start a new life. Imagine, when this horrid war is over, what it will be like.' And: 'You want, surely, to see poor mummy happy again?'

He swallowed hard. She knew – must know, as well as he – that the romance was doomed. That it was a question, rather, of pride.

But could no longer look into her eyes. Vera, he realised, had been too generous in her judgement. And his mother's attempt to blackmail him into acceptance of the unacceptable threw a shadow across his heart.

'Yes . . .'

Aware, however, of his true feelings, and seeing that Cecily now threatened to wake, she withdrew abruptly as from something bad.

During the following few days, she effectively kept herself from him.

Isolated, and of course hurt, Martin only hardened. That she should enforce a sense of guilt over what he felt to be an unfair issue seemed to him terribly wrong. Not for the first time, he felt himself to be sadly wiser than she.

She was eventually less indifferent toward him, but no real reconciliation came about between them. She was in any case too absorbed now to worry much about either child.

Then, again, the Squadron Leader came down.

And, again, Martin was forced to accommodate himself to a situation he found not altogether agreeable. A situation not only distasteful in itself, but in the atmosphere it brought with it. What – had he been an adult – he'd have described perhaps as tense.

It seemed, for instance, that his mother no longer thought it necessary to conceal from them – or from anyone – the exact nature of the relationship. Martin was astonished at the blatancy with which she now conducted the affair. Caring nothing for their opinion or for anyone else's. Either that, or she was extraordinarily naive. Or she may have believed that everyone save herself went about with their eyes closed.

Either way, Martin couldn't understand her reasoning. Everyone knew exactly what was going on – or they guessed. And he was constantly embarrassed by what Vera – and, apparently, the entire neighbourhood – regarded as her 'wild' behaviour.

★

Now – lying across the bathroom chair – the Squadron Leader's pyjama trousers. And (more deeply disturbing) a garment which must, he supposed, belong to his mother. Like a sort of bodice with knickers combined. In softest crêpe-de-chine, and trimmed with lace.

He stood a moment in the warm afternoon light (the pair had not come down to breakfast: had lunched early instead, and were gone now into the garden) and stared. It was as if he'd stumbled on a frightened – and, therefore, violently aggressive – snake.

The cami-knickers were in a subtle shade of peach. And so shamelessly luxurious in these times of utility wear they must be what Vera called 'black market'. They appeared to have been placed deliberately between the legs of the trousers; which lustfully embraced them. There was, too, a faint but unmistakable smell. Partly pleasant; partly not. Attractive in the broadest sense, like that of a rotting fungus. And peculiarly suited to the wet warmth of the atmosphere here.

Some sort of joke they'd enjoyed together in private. Now – either because they'd forgotten, or because they just didn't care – made appallingly public.

His eye detached itself at last – with difficulty – from this extraordinary spectacle, with its disturbing undertones, and wandered across the floor to the bath.

It had not been cleaned. A greenish stain indicated the level of the now absent water. The air reeked of an unwittingly concupiscent oil of pine.

'Bathe your beauty', ran the slogan on the abandoned bottle, 'in the haunting perfume of the rain-drenched pines.'

Conspiratorial drops of condensation wobbled apologetically down the wall . . .

Martin absorbed the aftermath of their little orgy in silence.

Obviously, they'd bathed together.

The idea of which, while it invited a certain salacious humour, nevertheless repelled him.

'Oh, look!' Cecily shrieked, clapping her open hand across her mouth. 'Mummy's knickers!'

She understood at once – and accepted without a qualm

– the full significance of the little tableau. Thrilled to it instinctively.

Martin, deeply shamed, turned away.

Saw, then, that his mother's bedroom door stood open. And, drawn back along the passage, looked in.

It was a large room. Bright, high ceilinged, airy.

It was finished in soft, opalescent blues and greys. Directly opposite was the big bay window with its floor length, blue brocade curtains. And, within the bay, the mahogany dressing table with its triple mirrors, its assortment of mysterious alchemies within their delicately tinted porcelain pots.

But though – in complete contrast to that in the bathroom – the scene here was calm and orderly, there was an atmosphere, too, of enigma. Which – epitomising, as it did, his mother's near total withdrawal – filled him with despair.

The one indication of impropriety was the chair which stood before the glass. Over whose shoulders was draped the Squadron Leader's smart blue jacket with its banded cuffs. The last thing one would have expected to see in so obviously feminine a room, it seemed somehow to leap at him.

His heart, too, leapt. Stood momentarily still.

He plucked up courage at last, went across. The two protectively outstretched wings over the breast pocket were like some powerful seal set before the entrance to a tomb.

He hesitated.

Then, abruptly, he put his hand inside and felt for the wallet. The leather at once warmed to his touch, like a live thing. His heart beat suddenly fast.

He glanced across at the door. But saw no one – not Cecily even.

He carefully withdrew the wallet. Opened it, and looked inside. But was disappointed. And, at first, startled. There was no picture at all. Or, rather, not the one for which he was looking. There was a picture only of his mother: a dazzling smile across her face.

He then realised that the Squadron Leader would not have risked displaying the other now. If he carried it at all, he would carry it secretly. Here perhaps? – tucked away inside.

Yes.

But the corner had fallen prey to fire – to an applied flame. (Martin could imagine him – the inevitable cigarette between his lips – setting it deliberately alight. Then, at the last moment – prodded perhaps by some gratifying memory – relenting.) But the photo was otherwise exactly as Vera must have seen it.

A woman about thirty. Very attractive. In a small hat, such as his mother sometimes wore, with a veil. And with a full fur collar turned up against her cheek. The features immensely vulnerable, deeply mysterious. Exactly as he had imagined.

Across the corner, in the same careful hand which had penned what was to be her last letter, was inscribed:

'For my darling Peter. With love, Ray. May God guard and bring you safely back to me.'

Martin stood for what seemed to him an age, transfixed.

What was it Vera had called him? – a philanderer. Though he had never heard the word before, it seemed to him now sharply inappropriate. Too kind, by far. He sensed, too, that this poor, sad creature was not the first to have suffered as a result of the Squadron Leader's deceit. His mother, too – who'd yet to learn that what is bad is not necessarily unattractive – would have her turn. And, should the errant hero survive another tour of operations, others yet to come.

He returned the portrait to its hiding place. Likewise the wallet. Then, on an impulse, went to the window.

There they were.

Together under the ornamental cherry.

She, laughing, was looking up into the tree. He – shrewd, and sure of himself – was watching her. He'd a special sort of smile for women. Light, lopsided, and with his eyes half closed as if against the smoke of a cigarette.

He'd just lit one now. Threw back his head and, tossing the match away, drew deeply at it, his cheeks hollowed like those of an emaciated despot. The line of his lips followed a cruel, scimitar-like downward curve. Or, at best, was blatantly cynical. But she, magnetized, looked now into his eyes like one possessed.

He dropped his jaw, allowing the smoke from his cigarette

to roll slowly over his open lips like some soundless wave
breaking upon the shore of a dream. Released, it hung like
a muslin veil lightly on the air between them.

He then took hold of her face, as he might that of a child.
Firmly, and with a forceful arrogance. And angling his head
– as Martin had seen him do before – like some cruel predator
about to strike, he kissed her vehemently on the lips.

Martin, unobserved within the deep fold of the curtain,
bit hard on his own.

That same evening, Martin – coming in at the gate – saw
him again.

He'd spent the greater part of the afternoon looking for
butterflies on a bomb site at the bottom of the avenue.
Buddleia grew there in profusion, and was smothered in
butterflies – even the rarer Swallowtail, which Vera had
forbidden him to touch. It was after six, and very warm
still, when he got back. But, here in front, the trees afforded
a fair amount of shade.

The Squadron Leader was out cutting the grass. He'd done
about half already: was going at it with a good deal of
enthusiasm, a newly lit cigarette jutting upward from the
corner of his mouth.

He caught sight of Martin as he turned at the far side to
come back across, and it was of course too late then to
escape.

'Ah! – hello there!'

Martin stood awkwardly on the path, his net in one hand
and a covered jam jar in the other. The front of the house
was splashed across still with sunlight, also that part of the
lawn nearest to it. But the bottom half was steeped in long
shadows thrown by the trees. There was a light, warm
breeze; and the shadows moved restlessly back and forth.
The air was sweetly pungent with the scent of severed green.
There was no sound except that of the old hand mower and
an occasional note from a startled bird.

'Hello,' Martin said.

The Squadron Leader rested his arm a moment on the
handle of the mower, took the cigarette from his lips and –

throwing back his head – gave out a wobbly smoke ring or two. He grinned.

'What've you been up to, eh?'

'I – I was looking for butterflies,' Martin answered. 'There are lots down on the bomb site.'

'Looks like they'd a direct hit there – when was that?'

'The year before last.' And, because he couldn't think what else to say: 'It's hot, isn't it?'

The Squadron Leader drew the back of his hand across his forehead.

'You're right there. Warmest day of the year, I'd say.'

'What about when you were in Egypt? – was it hot then?'

He put the cigarette back between his lips, pushed his shirt sleeves further up his arms.

'God, yes. It was really hot there.'

Martin wasn't sure about the Squadron Leader's use – or misuse – of the Lord's name. The emphasis he placed on it, the hardness he gave to it, seemed somehow blasphemous. In spite of which, however, Martin's interest was roused.

'Did you see any tombs?'

'I'd say. You can't miss them.'

'What? – are they . . .?'

'Everywhere, yes. And the pyramids of course are a terrific size.'

Martin thought a moment.

'Did you like it there?'

'I'd no option really. But it was very interesting – if you like old monuments, and that sort of thing. Trouble was it was so stinking hot. And, you know, it literally stank. If a dog died in the street, it was left there to rot. Smothered in flies. We chaps had to carry fly whisks to keep the dam' things off. Otherwise they walked all over you – all over your eyes and mouth. And, if you opened your mouth, they walked right in. Filthy.'

Martin wrinkled his nose.

But felt that this blunt speech was intended not so much as an indication of equality – man, as it were, to man – as of a thinly-disguised contempt. What was he after all but the infuriatingly curious, awkwardly male child of this man's mistress? A not altogether enviable role. Nor, it seemed, did the Squadron Leader intend that it should be. And this was his way perhaps – with Cecily absent – of putting him in his place.

Martin was both angry and ashamed. And there was, he knew, another side to life in places like Cairo. The father of one of his friends at school was in North Africa, and – wounded out of the war – told him all sorts of grown up stories. All about the night clubs, and things like that. And about the dancers. And how a chap had to 'look out', because half of them were spies.

'I told you, I think – I was posted there with the Squadron. Hawker Hinds, we were flying then. I expect you've heard of them? Nice little aeroplane. But not, of course, in the same league with what we have now. They were already hopelessly out of date then.'

Martin licked his lips. He could hear the Red Admiral he had in his jar beating its wings frantically against the paper cover.

'Did you go to nightclubs?'

The Squadron Leader looked straight at him. His face was virtually expressionless. He then dropped his eyes – thickly lashed, like a girl's – and his eyebrows shot suddenly up into his hair.

'Not very often. They kept us pretty busy you know.'

Martin was silent a moment. Then:

'Did you have lots of girlfriends?'

Again the Squadron Leader stared. Then, at last, he smiled a lopsided, faintly lewd smile.

'Naturally. We all did.' And: 'You know what the poet said: "A man's a man, for a' that".'

Martin, too, stared. He saw, vividly before his mind's eye, the haunting – because haunted – portrait he'd found inside the wallet.

'Mummy says you're getting married – to her, I mean.'

He knew at once that something was wrong. The Squadron Leader put the cigarette abruptly back into his mouth. And, with his eyes part closed against the smoke, brought the mower forward into the verge. A shower of bruised blades went up like confetti before sinking dispiritedly down into the grass box. The air was filled with their acid aroma.

'Yes. Will you like that?'

Martin adroitly avoided this question.

'What about your girlfriends? – won't they mind?'

The Squadron Leader swung the mower about and started off in the opposite direction. He laughed a short, hard laugh. But Martin bet he was glad he – Martin – couldn't see his face.

'I haven't any now.'

Martin daren't accuse him. Watched, instead, as he ambled after the mower, his wrists and forearms fluffy in a narrow beam of sunlight which wavered through the trees. He waited until, having turned, he came again toward him. Then:

'Why?'

The Squadron Leader was acting superbly. His eyebrows rose again.

'I don't know really. Getting too old perhaps.' He grinned. But the smile was gone as quickly as it came. 'No: I'd like to settle down now. This war can't go on much longer. We're bombing the hell out of them over there.'

Martin caught sight suddenly of the large gold ring he wore on the third finger of his left hand. He was, he knew, pushing his luck. But was carried now on a wave of recklessness.

'Did you get that in Egypt?'

The Squadron Leader ground again to a halt. He narrowed his eyes in a thoughtful sort of way. This child was a persistent little so-and-so. He ought, really, to give him a clout.

'What are you after old chap? There are no skeletons in my cupboard.'

Oh!, but he lied. Though why he deemed this necessary Martin couldn't imagine. There must be more to him than met the eye even.

'No, sir. I'm sure. It's just that – '

'That?'

'I just wondered. I've a schoolfriend: and his father has a ring like that. It – it was given to him when he married. As a sort of wedding ring I suppose. Only yours is different. It – it looks sort of foreign.'

It was like his words had inadvertently revealed a brilliant truth. But one which, like a gem within the rock, remained part hidden still.

The Squadron Leader smiled. His features, it seemed, broke into a thousand enigmatic fragments – each a part of the puzzle, but none a perfect fit – which flew then in all directions. So that the garden, shocked, stood momentarily still. The trees, even, ceased to move. Nor was there any sound.

'And so?'

Martin, equally shocked, swallowed hard.

'N – no.' he stammered. 'Nothing.'

The Squadron Leader looked at him a moment. One eye part closed against the smoke of his cigarette. The smile was gone. And there was a sort of archness about him now that Martin found suddenly unnerving.

An atmosphere, briefly, of darkness. Like during an eclipse. As if the sun had gone. Only it hadn't. Something huge. Overwhelming. Martin, barely able to regard that bleakly cruel countenance, shuddered.

'I – I ought to go now. Vera will wonder where I am.'

The Squadron Leader's chin came down a fraction. As if it were brought down by the gears of a machine. His lips broke soundlessly open. He smiled. Sort of.

'See you later then.'

'Yes,' Martin eagerly agreed. 'I expect so.'

Alone at last in his room, he opened the window and set the butterfly free.

The following day – Saturday – Vera took them to the cinema. It was a Marx Brothers film. There were a lot of crazy goings-on, a lot of laughs. But Martin was particularly struck by the sad, speechless features of Harpo with his round, wonderful, child-like eyes, and his tight blonde curls which reminded him of wood shavings on a workshop floor.

But Cecily was bored by their antics. She wanted beautiful ladies in beautiful dresses; or the deep, esoteric romance of a story like 'Rebecca'. Which she hadn't really understood, but to whose dark passions she had instinctively thrilled.

On the way home, each holding on to one of Vera's hands, they argued furiously over their next choice. Until, her patience exhausted, she finally shut them up.

'For goodness' sake stop it! Or there won't be a next time – and that's for sure!'

It was this little incident which gave rise, later, to a furious row between them. They ate their tea more or less in silence, Vera tut-tutting all the while and accusing each in turn of a 'show of temper'. Which didn't of course help. The atmosphere only grew more explosive.

'I think it was a silly film!' Cecily blurted out as soon as they were alone together in the summerhouse, to which Vera had packed them off 'until such time as their tempers should have improved'. Then, and then only, they might return to the house.

Martin glared. He knew at once that this was only the bait for a full scale fight; but rose to it regardless.

'At least there weren't a lot of soppy love scenes. When I've saved some pocket money I'm going to see it again – so there!'

'No you're not! It's my turn – so there!'

'You're stupid!'

'So are you!'

'Not as stupid as you! All you care about is silly dresses and showing off!'

She turned furiously on him.

'You're jealous! You're jealous because Peter likes me better than you! I'm going to tell him when I see him. I'm going to tell him about all the beastly things you've said – so there!'

Martin – dazzled by this display of pure rage – was momentarily stunned. Her accusation seemed to him so ludicrous he couldn't at first think of a suitably scornful reply. Then:

'I don't care if you do. He's a fibber, like you. I know, because he fibbed to mummy about the other lady. He said he'd never see her again, but he's got a photo of her in his wallet!' And then, in a sudden flash of inspiration: 'And he'll never be your daddy, because he's married already!'

The enormity of what he'd just said filled him at once with superstitious dread. It was, of course, a lie. Or, if not a lie — for it certainly didn't feel like one — then what his father might have called a shot in the dark. Something he sensed to be true, but couldn't possibly prove. Any more than he could say why he sensed it to be true.

But, having now escaped his lips, it was no longer a mere figment of his imagination. It was a fact. And there was no going back on it. What was said could not be unsaid.

Cecily, her anger forgotten, looked at him in amazement. Her expression now was as blank as his own must have been just a moment ago. She couldn't have been more surprised had he leapt suddenly, fully formed, from out the pages of a story book. And, clothed in his lie, he in fact felt like he was ringed around with some other-world aura, dull rather than bright, like black sheet lightning.

It was she who recovered first.

'What lady?'

Martin, already deeply penitent, hung his head.

'I'm sorry. I didn't mean it. Honestly . . .'

Again she stared. Until, at last:

'He will be my daddy though. And yours too. He said so.'

But there was an uncertainty to her tone which made him suddenly afraid. Suppose she were to seek verification of this — from either their mother, or from the Squadron Leader himself?

'Yes. I know. Don't tell anyone what I said — I'll give you that little picture in my prayer book if you promise not to say anything.'

Her eyes lit again with excitement. She'd wanted the picture for ages, but he'd refused till now to part with it.

'All right. I promise.'

He went straight upstairs and took the prayer book out from under his pillow. The tiny portrait, bordered with gold, was slipped in between the pages. The Virgin with a sword through her heart. Our Lady of Sorrows.

He looked at it a moment. Felt that his own heart was similarly assailed.

Cecily watched as her mother sat down at the dressing table. She'd twisted herself round inside the curtain, and only her head was visible.

'Darling! – I've told you before: don't do that. You'll have the whole thing down. Come out at once, and put it straight.'

She slowly unwound herself, and stepped gingerly out. As always when her will was opposed, she was pouting and truculent.

She stood a moment at her mother's side. Then reached out suddenly and picked up one of the little cosmetic pots she so admired but had already been told she mustn't touch.

'Is this what you're putting on?'

'No darling. That's face powder. This is cold cream. And look – must I tell you again? Don't touch!'

Reluctantly, she returned the pot to its place.

'What will it do? Make you pretty?'

'Why? – aren't I pretty already?'

'Yes.'

But it was a dutiful rather than enthusiastic response.

Her mother looked quickly at her. Cecily, her lashes apparently glued to her fat red cheeks, poked her finger through the pattern in the lace runner. Her mother spoke impatiently, without any real sympathy.

'What's the matter darling? Aren't you well today?'

'Yes,' she said again. And, abruptly: 'The other lady is pretty too, I expect.'

Her mother sat a moment like one turned suddenly to stone. Until at last, her voice so altered it was like that of another person altogether:

'What other lady?'

Cecily – mesmerized both by her own power at this instant, and by sheer terror of the storm it was bound to unleash – looked up at last.

'The lady in the photo . . .'

Her mother slowly replaced the pot of cold cream,

screwed on the lid. Her complexion was glazed and greasy;
her movements mechanical, like one in a trance.

'Which photo Cecily?'

There was no warmth to her tone. Only a coldly
controlled rage.

The child at once burst into tears.

'Martin told me. He saw it in the wallet. And Peter can't
be my daddy anyway, because he's married already.'

Her mother looked sharply at her. Her eyes blazed.

She said nothing. But got abruptly up and went to the
wardrobe. She tore open the door, seized on the jacket
hanging inside, threw it down on the bed and began a frenzied search for the wallet.

Cecily, in floods of tears, fled.

Martin had gone up to fetch his football when she burst
howling into the room.

He'd barely taken this apparition in when he heard his
mother go tearing down the stairs, screaming out at the
same time for the Squadron Leader.

He at once realised what had happened. Froze. The magni-
tude of the crisis bore down on him like a landslide. Invisible,
yet crushingly palpable. And with such terrible force that,
momentarily, it took his breath away.

The Squadron Leader must have been in the garden, for
he didn't appear at once. Instead, Vera came through from
the kitchen to ask if everything was all right. She sounded
alarmed; quickly wiped her hands on her pinafore as she
peered nervously along the passage.

His mother snapped out a furiously incoherent reply. At
which point the Squadron Leader must have appeared, for
he heard his voice – equally anxious – at the back of the
house.

They went together into the drawing-room. Within a few
seconds of which Vera came quickly up the stairs and into
the bedroom. Pulling her pinafore off over her head, she
cast it aside.

'Get your things on please – we're going down to the sea.'

This on a Sunday, in the middle of the morning, with preparations for luncheon not yet complete!

And then, under her breath:

'No child should be exposed to that sort of thing. It's not right!'

Martin wouldn't have dreamed of disobeying her. A trip to the sea seemed at this instant an excellent idea. He'd never, in all his life, felt so afraid.

She dressed them abruptly, forgetting even to insist that he wear his school tie. Then, having looked quickly out the open door, she rushed them helter-skelter down the stairs. It was like during an air raid: the same panic, the same mad urge to escape.

Even so, as she hustled them along the passage toward the rear of the house, his ears caught something of the terrible confrontation behind those two heavy doors.

His mother's voice was raised. Her tone coarse and abusive. Barely recognisable. Certainly it was not the tone she used with strangers, with those she wished to impress. But, at the same time, shocked through. Broken.

'You? – tell the truth? Never! Not in a thousand years!' A terrible pause. 'I curse you Peter. I curse you for what you've done to me and to her too.'

Martin, sick to the pit of his stomach, stumbled through into the kitchen. Vera, too, was white as a ghost. Mechanically, she pulled on her hat and coat and went out with them by the back door.

But suppose, Martin wanted to ask, she kills him? Suppose, in her blind rage, she takes him by the throat? What then?

But daren't. For fear that, once spoken, the words might somehow raise the deed.

They spent a damp, cheerless couple of hours walking along the beach. The day was overcast; the air flecked with spray. A thin mist stole in over the sea and up the empty beach with its stretches of barbed wire, its posted notices warning against the presence of mines. All was part obscured, adding to the dream quality of the day and its dramatically cataclysmic events.

They three. Each apparently guilty, yet not guilty at all.

'Do you think we should go back now?' Martin asked at last. 'In case . . .'

And Vera, who'd failed to interest them in the small shells and strips of seaweed she picked up out of the sand, stopped and looked at her watch.

It struck Martin then that she was probably just as afraid as he. She didn't really want to go back, any more than he did. For each, of course, must to some degree or other face the music; and Martin was sure his guilt was greater than either hers or Cecily's.

'I didn't,' he said, looking suddenly up into her pinched little face all drawn together with distress, 'mean it to happen. I didn't tell anyone what you said – I never mentioned it, I promise.'

She looked at him a moment. He could feel the hot tears at the back of his eyes.

Her mouth was tight still. But she nodded abruptly.

'That's all right dear. I'm not blaming you. I blame myself for having spoken about it in the first place. I don't know what your mother's going to say to me – I'm sure I don't. But it was bound to come out in some way or other. I should have realised that.'

When they got back, however, the house was silent. The Squadron Leader had gone, his car too. And their mother, exhausted no doubt by her outburst, was in bed.

An ominous stillness hung – literally, it seemed – over the place. For the rest of the day they went about like mice.

The following morning came the inquiry. Or inquest was perhaps a better word, since the series of interviews held after breakfast seemed cloaked in a black formality.

His mother, when at last he was called into the drawing-room (where the air was thick still with the effluvia of yesterday's terrible scene), was deathly pale but calm. Her calm so deep it sank – not only down into her own roots – but into those of the chintz armchair in which she sat.

Her back was to the window. When at last she spoke, her voice, too, came it seemed from some greater depth than that of her mere physical self. In her short sleeved black frock (she was again a widow), and with one white hand on either arm of the chair, she was like a small but powerful cult figure. A goddess of some sort.

She looked at him a moment. Her gaze was hard and shrewd, as though he were someone she disliked intensely.

Then, distantly:

'We shan't,' she said, 'be seeing the Squadron Leader again. Which may please you perhaps: I don't know.'

She paused.

'I've spoken to Vera. There was, it seems, some talk. Between herself and you, I mean – which was foolish. And it was this no doubt which prompted your curiosity.'

Martin, standing before her with his hands behind his back and what seemed like a mile of richly patterned Axminster between them, felt his cheeks begin to burn. A sense of outrage at being held responsible for what was after all inevitable tightened inside his stomach. But – not accustomed to speaking in his own defence before any adult, let alone his parents – he remained silent.

He was conscious, too, of his bare knees below the jutting line of his grey knickerbockers. It was early yet, and there was no sun here at the front. The air was as cool as his mother's stare. There was also a faint whiff still of the Squadron Leader's cigarettes.

'It was very wrong of you, however, to have looked inside the wallet. You'd no business to touch what didn't belong to you. I hope you will always remember that; and the terrible heartache the whole thing has caused me. Apart from which it was in one sense fortunate, since it made me aware of the terrible things which were going on behind my back before it was too late.'

Again she paused. Martin chewed his lip apprehensively. Would he perhaps be condemned to spend what remained of the holiday back at St John's, alone save for one or two others – who having lost either one or both parents – had no home to go to? Or, worse perhaps, must he suffer instead her powerful disapproval here at home?

Neither, as it turned out. But the actuality was equally bleak, since it put a similar distance between them.

'I'm sending you both to stay for a week or two with

Vera. You must understand that I've had a terrible shock: and that it has set me back considerably. But I'm going to warn you – do not, please, speak of this business to anyone. I've warned Vera too. She is lucky, under the circumstances, to have retained her position.'

Martin was stunned. She had conducted the affair with so little discretion it couldn't in any case have passed unnoticed, but was acting now as though there were some sort of conspiracy against her.

Confused, he dropped his eyes.

She took this, of course, as an acknowledgement of his guilt. Inclined her head slightly.

'Mummy understands,' she assured him. 'But please: don't ever let anything like this happen again. I've been deeply hurt. How deep, you will never know. But you are, all of you, responsible in some way for this. Now: send Cecily in, will you? I can't of course speak to her in the same way I've spoken to you. But she, too, must be made to understand.'

And, commandingly:

'A kiss darling, please. All is now forgotten and forgiven.'

Martin, as he advanced in compliance with her wish, rejected this blatant falsehood outright.

He knew also that – though the approach might perhaps differ slightly – Cecily, too, would be made to feel her complicity. The part she had – however innocently – played.

If only because she had dared – similar, as she was, to her mother – exhibit her partiality for the shamed hero.

Having somehow taken in all the lines he normally cast from out the deep centre of his being, Martin set his false seal upon her regally gratuitous cheek.

Everything was very different at Vera's. As they'd discovered on an earlier visit, just after their father died.

She lived almost on the sea front, in what they felt to be a very 'down' area – though, physically, the row of narrow terraced houses (of which her parents' was one) stood on the side of a hill, and so was neither up nor down. She lived there alone with her elderly, working class, but stiffly respectable parents. The front hall was narrow as a coffin, and there were stained glass lights over the door.

Martin and Cecily spent most of their time indoors because the children all around – and there seemed to be hundreds of them – thought they were stuck up and cissy and spared no effort in letting them know this. Cecily's name in particular, with its hint at Victorian propriety, attracted abuse.

They had of course to be very quiet. Neither found this too difficult, however, since the same was expected of them at home, but it did rather limit their activities. Both loved to read, but there were no books at Vera's and they hadn't thought to bring any with them.

The one highlight of an otherwise dull, even miserable fortnight, was when Vera's sister came down for a few days from her Midlands home.

Her name was May. And she was married to a soldier. He was with the Eighth Army in North Africa and she, in the meantime, seemed to be enjoying herself enormously. She brought a boyfriend or two home with her, and Martin only marvelled that neither her parents nor her sister seemed aware of what was going on. Vera, who'd been so quick to spot what was happening elsewhere, was curiously naive with regard to what was happening here. Or she preferred it that way perhaps.

May was also an outrageous gossip. And it wasn't long before she winkled out of Vera the whole story of what had transpired 'up at the house'.

They were sitting together one evening in the cramped little kitchen with its old-fashioned range under a narrow mantel crammed with seaside bric-à-brac and silver framed photos from the First World War.

The door was partly open. About to go in, Martin hesitated. He knew at once what they were talking about. By instinct, rather than from what he'd heard. Withdrew slightly, so they shouldn't see him.

May – to Vera's obvious distaste – was smoking a cigarette. She also wore thick lipstick which came away in scarlet half moons on the rim of her cup.

'Come on love,' she said. 'They're all talking about it up there – Mum said. So it's not exactly a secret.'

And, when Vera still demurred:

'I'm your sister, aren't I? You can tell me.'

'Well, you know, I shouldn't really. It was a nasty affair – that's why the children are here: to give it time to blow over.'

'She'd a boyfriend, hadn't she . . .?'

Vera stiffened visibly.

'Well, no. Not in that sense. They were to be married – or she thought they were. The real tragedy was that – apart from the fact that he was carrying on at the same time with at least one other woman – he was married already.'

Martin admired her loyalty, after what she'd been through.

'Well, I never! And he'd the cheek to propose to her?'

Vera dropped a single lump of sugar into her tea, took up a spoon and stirred it vigorously.

'I don't know about that. In a way, it was she who proposed to him. She knew already what he was up to, but was determined I think that of the two – herself, and this other woman he was carrying on with – it was she he was going to marry. But she knew nothing of course of this earlier marriage – not at the time. And, when at last she found out about it, it came I'm sure as a terrible shock to her – as it did to me. But mind: I knew all along something wasn't right.'

'He hadn't got a divorce then?'

'Oh, no. What happened, as far as I can gather, is that she left him. Walked out one day and went back to her family. Can't say I blame her either, if he was up to the same tricks then as he is now.'

'Were there any children?'

'Not as I understand it, no.'

'So – what happened? Did he meet her during an air raid or something?'

'Lord, no. Nothing like that. They were married before the war started. He met her in Egypt, the Missus said. She was the daughter of some big bug on the administrative side. They were introduced at one of these function things, and there was a whirlwind romance – of which, apparently, her father didn't approve. The Missus told me all this herself. She didn't wonder, she said, seeing the sort of man he was. There's a lot, of course, that I don't know. And don't suppose I ever shall.'

'Sad though. It makes you wonder what'll happen to him now. I mean, it would be terrible if he went off and got killed or something . . .'

'Never! – he'll survive this war, I'm sure. And carry on after where he left off. No: it's the children I'm sorry for. The whole affair must have upset them dreadfully. The Missus, too, of course. But she went into this, you know, with her eyes wide open. In a sense, she's only herself to blame.'

Martin heard all this with mixed feelings. Best expressed, perhaps, by what came after.

'She has my sympathy, naturally. No doubt about it. Bit of a so-and-so, he was. Very sure of himself. Not that he was particularly handsome: no – I wouldn't say that. Forceful, rather. But he met his match, I think, in the Missus. Still . . . She'll not forget him easily – I know that.'

'Smoke,' May agreed, as she stabbed out what was left of her cigarette, 'gets in your eyes.'

THE SUN IN HORUS

'I – I didn't expect you'd be here,' she said.

He stared.

'I was just on my way out. Is something wrong?'

She took her cigarettes out of her bag. Went across to the fireplace.

'No. No, I – I've this awful headache, that's all.'

'You look like nothing on earth. Do you feel all right otherwise?'

She lit a cigarette. Her hand shook slightly.

'Yeah. It's probably just my monthlies.'

'You wouldn't like me to stay . . .?'

'Darling, no. Don't worry about me, please.'

He took his briefcase up off the table. Glanced her over. She wasn't sure how to interpret the look. Concerned, certainly. But baffled too. A mite more penetrating than was usual for him.

'I'll see you later then.'

'Sure.' And, abruptly: 'Uh – at about what time?'

'In time for dinner I hope.'

She turned away.

'Okay.'

'Will you be here?'

'Yeah.'

He hesitated. Came across and kissed her gently on the back of her neck.

'I'll look forward to that.'

She stood motionless. Straight as a stick.

'You'll miss your appointment . . .'

'Yes. But you worry me darling. You're doing too much.'

She forced herself to turn around. To meet his gaze. It wasn't easy. Warmly humorous as always, there was an element, too, of something less comfortable. Or comforting, as the case may be.

'Hugh, please . . . I'm perfectly all right.'

'If you say so.' And, smiling: 'Behave yourself.'

She blinked.

'Yeah. Sure.' (So what did he mean by that?) 'You too.'

Watched him go.

Stood a moment like one waiting to be shot.

Then, when she heard the front door, wheeled suddenly about. Threw open the drinks cabinet and grabbed whatever came to hand.

Brandy.

She poured herself a shot and drank it down in three or four gulps.

Instantly . . . relaxed. Like a stricken predator just fell from her back.

She filled her glass again, took it across with her to the window.

Her passing image in the huge mirror over the mantel. Shadowy in the pale light. Her face like death. (But felt, now, the Life which rose from her belly to her brain. The sun in Horus. And Hathor, was it?, who became so drunk she drowned the world in blood. (But had got it wrong, she at once realised.)) Her hair cut like a boy's. Short back and sides: curly on top. A melancholy, incipiently depraved, but fatally attractive youth from some past age – Attic? Renaissance? – at once more civilised and less scrupulous than her own.

'What is it about you?' he'd asked her once. 'You even smell like a boy.'

Was herself conscious of this warm animal odour which so fascinated him. The faintly spicy aroma of the pre-pubescent male at one still with his mother, a part still of her body.

Was proud of herself. Of her sexual ambiguity.

She went first to the hi-fi. Selected a tape, slipped it in and shut the cover down.

Mozart.

And, somewhere inside her head, an October garden. Ineffably sad. Sinking, with the sun, back into the soil that spawned it.

Went then to the window, leaned up against the

embrasure. A warm breeze off the street played mysteriously
– because invisibly – with the drapes. Lifting them lightly,
like the skirts of a dancer.

Fifteen years of marriage. And he still the same. Warm.
Dependable. Concerned. More than just a good husband. A
very good friend.

Whether or not he had at any time been unfaithful to her
she daren't ask. Not because she didn't care: but because –
unreasonably, in view of her own infidelities – she'd have
been hurt.

Yet this reluctance to look too closely into each other's
affairs – an unwritten, but no less tangible law – seemed in
fact to work the opposite for him. Bound him to her more
closely. Had anyone asked did she think he had at any time
taken a lover she'd have been obliged to answer no.

Really, she should have been happy. She had in him the
ideal partner, and yet . . . Yet she was like an erratic
compass; always pointing off in another direction.

One male. One female. In that order. Each rather good
in his (or her) own way. But not specially memorable. Or
she'd asked too much perhaps?

Her career, however, completely satisfying. Intelligent,
ambitious, she had, too, the right amount of drive and determination – cheek, Hugh called it. Backed by a strong self-
interest, and characteristic Yank panache.

But this too – though she'd never have settled for anything
less spectacular than success – a mite predictable at times.
(Her sure-fire instinct for a potential high achiever seldom
failed.) So that, among her colleagues, she was seen as something of a legend already. At just thirty-five.

But, apart from all this . . .?

Ought, she supposed, to have felt at least a little guilty.

For not having put more into her marriage. For her purely
friendly feelings toward a man who had given her so much.
For having given him so little in return. (Knew, for a start,
he'd wanted children.) For not having loved as he had
loved . . .

And for the gratification this gave.

★

Her most jealously-guarded – one might say her most ambitious secret, however, had nothing to do with sexual infidelity, or with what might be seen as her poor performance as a wife.

Not that she believed this secret to be in any sense shameful. (She was weak perhaps – oddly, for she was also strong.) Rather – like sex, or going to confession – it seemed appropriate that she keep it to herself.

She'd always – as a child even – been fascinated by intoxication as an experience in itself. By ritual intoxication. By that 'holiday from reality' of which Huxley spoke. But more than just a holiday. An act of worship.

Social drinking wasn't the same thing at all. Was not a preparation even. For preparation – as in all religious ceremonies – should consist of abstinence, of purification. A cleansing of the House in preparation for the Guest.

Drunkenness was for her a state of grace – like the Catholic Communion. A condition in which the god – the wine itself – took residence briefly within the limits of one's physical frame, now the temple, and sent the soul off on an ecstatic journey of discovery.

In other words, a sacrament.

There were many things she liked doing. Driving; reading; cinema or video; music – and, of course, her job. All of which gave her pleasure of one sort or another.

But none so much – since she was first free to indulge in this way – as drinking herself insensible. Business lunches, dinner parties, office or domestic celebrations – all these offered a legitimate excuse for what she thought of as irreligious drinking. Drank on average one bottle of wine, or half a bottle of spirits a day in this way. But it was incidental. She was a serious rather than a social drinker. And, once or twice a week, she'd shut herself up, put on a tape or disc of her favourite music, open a bottle of her favourite wine, and get as drunk as she was able in the time available.

A Dionysian celebration. But without the frenzy. In fact, a rather civilised affair. Raised to the level almost of Roman Catholic ritual. (She was sent, as a child, to convent school. Would she ever forget?)

Crazy.

Since it meant, too, that she must lie and cheat like a common thief. Was reduced, automatically, to the same level.

Alcoholism, she knew, had nothing to do with either class or intelligence. But she was not, she felt sure, an alcoholic. Shrank from the word. From all its implications. Fumbling, incontinent, apparently sexless creatures of indeterminate age writhing around on the floor of a police cell somewhere. No. She was in charge still. On top. In everything.

Therefore, in this.

But could not, she suspected, have convinced her husband these blinds were a matter of choice rather than of necessity. And so refrained from discussing it with him. Drinking in his company became, as a result, increasingly hazardous – something she tried now to avoid. Which wasn't actually difficult. They spent on the whole very little time together.

But there were awkward moments. Like just now when – unexpectedly – she'd found him at home.

Or, more simply, like when he wanted to kiss her.

Ways to avoid this.

Resorting, at best, to the most fragile excuses. 'I'd garlic with my lunch.' Or: 'I've another cold coming. You don't want one too.' But could see that he was beginning to feel it. To doubt himself. Or he thought perhaps that it was she who was to blame? – that she had lost all desire and was becoming frigid. Which was certainly not true. She was a sap still for erotic experience. Prided herself on an apparently endless orgasm once she started.

Not that Hugh was ever exactly erotic – no more so than a teddy bear. Though every bit as comforting.

But now . . .

This room.

Their room.

Her room. (The entire ground floor flat, her.) One of two. Very large. The other, across the hall, partitioned off to form both bed and bathroom.

The Front Room. (Not strictly, since it went from front to back. But The Front Room, all the same.) The light uncertain. A blue, Impressionist light. In whose shadows were part submerged the major features of this enormous space.

The full length Jacobean dining table. Dark oak, polished daily to a coldly autistic sheen by their French maid, Elise, who'd have gone gladly to the ends of the earth for her. To the moon even. (But the French, of course, were like that. Wonderfully warm. Altogether uncomplicated, or apparently so.)

The imposing fireplace, directly opposite as one entered. Flanked on either side by shaded table lamps, and in whose empty grate the iron fire dogs crouched in mute anticipation of a crackling log or two.

To the left of which, the 'Chinese' escritoire (antique lacquered writing cabinet: gold borders on a red ground, eighteenth century, German) and bookcases. The 'Napoleon' desk. The huge tapestry where, once, a window had overlooked the small, walled garden at the back. Bricked in now, so that the light came from the front only.

And to the right of which, the leather chesterfield and two big chairs against the window. An occasional table, topped with glass. Further bookcases. The hi-fi.

All of these at first glance dominated.

But then . . .

The great glass over the mantel. In which, dimly, all was seen again.

And the Afghan carpet – rich shades of blue and brown. And the many objets d'art. And – absorbing something of this ambience, but with a lucence all their own – yellow roses . . .

Daily, from Moyses Stevens, for fifteen years. From him.

She had herself the undoubtedly charming, yet somehow incomplete quality of these hybrid flowers. Like them, she was straight, strong (though slightly-built), glossy, sophisticated. Perfectly presented. Her eyes, too, echoed this still perfection. Light brown, yellow-brown, like autumn leaves. Their expression rather crisp. Brittle even, according to the light – or to her mood. For, when melancholy, they were deeply diffused: cloudy, like old wine.

The flowers had one flaw only. They were scentless.

Here now, in her glass, all the fire of the sun. (Held it a moment to the light: an Elevation?) The god, here in her glass.

Drained it solemnly before going again to the drinks cabinet. Muscat de Beaumes de Venise. Perfect.

And the clarinet concerto. Whose beautiful slow movement, with its sombre orchestral cadences, now began.

Was sick in the bathroom when she heard the front door.

Hugh!

A last ditch attempt to collect her senses.

But – Elise. Where was she?

No, it was Elise. Back, as arranged, to complete the Corfu fish recipe she'd started on earlier.

Did not, however, enter. But spoke from outside.

'Madame?'

Put both taps on full. Wash it all away . . .

But the floor pitched and rolled still under her feet. And her eyes . . . a couple of indicators gone berserk. Back and forth. Back and forth. Right off the clock, and still not able to focus.

And her throat so raw . . .

'Madame? – what is it? Are you all right?'

'Sure, yeah. Something I ate. Or some kinda bug maybe . . .'

'Oh, Madame! – let me get you something.'

'No, no. It's okay. I'm all right now.'

All smartened up, bright and deceitful at the dinner table. (But God! Elise must have seen. She wasn't stupid. And the smell. There must have been a terrible smell.) But like her inbuilt computer had gone crazy. False information through her poisoned circuits . . .

And now, like a bolt from the blue, his announcement.

'The Old Man will be over for dinner one night next week. He and his wife, and one or two others.'

'Oh!' And: 'Uh – yeah. When?'

'Thursday I thought. If that's all right with you.'

'Sure. I – '

'Yes?'

'No. I – I was wondering about Elise. Wasn't that her night off?'

'Darling, I've no idea. I leave all that to you. But we could always – '

'No, no. Forget it. I'll have a talk with her.'

There was a short silence. During which, as he removed the bones from his fish with the skill and patience of a surgeon, she quickly scrutinised him. Searched for some flaw in his otherwise calm expression, some clue as to his thoughts. Nothing, however. As bland, equable, and apparently untroubled as always.

So that his next words came as something of a shock.

'Did you get over your headache? You didn't look at all well when I left.'

'Oh, yeah. It was my monthlies, like I said.'

He looked up suddenly.

'Again?'

'No! But that's what it was – I always know.'

'I was going to say – it's only a couple of weeks since the last one.'

She glared.

'I oughtta know. It's me who's having them, not you.'

He was silent a moment. Then, just as she was starting to feel she'd over-reacted:

'I'm aware of that darling. But I worry about you. It seems you're under some sort of pressure at present. I wondered if perhaps you'd something on your mind.'

She dropped her knife and fork. Lit a cigarette.

'Nonsense! I'm fit as a fiddle. Really, I don't know what all the fuss is about.'

'You're not eating . . .'

She nodded.

'I've an upset stomach. You know I always get an upset stomach with my period. Ask Elise.' (God!, what was she saying?)

'But you just said – '

'Hugh, please. I'm ovulating. Right now, I'm ovulating.

Does that make sense to you? For some women, this bit is the worst. Can you get that into your head?'

'I'm sorry. I didn't mean to pry.'

'So what am I supposed to do? – stand up and make a speech, or wave a flag or something every time I expect a period?'

He stared.

'No. Of course not. But you are my wife. And I love you. Something you've never seemed able to get into your head.'

She dropped her eyes. Put her knife and fork straight. The smoke from her cigarette shuddered up toward the ceiling – lost now in shadow. A soft evening light through the tall windows set up in triptych like in a church. The sky across the street flushed pink, against which a silhouette landscape of slates and chimney stacks. Here, the cloth – white damask: likewise the napkins – similarly tinged. (Elise had set the smaller table near the window, as she always did when they ate alone.) Most else in semi-darkness. The bookcases; the mantelpiece. The glass a great pool. Mysteriously shadowed depths.

'Yes,' she said at last. 'I know. And I love you too.'

Which was not, actually, a falsehood. She did, in a sense. And needed him – more, perhaps, than she cared to admit. Bright, slight, and strident as a trumpet solo, tremendously self-assertive, she was also highly strung and given to moods of melancholy, of diffusion. Not, oddly, as regards her work. But in the handling of her own affairs – her 'sentimental side', as she called it.

He looked at her a moment.

Then, reassured, he smiled at last.

'Take care of yourself darling. That's all I ask.'

She, too, smiled.

'Sure. I'm not exactly stupid. I feel like I'm doing too much, I'll take a rest . . .'

'I wish we could take a rest together. That's what we both want, I think. Which brings me, however, to what I have to say next. They're sending me to Johannesburg for a couple of weeks: I want to be sure you'll be all right while I'm away.'

Her heart leaped. Soared. She felt like a hawk flown from the wrist. Dare not, of course, let him see this. Because she was also genuinely sorry. Would miss him in a sense, as she always did.

'Hughie – what am I gonna do . . .?'

Same old whine.

Same old grin and bear it.

'I'll just have to wait, I suppose. Again.'

'Darling, you'll be so busy I'll have come back before you know I've been away.'

She smiled.

'Yeah. True.'

Before then, however, this dinner party . . .

She sat with her client at a corner table next the window. It was somewhere around two. The place was packed still.

'I feel we should go for this while it's good. Rossi has made us a very generous offer.'

Dark mahogany. White cloth. A half curtain across the window. Lace; finely woven. Through which, the wet street. Umbrellas. Here, a subdued drift of conversation. The odd word or two. Islands in a vast ocean. Drift, too, of cigarette smoke; both elusive and pervasive. On the table, her part-eaten meal. His empty plate. Bottles. Her empty glass.

She lit another cigarette. Refilled her glass. Her head was light as a feather already, her brain nearly numb. In spite of which – if only because she was on familiar ground – she remained convincingly intelligent.

'So – what do you think?'

He blinked. But, behind the glasses (young; college type; very blue eyes), this guy was far from stupid.

'I think you're right.'

She flicked the ash from her cigarette.

'We'll not get a penny more out of him – of that I'm sure. Only snag is, once he has the option you're tied to him. But – at this stage anyway – it seems like a fair deal.'

'Good. I'll leave the rest to you.'

She emptied her glass. Sought the Cameriera's eye.

'Okay. Soon as I get back, I'll put it through.'

That last glass. . . A mistake. But talking still like an intelligent machine.

At her elbow . . . slim young man in black. Very good looking. Oddly penetrating stare.

Reached down for her bag. (Christ! – like the table came up and hit her in the face.) Opened her wallet. Slapped down the little green card.

He treats this with due respect. But she's not too clear about what happens next.

Now, suddenly, out on the sidewalk. She pumps young Aldridge's hand.

'I'll give you a ring, okay?'

Traffic tears past. Raining really hard now.

He offers his umbrella.

'Thanks, but no. I'll call a cab.' Laughs awkwardly, like a schoolgirl. 'I mean taxi. I still can't get used to that. Where I come from, it's a cab.' (God!, did it matter?)

Whether or not he understood, she didn't know. But like his smile just sort of faded into the rain, and . . .

Cab almost takes her nose off as it comes into the kerb.

Gave her home address.

Was woken by the doorbell.

Sat slowly up. Looked at the clock. A quarter to five. Her brain felt sore all over.

She got off the bed, reached for her jacket. Her things . . . everywhere. She'd had, she remembered, another one or two drinks when she got back. After which . . .

Nothing.

But who in hell? Hugh wouldn't be here till late. He'd his key, anyway. Elise too.

She opened the door, went out into the hall.

The greater part of which, as for most of the day, was lost in shadow. One window only, up on the landing. The light had first to travel down the stair. And, when at last it reached the bottom, was so diluted – or polluted by all it had picked up on the way, it touched only tentatively – mysteriously even – on everything below.

The house was old. Was now split up into flats. Theirs –
here on the ground floor, with its large entrance – was rather
impressive. They'd maintained – and, in some respects,
improved upon its more attractive features when they'd
taken residence here soon after their marriage at the nearby
Brompton Oratory. (They had, too, a lovely old cottage in
wildest Sussex.) Chequered tiles; old mahogany; the magnificent stair with its wrought iron banister and mahogany
handrail which curved back upon itself at the bottom.

As one entered, the bedroom was on the left. Lounge and
stair on the right. Directly opposite was the kitchen. (All
were connected internally, so as to avoid embarrassment.
Lounge into kitchen; kitchen into bathroom; bathroom into
bedroom. For the hall, of course, was a public highway.)

The walls here were part panelled, part papered. Either
side of the kitchen door – this room, like all the others,
opened also onto the hall – was a mahogany plinth graced
with two rather impressive figures modelled on Greek orig-
inals. On the immediate left was an old mahogany hat stand
with glass and telephone table built in.

It was into this muted, rather nebulous light that she now
emerged. Grateful for its discretion, for the dignity which
this conferred.

The opalescent glow of the white tiles: the near disappear-
ance of the black. (Reminding her, as always, of their honeymoon in Venice. The rented palazzo with its part submerged
façade, its crumbling cornerstones, its Renaissance
windows.) The heavy, panelled doors, with their brass knobs
and locks . . .

Still wondered what right she had, as a relative stranger
here, to all these years of conspiratorial silence. To those
long, summer afternoons; to the measured hours struck
sonorously off by that same clock she saw now on the wall.
(While, distantly, the passage of a horse drawn cab.) To this
unchanging tradition.

She crossed to the door. Hesitated.

Reached at last for the handle, and drew it slowly open.

Knew him at once. But couldn't think for a moment
where she'd seen him before.

'I, uh – yeah?'

'Mrs Stone?'

A pronounced accent. Young. Fairly tall. Conventional haircut, slicked back. Penetrating stare – but reticent, too. Like all this was just as painful for him as it must be for her.

God, yes. The restaurant.

'Yeah. But – who are you?'

'I am from Mario's. You were there for lunch today.'

'Yes. Yes, of course. But – '

He held something out. Shocked, she could only stare. Then, recovering at last:

'My bag! I – I must have left it behind.' She laughed awkwardly, took it from him. Aware, at the same time, of her appearance. Her crumpled clothes; her tousled hair. God!, whatever – 'Thank you. I, uh – it's very good of you.'

'Will you check please to see that all is in order?'

'Sure.'

She went quickly through the contents. Comb, cosmetics, fragrance. And her wallet, credit card, cheque book – all untouched.

But blushed furiously. And he staring all the while like she just crawled out the cheese or something. A passionate Continental interest in what he must sense to be an odd situation. Such forgetfulness, after all, gave indication of an unusual state of mind. An aberration.

She looked suddenly into his eyes.

'I – let me give you something. After all, I – '

'Oh, please. No.' And: 'The pleasure is mine. Only forgive that I must examine the contents to see if they will tell me who is the owner.'

'No. That's all right. It – it's most kind of you to return it. Really, I didn't know...'

Hadn't missed it even when – But Aldridge, she remembered, had paid off the cab. So she'd had no need of it.

'I do thank you, really. And I insist you take this.'

Put a five pound note firmly into his hand.

'No, please. I'd be awfully upset if you refused it. I was lucky to get the bag back at all. I'm so forgetful: that's my trouble.'

A weak smile. And a weak excuse. Which he immediately recognised as such, but was too polite to comment upon.

Only looked. In that peculiarly penetrating, rather sad sort
of way he had. (Candlelight; the musical blur of mandolins;
the Rio dei Palazzi by moonlight . . .)

She dropped her eyes suddenly. Fumbled with the clasp.

'Thanks, anyway.'

'Thank you, Signora. You are too generous.'

She looked again into his eyes. Smiled.

'You're welcome. Goodbye.'

But, even as she closed the door, knew it was he who'd
ultimately come off best. That the money she'd given him
did not neutralise the damage she'd done herself in his eyes.

Her cheeks burning still – both from the wine, and from
embarrassment – she went to the telephone. Grabbed the
receiver and drew the dial abruptly down.

'Mags? – thank God!, you're there still. I'd have called you
sooner, but was held up. The Rossi option: put it through at
once, will you? Tell him I'll be on to him personally first
thing in the morning. What? Yeah. Thanks . . .'

It wasn't till she'd put the phone down that it occurred to
her it was perhaps a little unusual – this visit to her home
when, normally, the bag would surely have been passed first
to the management . . .

Blushed again. Was only thankful there was no one here
to see.

The room . . . its dimensions very grand. Had an air, too,
of this – of grandeur. The two lamps only: the curtains pulled
across. The ceiling withdrawn, but perceptibly present. Like
clouds across the moon. Seemingly far, yet not.

And, again, Mozart. But not so loud as to intrude upon
the conversation. The warm hum of which went back and
forth like. . . Individual words like tennis balls across the
table, wittily returned. Same concentration as during a game.
Same dedication. (But to the social graces.) Same competi-
tive urge. Same need to shine.

She wondering meanwhile whether she might take another
drink without appearing drunk. There was a bottle at her
elbow, of which . . . increasingly aware. And to which her
eyes returned subversively, as to a lover . . .

'What about you Viv?'

'Huh? Oh – yeah. I . . .'

At the far end – Hugh. His image softened by the glow of the candles, he looked like a kindly country doctor – or veterinarian perhaps. Philanthropic, anyway. Caring. Hair fairly thick still; shot with grey. Rather heavy, good-humoured features.

But was saved – not by the bell exactly – but like they rang a bell in her mind, those few words addressed to her, so that she was instantly aware of what it was Robert had said.

Mozart . . .

'Music for indoors – chamber music, I guess. Though not in quite the sense we might apply this term today. But, like one imagines Handel heard in the open – I've never actually done this, but I can imagine it, you know? – or in a hall, or church, well . . . so Mozart seems to belong inside.'

(God!, this was her? Hadn't realised she could still be so boring, hence so sensible.)

Robert:

'Mm. My feeling exactly. Sylvia thinks not, however.'

His pretty wife . . . Who now laughs a little, as is expected of her.

'Oh, I know what you mean. It's just that I can't imagine the Requiem, for instance – or the concertos even – well, in here. I mean, how would – '

Hugh:

'But orchestras were rather smaller then. And the piano, you know, had a smaller voice than the modern instrument.'

She:

'Sure. I can't hear Mozart without I have a mental image of those opulent Baroque interiors – I mean, I know that not many people at that time enjoyed such luxury. But, for me anyway, his music seems to reflect this conscious style. Civilised, orderly – and of course deeply personal, rather sad. Weltschmerz: isn't that what they . . .?'

Sylvia:

'Oh, yes. I agree. It's like everything.' (But wasn't sure what she meant by that.) 'This room, for instance, is unmistakably you. No – really. Everything about it. Tasteful, a touch eccentric for these times. You seem in some sense part of it – or it seems part of you. A reflection of sorts, like you were saying. And equally enigmatic.'

She was right, of course. She was an indoor rather than an outdoor person. Insofar as she ought, she knew, to be viewed against a landscape of elegant interiors – and all the artifice that these implied. An exaggerated, a Baroque formality. Bright but false.

And:

'Don't you think, darling, that Vivienne is somehow mysterious?'

'Yes. I – '

'Well, thanks. But really I don't feel I qualify . . .'

'But isn't it so Hugh?'

'Absolutely, yes. It was Viv, of course, who insisted on preserving the character of the place – rightly, I now realise.'

Sylvia, to her:

'Perhaps you lived here before. In another life, I mean. Did you get that feeling when you came here first? – a lot of people do. Déjà vu, or whatever it is.'

She reached at last for the bottle, filled her glass.

'No, I don't think so. But there was a certain sympathy. Old places have this sort of appeal, I think. That's what's so beautiful about England.' She lit another cigarette. Almost took her nose off with the flame. Hadn't realised she. . . But otherwise fine. Exhaled aggressively through her nostrils by way of compensation. 'I'm a dedicated Anglophile – I think I told you. I really love everything about the place. And I'm not tired of it yet. No, really. I've been all over Europe, but I – '

Sylvia:

'What part of the States are you from?'

'New York. I was born and bred there.' Laughed a little. 'And I still hate it. I always wanted to come to England – ever since I was a child. I used to read about it in history books – about the kings and queens. And. . . Like it was all so real: so vivid in my mind. I especially wanted to come to London. But I never dreamed I'd actually live here one day . . .'

'What brought you over at last?'

She smiled.

'Gentleman sitting just across. He was in New York on business. We met at . . .'

But wasn't sure she could be understood still. Her tongue seemed to have stiffened, and she'd difficulty forming her words. But they were listening still – both of them. Didn't seem to have noticed anything.

'And. . . Well, we fell in love. And I was determined we'd marry in London, so we did, and . . .'

'Lived happily ever after!'

'Well, yeah. I guess so.'

Her elbows on the table, the smoke from her cigarette wavering up before the supernaturally still flames of the candles, she glanced slyly in Hugh's direction.

He was not, however, looking at her. Toyed instead with his knife and fork. His expression serious, rather withdrawn.

So. . . What had she said?

An awkward silence.

The distance between them more than merely geographical now.

She took up her glass. Drained it abruptly. They were looking at her expectantly, Robert and his wife. A wild attempt to make out they hadn't noticed whatever it was had passed between their host and hostess.

Wasn't entirely sure herself.

Unless . . .

'I – uh, I go home occasionally, however. To see my parents – that sort of thing. I expect . . . I mean, it's still my home. The place where I was born.'

'Have you any brothers or sisters there, or just – '

'No. No, no. I . . . just my parents.' She laughed again. Helplessly. Like she was about to cry. 'I'm an only child. I – I'd have liked a brother.'

But difficult to explain. And they, in any case, a little embarrassed suddenly.

So hell.

Emptied the last of the wine into her glass.

Somebody shouted out:

'Oh!'

Hugh:

'Elise! – a cloth!'

'No. It's nothing. I . . .'

Elise. At her elbow, mopping up.

'I – was that me? I'm so sorry darling. I hadn't realised there was that much left.'

'Is all right madame. There!'

'Thank you. Yeah, I was saying. Mm . . .?'

Sylvia. Talking about her brother. Would have liked a sister really. Brothers weren't quite the same. But there.

She dragged at her cigarette. Sylvia's face bobbing about behind the smoke like a toy balloon in a gale. Didn't really understand what she was saying. Hard to follow . . .

'Yeah. Men can be so bloody thick.'

A pause.

Sylvia:

'Well, I didn't mean that exactly. My brother-in-law, for instance, is one of the nicest people I know.'

On in the same vein. Harmless crap. A desperate attempt to hide her embarrassment.

But –

God, what was it?

Suddenly so –

Silence. Everyone aware, it seemed, of what was about to happen. The air electric.

Sylvia:

'Vivienne! – what is it? Are you all right?'

Robert:

'Quick! – get her to the bathroom!'

Somebody . . . by the elbow.

Rushed with her across the hall like she was a piece of scenery shunted off between the acts.

Hang over the basin. Her arm out in front; her palm against the wall. Desperately apologetic between scalding eruptions. All over the place . . .

'I – I'm so sorry. Musta been something I – oh, God!'

Friday.

Breakfast at half-eight. She with her casual expression. He very quiet. Hardly a word from him since he got out of bed.

Until, folding his newspaper and setting it carefully aside:

'What the devil got into you last night?'

Mock astonishment.

'Me? What do you mean?'

He looked quickly at her.

'What I say. You were drunk.'

She took up her spoon, stirred her tea. For the second time, she realised. Quickly replaced it.

'Nonsense!'

He stared.

'I beg to differ.'

No point in arguing further. She hadn't a leg to stand on. Smiled instead. Shrugged her shoulders.

'Could happen to anyone.'

'I've never seen you quite like that.'

'Okay. I'm sorry. I'd a hard week: too much on my mind, I guess.'

'That's not exactly an excuse darling. The Old Man was shocked – naturally. He's a bit of a fuddy-duddy at the best of times. And Patterson, too, was terribly embarrassed – in fact, everyone was. Myself included.'

'Look: I said I was sorry. What more – ?'

'And I didn't know what to say. I've never felt such a fool in all my life.'

She glared.

'So: what did you say?'

'Something you ate – what else?'

'Which was probably – '

'But they could see damn well it was the drink.'

She felt suddenly furious. Rushed instinctively to her own defence.

'Oh, come off it! You know me well enough to realise this wasn't exactly typical.' Made at the same time an effort to calm down, afraid her anger would give her away. 'It was Robert's fault really. He would keep topping up my glass.'

'So the answer would have been to seat him somewhere else? – I'll remember that next time.'

'There's no need to be sarcastic. There won't be a next time. God, anybody'd think I was an alcoholic!'

Knew at once she'd said the wrong thing.

He looked oddly at her.

'What do you mean?'

'I – well, you're so damned exasperating. I didn't of course mean it literally.'

They stared at one another momentarily. He suspicious. She belligerent.

Then:

'Look darling: I know you haven't been feeling well lately. There was that business the other afternoon . . .'

'What business?'

'I was on my way out, remember? You came in looking like death. I was very worried about you.'

'God – have we got to go into all that again? I told you: it was my period. No man, I grant, can even imagine what it's like. But I can't believe, the way you go on, that we've been married for fifteen years. I mean, how many periods is that for Christ's sake?'

'Yes. All right. But then, later, you'd a tummy upset. Something you ate, Elise said. She was quite distressed. Especially since she wasn't here when, as she put it, Madame was in such a way. She came in, she said, and found you doubled up. Now – last night – you're sick again.'

She looked blankly at him. But her brain was working overtime. She had to kill this thing dead.

'So, now, I can't get an upset stomach? Okay – if you want the details. I'd a headache, remember? And I took a couple of Distalgesic. I'd eaten almost nothing – you know how sensitive my stomach is to medicines – and I brought them back. It was just as unpleasant for me as it was for Elise – if not more so. But I didn't say anything about the tablets because I knew she'd scold me for not eating anything. You know what she's like: you miss a meal, you're dead already. Now: can we talk about something other than the ins and outs of the hen's backside? Or her menstrual cycle, or whatever else?'

'That wasn't necessary. But it does seem that you're constantly upset – if not by one thing, then by another. And you don't look well: this is what worries me. Not what I hear from Elise – but what I see with my own eyes. If you've something on your mind darling, you must tell me. Or at least promise me you'll go to the doctor.'

'The doctor! – whatever for? Really, this is getting ridiculous!'

'I've just told you why. Now, please: do as I say for once.'

'What, see a doctor because I brought back a couple of tablets? I wouldn't waste his time. He'd think – '

'No. See a doctor because you don't look well anyway. Or, if you're worried about something, then tell me.'

'Look: all this was incidental. I'm fit as a fiddle – I promise you. I've been a little tired, I admit. And maybe a bit peaky because of that. But I certainly don't need to see a doctor. And I certainly have nothing on my mind. Other than work, that is. But I wouldn't let that get on top of me – I'm used to it.'

She reached out suddenly. Put her hand over his.

'But thanks, anyway. And please remember that, if something was really wrong, you'd be the first one to know.'

He looked at her a moment. Then:

'I hope so.'

She smiled. But felt, somehow, that he wasn't entirely convinced.

'Hugh: I promise.'

He glanced at his watch.

'I must go.' Rose suddenly. Patted each of his pockets in turn, as he always did. 'You won't go getting up to anything while I'm away . . .?'

'Huh?'

'When I'm abroad, I mean. I'll be worried stiff about you.'

She thrust her fingers in through her hair and took a deep, exasperated breath.

'If it'll make you any happier, I'll call you every night. So long as you foot the bill.'

He was back just after four. It was raining hard.

He left his umbrella on the hallstand, where it dripped disconsolately into the pan provided. About to cross to the lounge, he saw the kitchen door was open. Looked in.

It was Elise, however.

'Ah!, M'sieur: I am just back with the shopping.' Rolled her eyes expressively. 'What an afternoon!'

'Not very brilliant, I agree. Did Madame say what time she'd be back? – I forgot to ask her.'

'She didn't say what time exactly, no. But she did say she would be in for dinner tonight.'

'Oh; good. Meantime I'll sort out a few things to take with me on Monday.' And: 'What's all that for goodness' sake? We're not having another dinner party, surely?'

She smiled.

'Ah!, no. But I saw that the cabinet was getting low, and I know that Madame prefers the Muscat.'

Prefers . . .

He didn't know why, but he felt there to be something a little over-delicate in her choice of expression. As though she hoped in this way to diminish, or altogether obliterate, a not completely pleasant fact.

He stood a moment, rather foolishly he felt. Looked at the half dozen or so bottles on the draining board. The light passed through them from behind. And, alongside the fresh vegetables – onions, courgettes, field mushrooms – she'd taken from her basket, they looked innocent enough. Rather charming, in fact. Like a still life painting. Or an advertisement in a quality magazine.

And yet, for some reason, they alarmed him . . .

'But, good God!, we don't need all those.' Then, seeing her startled look: 'Or do we?'

'Well . . . I don't know. I just thought – well, really, I didn't think. I had forgot there would be no one here. I am sorry . . .'

'No, no: not at all. It doesn't matter. Stock's as good as money, they say.' He made to leave. Stopped suddenly. Turned again to face her. 'Elise, I – ' Embarrassed, he scratched his ear. 'I wondered – '

'M'sieur?'

When Madame was unwell – had she been drinking?

This was what he wanted to ask. But couldn't.

'Er – no: it's all right. You're far too busy just now. Another time will do.'

'Oh, but if it is important . . .'

'No, no. Not at all. Just carry on as you are.'
Left abruptly. Took his things with him into the lounge.

'I'll drive you there if you like.'
'What – to Heathrow?'
'Sure. And go on to the office after.'
It was past eleven. She sat at the dressing table, prior to taking a shower, and removed her make-up.
He didn't answer at once. Then, loosening his tie:
'I'd rather you didn't tire yourself darling. I can just as easily get a taxi.'
She paused. The cleansing tissue hung fire momentarily. He thought she was going to be cross. But she wasn't. Not visibly so, anyway. Began again to wipe the stuff off her face.
'Oh, come on. It makes no difference to me. And it'll save you all that hassle at the last minute.' She wiped her hands quickly, got up. 'Right: I'll just – '
He came across. Took her gently by the shoulders. She looked at first surprised. Then defensive.
'What did we do fifteen years ago today?'
She smiled.
'Flew off to Italy.' On a belated honeymoon. They were both too busy for a couple of weeks after the wedding. 'Venice. I was really excited. I'd never been to Europe before.' Laughed a little. 'I must have been awfully green.'
He pushed his fingers in through her hair. Kissed her lightly on the lips.
'I'm not so sure. You were clever enough to – '
She rapidly extricated herself.
'Okay, okay. We won't go into that now. If I don't get some sleep, I'll overlay. Then where will we be?'
'In bed asleep, I imagine.'
'Yeah. And your plane will have left without you!'
Then, under the shower:
He'd taken it in good humour – as, indeed, she'd intended he should. But how much longer could she go on denying him in this way without creating an irreparable rift between them?

Venice.

Those magic nights. He so anxious to please, to do whatever she wanted. Too anxious perhaps.

What she'd felt during those two idyllic weeks wasn't easy to analyse even now. Certainly she wasn't disappointed. But there was something about the place itself which accentuated his Englishness. And, though it was this which had so fascinated her in the first place, made him seem – as a lover, that is – if not exactly dull then definitely understated. Which was not of course without its own charm. Still waters ran deep – of which the daily gift of flowers was a constant reminder. It was her fault, no doubt. She was too selfish. And, as far as her personal relationships went, too intellectual perhaps. Too introspective. Always looking into the mechanics of the thing… Also, she was sensual rather than sexual – which was why her Sapphic affair had seemed so promising. In her husband she had without doubt found an ideal – if not perfect – companion. For, unlike her, he was not overly intellectual. (Music was his one passion.) He'd little or no sense of the past, and a great deal of what they'd seen together in Italy was lost on him. But they were tolerant of each other's differences, and willing to learn, and so in a sense were well matched.

But she'd yet to find her ideal lover. He, or she perhaps, remained for the present –

She stood suddenly still.

Turned off the water.

The silence was extraordinary.

'No, no. You go on. I'll follow after.'

And, when her colleague had left:

'Waiter! – my bill please.'

He came again from the shadows. (Not dark exactly over there. But, here at the window, her eyes were so accustomed to the light that – what with the smoke and everything – all else appeared obscure.) Same blandly professional expression. Same deeply personal stare.

'Signora?'

'My bill.'

He'd come forward as soon as she entered. ('We'll go to Mario's. It's grand in the way hotels once were, but on a rather more intimate scale. The wine is very good: and they're not overly expensive.') She'd acted, however, like she didn't know him from Adam. Had treated him throughout the meal in the same way. It was the sort of thing she did so well – her best business manner. (Which had her work subordinates either all of a dither or stiff with envy – depending on how they reacted to her on a personal level.)

Now – resigned, it seemed, to remaining unrecognised – he waited as he was taught to wait, in more senses than one: attentive; respectful. But behind this professional screen his eyes – ever alert – observed her with a passionate interest.

Her heart beat suddenly fast. But she gave no outward sign of this.

'Okay if I pay by cheque? – I don't have my card on me at present.'

'Si Signora. Of course.'

Felt his eyes on her as she scribbled across the open page, but kept her own on what she was doing.

'Rain again, huh?'

A pause.

'Er – si Signora. The weather is not good.'

'What's your name?'

A rather longer pause. Sensed his surprise. And, of course, his excitement. Then, with a strange simplicity, like he'd known all along she'd ask him this:

'Enrico, Signora. Enrico Muraro.'

About to write in her signature, she hesitated. Looked up suddenly.

Was seen, she knew, to advantage. Her image soft; part burned out against the light. Her clothes – silk suit, in softest amethyst – immaculate, blatantly expensive. Her hair – just recently trimmed, and touched up with a lightener – charmingly disordered, like the wanton curls of a shepherd boy. The total image, spiced with a darkly warm scent (Russian Leather: animal, yet remote), both ambiguous and powerfully feminine.

With her cigarette between her first two fingers still, she

took up her glass. Swallowed quickly. He stood like one
under a spell. Stared.

Her own expression. . . Distant.

'That's nice.'

It had, indeed, a lyrical ring. But she was not, at this
stage, prepared to elaborate. Set her glass abruptly down.
Put her signature to the order with a flourish, ripped it off.

'Okay?'

'Er – si Signora. All is correct.'

'Good. Oh – just a minute.' Ransacked her bag for her
wallet. 'Here!'

He bowed respectfully over his open hand. The note
contained – but only just – between his fore and middle
fingers.

'Mille grazie Signora.'

She flashed him a brief, but one hundred per cent effective
smile. The coup de grâce, as it were.

'Thank you.'

It was the closest she'd come to propositioning a man in
all her life.

Rose suddenly, and walked out without looking back.

Her cheque book remained where she'd left it: on the
table.

He waited till she'd gone. Seized then like a hawk on this
piece of property. He wasn't sure whether it was intentional
or not – her having left it behind. But thought that it must
be. For surely she wouldn't make the same mistake twice?

Here, anyway, in his two hands was his passport. His
means of entry.

Deposited it, as soon as he was able, alongside his personal
effects in the men's room.

Carefully turned the key in his locker door.

Found that he was smiling.

'Forgive me. I would have called during the day, but I wasn't
sure I would find you at home.'

She looked blankly at him a moment, her mouth open. It had gone eleven, and was raining still.

'Oh – good evening.' And, when nothing came of this: 'Is there something I can do?'

He didn't answer at once. Slipped his hand inside his jacket and took out the familiar plastic wallet.

'You left your cheque book, Signora.'

She stared. Smiled at last.

'Oh! I – I don't believe it!' And, laughing: 'I'll forget my head next time.'

He looked penetratingly at her. Had her sussed all right. But refrained at this stage from speaking his thoughts aloud, for he didn't of course know which way the wind was going to blow.

No point, however, in tormenting him further when his eyes so blatantly informed her of what was in his mind.

'You'd better come in a moment – it's so wet out there.'

She stood back, and he stepped hesitantly in. Looked around like it was a well-rehearsed scene in a movie. She was conscious, too, of the falseness of her own behaviour. All she wanted actually was to put a match to him and see him go up in flames.

'Is very nice . . .'

She closed the door.

'Just across.'

He followed her into the lounge. His hair was slicked back with oil or pomade, and the water ran off it literally like off a duck's back. He took out a spotless kerchief and mopped his face with it. Looking, again, all around.

'You live here alone Signora . . .?

She poured two large brandies, screwed the cap back on.

'No. But my husband's away at present. He's in Johannesburg.' She put her head a little to one side. 'He's marvellous really. Makes me feel such a cow!'

He came forward at last. But remained, still, at a respectful distance. She brought his drink across; handed it to him. He reminded her, she didn't know why, of a refugee from a black and white movie. The suit perhaps? – which he wore with typically Continental elegance. His shirt – like the kerchief – was spotless, and he'd his black bow tie on still.

(Had just come off duty perhaps?) He wore, too, a watch with a steel bracelet, and his wrists were those of a grown man – strong, and with a soft covering of hair. Conversely, his features were those of a youth still. He'd pimples, and was obviously having some difficulty using a razor – partly, no doubt, because of this. His hair was black as jet. His eyes were the colour of conkers: a warm, golden brown. Rather darker than her own.

She smiled. Touched her glass against his.

'Cheers.'

He inclined his head.

'Grazie Signora.' And, in almost the same breath: 'Scusi – but you are from America?'

She went across to the sofa and sat down. Put her head back a little and looked warmly, humorously at him.

'New York. How did you guess?'

'The accent, of course. And something about you . . .'

She laughed.

'I'm very New World I'm afraid.'

'But not completely. Something, too, of the Old.'

Smiled.

'England must have rubbed off on me.' And: 'Please: come and sit down. Tell me something about yourself instead.'

He at once obeyed, like a small boy summoned by the teacher. (Sat, however – not on the sofa – but in one of the two deep armchairs.) Or like she was his mother perhaps? A certain deference. . . But looked, at the same time, deeply into her eyes. No man, surely, ever looked at his mother in quite this way? But ready, too – like a soldier – to comply with her every command. His eyes alone dared. His eyes alone sought forcibly to penetrate the invisible barrier of social reserve.

'Signora is too kind.'

'Tell me: how old are you?'

This, of course, embarrassed him a little. But he was too polite not to reply.

'I am nineteen.'

'Which part of Italy are you from?'

'I was born in Rome. My father is wine waiter in a hotel there. But my mother came from Venice.'

She looked at him a moment.

'Oh!' And: 'How strange.'

'Strange?'

'Well – I didn't mean it like that exactly. What I meant was, I know it well. I went there for my honeymoon.'

He sat a little forward, his elbows on his knees. And against the light – she'd the lamps on only; a down-directed, warmly subdued glow. So that she sensed more of his expression than she actually saw.

'Ah, yes. It is for lovers . . .'

Though not, perhaps, for husbands.

She finished her drink quickly – her third in half an hour. Got up and went to the mantelshelf for her cigarettes. Her lighter, she knew, was on the coffee table. Where she'd deliberately left it.

She put a cigarette between her lips, felt along the shelf.

' 'S funny. I was sure I'd left my – '

'Here Signora.'

He picked the lighter up and brought it across.

Did not, however, hand it to her. Flicked it instead, and held out the flame.

'Please. . . Allow me.'

'Oh! – thanks.'

Leaned forward and took a light. Threw her head abruptly back and blew the smoke out through her nostrils.

Again their eyes met. No masks now. Bare flesh, face to face. Red with passion. Her eyes softened, blurred. She put out her free hand, slipped her fingers in under his collar. Their lips approached. Touched. Withdrew. His dark, intelligent eyes burned into her own. The low lamps; the late hour; the warmth of the drink . . .

She dropped her cigarette in the grate and took him by both lapels.

Their lips smudged. Lost shape a little. Merged.

But, after showering with him the following morning . . . What sort of gesture was this? What exactly was she trying to say?

Her orgasm had died on her. Abruptly. But put this down to 'feeling tired'.

Other than which aberration, it was all she'd hoped it would be. He was sweet; rather ingenuous. Or 'natural' was perhaps a more accurate expression. She was certainly his first; and he'd that dew-fresh youthfulness she so adored.

But there was one thing she wanted more than him just now: a drink.

At only ten a.m.

She followed him back into the bedroom. Stood before the glass in her short wrap and bare feet. Nervous, she grabbed for her cigarettes and lit one. Turned the lighter slowly round in her hand. Was aware, suddenly, of her reflection. Her hair wet still, lots of curls, she looked sulky and – yeah – dead scared. Sexually, rather ambiguous. Two youths together in the changing room . . .

He'd most of his clothes on already. Reached now for his jacket.

'Signora – who are you? What is your name? Rather, your Christian name.'

She replied without turning, her eyes fixed on the tip of her cigarette. The smoke broken, like her nerves. She had to grasp the elbow of this arm to keep the hand from shaking. There was now just one thought in her head: to get rid of him as fast as she could.

'Vivienne – two n's and an e. I work for an agency: talent scout, of a sort.'

'It sounds very interesting.'

'It isn't. Well, it is. But I can't talk about it now.' But then, because there was an unintentional edge to her voice, and she certainly didn't want to hurt him: 'Another time perhaps.'

'Signora – would you like some breakfast? If you tell me where to go, I will prepare it for you.'

'No. You'll have to leave I'm afraid. I've a lot on today, and my woman will be here shortly.' (A lie. She'd given her the day off. Purposely.) 'It wouldn't do for her to find you here.'

Sensed his dismay. Furthermore, his objection to what he obviously knew was an untruth.

'I would like to have done this for you. I am a very good cook: you would be surprised – but pleasantly, I think.'

She threw down the lighter, turned.

'Look: for once you're gonna have to forget you're a waiter. I can't afford for Elise to find you here.'

'But, just a moment ago, there was no hurry. Now . . .'

She glared.

'Yeah! – now there is!'

But could give him no explanation for this sudden urgency – any more than she could herself. Except – desperate. Again. Like when she'd come in and found Hugh at home still.

He came across. Stood before her like a matador, tall and proud. But refrained, thank God, from touching her. Had he done so, she would – she felt sure – have exploded.

'Signora – is something wrong? Have I done something to upset you?'

She smiled. Sort of.

'God, we've been in bed together all night and you're still talking to me like I'm your mother!' And, when he drew himself up still further, his expression consciously pained: 'Do what I ask Bambino, please.'

'But – '

'No!'

He asserted himself suddenly. A spark of Latin fire.

'So: how long before I see you again? I cannot leave until I know this.'

She took a deep breath. Then:

'Okay. You leave me your 'phone number, and I'll give you a ring. More than that I can't promise.'

He took out his diary. Tore out a leaf, and wrote his number on it. And, handing it to her:

'You told me this was different . . .'

She carefully folded the piece of paper and slipped it into her pocket. Looked, at last, into his eyes.

'It is. Very. And – next time – I'll make sure we're not disturbed. Remember, I didn't know all this was going to happen.'

He didn't, of course, believe her. But said nothing, until:

'How long?'

'I told you: when I can. But I'm a very busy person.'

He took her hand. Touched it with his lips.

'I understand. But I will live only for this moment.'

She kissed him lightly on the mouth.

'I'll see what I can do.' And: 'You can use this door. It'll take you straight out into the hall.'

She stood a moment. Listened. Then, when she was sure he'd gone, went through to the lounge.

To the drinks cabinet. Opened it and took out the brandy. Did not, however, fill her glass at once. It was important she convince herself first she didn't actually need it. Fancied it, rather. Fancied a drink – why not? The nervous feeling she'd had, the little panic worm in her gut . . . a passing thing. But, since she had the stuff to hand, she'd pour one anyway.

Then, she'd go cook herself some breakfast.

Couldn't make out at first what was happening.

But like someone had forced her over onto her side and was pressing down on her shoulder. Like being woken out of an anaesthetic. Her mouth blocked, like with a wad of something. Her throat on fire. And literally gasping for breath.

This mess . . .

God – what was it? Where was she?

'Madame! – oh, Madame, please wake. Please.' And: 'Mon Dieu! What shall I do?'

Mon Dieu . . .

Elise.

But . . .

'Oh, Madame! – you are awake! Now, please, let me help you.'

On the bed. Since when, she'd no idea. Her mouth full of scalding debris. Everything . . . smothered.

The little woman now took her under her arms and dragged her up into a sitting position. She didn't even try to resist.

'Thank God, thank God! Another moment and I would have been too late.'

Now, at last, she realised what had happened. She was

drunk. Had somehow got herself to bed. Where – had it not
been for Elise – she'd have choked on her vomit and died.

Shocked almost out of her mind, she broke down and
wept.

Was swept then by shame. For it must be more than
obvious what had happened. To Elise even, brought up
though she was in a convent, from where she'd gone straight
into service.

'I – Elise, I'm sorry. I don't know what . . .'

'Now! – into the bathroom. And I will see what I can do
here. Then, when you are ready, I will make you some
coffee.'

She crawled obediently off the bed and stumbled across
to the bathroom. She'd the wrap on still, but the belt had
worked itself loose and dropped down now over her hips.
She felt helpless. Terrified. Like a child woken out of a
nightmare. Avoided her reflection in the glass for fear of
what she might see. Her head felt like it was about to burst
– she must have been blue. Was only now starting to breathe
normally.

The earlier events of the day – bathing here with her lover,
in this same room – seemed light years away. So what had
happened? What had got into her for God's sake?

A fluke.

Her mind was occupied, and . . . she'd drunk too much
without really thinking.

Simple.

'I – I don't know. I – '

Elise, holding on to the coffee pot like it was a cat or
some other small creature, deeply embarrassed by it all now
the emergency was over. As, of course, was she. Felt,
however, that she owed her some sort of apology.

She sat at the kitchen table, toyed with the spoon in her
saucer. The coffee was scalding hot and aromatic, but her
stomach felt like it just couldn't take it.

'I'd a lot on my mind, and I guess I must have drunk too
much.' But, hastily: 'How, I don't know. I mean, all I had
was – no: wait a minute. It must have been the tablets. I
remember now: I took some pain killers. I'd slept badly, and
I'd a headache.' (All of which was true.) 'So I took a couple

of Panadeine. Then I went into the lounge. . . And I – I
wasn't thinking, you see. And I must have taken a drink
without . . . Well, without thinking, if you see what I mean.'

Made a poor attempt to laugh.

'But, Madame, you must be careful. You must promise
me that in future you will think first. I cannot – I dare not
imagine what would have happened had I not – But, you
see, it was an act of God that I was prompted to look in
when I did. I was at the Oratory, for mass you know, and
I was just leaving when I – '

'Yes. Thank you. Thank you Elise. I don't know what
I'd have done without your help.'

'Drink the coffee, Madame. It will steady you.'

She shook like a leaf still. Both from the after effects of
alcohol, and from sheer shock at what had so nearly
happened to her. Was obliged to use both hands to lift the
cup to her lips.

Elise had not, of her own accord, referred to the incident,
but she sensed the woman's unspoken fear. This was the
third in a string of such incidents of late, and she was no
doubt in dread of another.

She plucked up courage. Adopted what she hoped was a
convincingly responsible manner.

'Elise: look at me.'

And, when she turned from the sink, her expression suitably masked:

'There's no chance it'll happen again. So, please, don't
worry.'

But – an echo here of a similar pledge given her husband
at the breakfast table. An echo, too, in the lie she'd told:
that it was the fault, rather, of the tablets she'd taken.

Was surprised, however, at the frankness of Elise's reply.

'Madame – it is not perhaps for me to say, but this is three
times now. . . And, of course, I do worry – M'sieur, too. I
know that he is concerned.'

Could feel her face freeze over.

They looked at one another a moment in silence. Then,
at last, Elise dropped her eyes. (Had of course no option.
For, as an employee, she was in a difficult position. A stroke

of luck, all the same. For she'd felt her resolution start to waver.) Turned again to the sink.

It happened that Enrico put up at a hostel for young men run by some sort of Catholic organisation.

So that there was a good deal of confusion before she was able at last – not, actually, to speak with him: he was back on duty already – but to leave a message.

The gentleman who answered the 'phone – he was a priest perhaps?, or something of the sort: certainly not a layman – spoke, like Enrico, with a marked accent. He was also very suspicious.

Was she a relative? If so, he could –

No, no. Just a friend.

And, when the 'phone suddenly frosted over:

'Uh – of the family, that is.'

'Signor Muraro has no family here Signora. They are in Italy still.'

'Oh! – I see.' Duly chastised. Could feel herself start to blush even. 'Well . . .'

'What name shall I give Signora?'

(Dried up, disgusting old hypocrite.)

'Stone. Mrs. I'll leave my telephone number, just in case. See that he gets it, huh?'

A pause. Which, at this distance even, more than made its point.

Then:

'Naturally Signora. Goodnight.'

'Thank you.'

Slammed down the receiver. Glared at it a moment.

'There was this old guy answered the 'phone. But really cagey, y'know? I don't know what he thought I was after.'

He looked a moment into her eyes. Smiled at last.

'I do.'

She laughed a little. And again. Chased his lips with her own.

'Bambino . . . je t'adore – or whatever that is in Italian.'

And, smiling: 'I'm sorry: I have a French maid. And she – well, she talks French . . .'

His turn to laugh.

But meant what she said. He'd given her enormous pleasure this last hour or two. Was a sensitive, intelligent lover, like most Latins – or so she imagined. Certainly he came close to filling the gap in her venereal experience: just as she'd known he would. For he was unusual, and stylish too. Rather like a woman. She'd but to suggest, and he knew exactly what she wanted.

He lay on his back. She, on her side. Each fitted the other as neatly as two pieces in a jigsaw. It was so quiet she could hear the movement of her watch on the bedside cabinet. Curiously amplified. As was their every small shift of position.

'Signora?'

'Mm?'

'Have you done this before?'

'What?'

'I mean – have you other lovers?'

'No.' And: 'Only my husband.'

He thought a moment.

'What, then, made you take a lover now?'

'Oh, I don't know.'

'Your husband: what sort of lover is he?'

She was torn between loyalty, and a desire to excuse herself. For of course, the real question was – what sort of lover was she? Saw, with terrible clarity, her own short-comings with regard to this.

She turned slowly over on her back. Pushed her fingers in through her hair.

'Adequate. But we've been married a long time . . .'

'How long?'

'Fifteen years. But please: I don't want to talk about that.'

He studied her profile in the low light of the bedside lamp. Could feel his eyes – literally, it seemed – bore into her. Distantly: sounds off the street. The occasional passing car. Here: gentle movement of the bed hangings. Four poster, in the French style. Brought together at the top in a sort of coronet. Cream and brown. Mahogany frame furnished in cream silks. Dark brown duvet . . .

'But I know nothing about you.'

'Well. . . What is there to know? Not a great deal.'

'You are a mystery?'

Smiled again.

'Oh, no.' And: 'I wish I was. No: I'm very ordinary I'm afraid. My one real vice is that I smoke in bed.'

'You shouldn't!'

'I know. It's really not good for you. I have a doctor friend, and he – '

'Not good for the bed! – suppose you set it all alight? No: but there is something about you. Something different. You seem at first very extrovert. But you are also in some sense withdrawn. People must find you fascinating.'

'Still?'

'Oh, yes. In fact, I would guess that you are more attractive now than, say, ten years ago?'

Actually, he was right. As a younger woman, she hadn't half whatever it was she had now. At thirty-five she was more confident, less scrupulous, and more successful as a result. (Success, however, brought a degree of loneliness. Nobody really liked successful people. And there was a lot of jealousy – especially from men.) Certainly, too, she was better looking. Her features more developed, more inter-esting. She was slim still, boyishly so, but wore her clothes better. Was altogether more pleased with her appearance.

And yet . . .

'What did you mean, withdrawn? No one ever told me that before.'

'I don't know.' And: 'Are you sure there has been no one else? – no other lover?'

She moistened her lips. Looked up into the soft folds of the canopy.

'Oh, all right. Yes.'

'There – I knew it! I knew that you had a secret!'

This persistent romanticism both irritated and alarmed her.

For, of course, he was warm.

But, thankfully, not warm enough. In fact, only slightly so.

'I'd hardly call it a secret. I mean, all my friends know about it – though not, of course, my husband.'

'Your husband must in any case be more to you than a friend . . .'

She thought a moment.

'Mm.'

'And this other – who was he?'

'A young man, like yourself.'

Said nothing, however, about an older woman. Felt sure this would not have fitted in with his idea of her at all. He did not, she knew, entirely like the idea of a previous male partner – quite the contrary. But was fascinated, all the same.

'But yes: this accounts for it. For your sadness sometimes. Was it an unhappy affair? – I sense that it was.'

She thought it wiser to go along with this, though neither of her two affairs could strictly be classified as such. Any more than could this one.

'Uh – yeah. A little. Most love affairs are, I think. I mean, like all good things, they must come to an end sometime . . .'

He raised himself suddenly on his elbow. Looked down at her. And, in what appeared to be a flash of inspiration:

'And what about your affair with life?'

She felt trapped. Sat up abruptly.

'Oh! – fine!'

'What is it? Aren't you well?'

'I have to go outside, that's all.' She got out of bed, dragged on her wrap. Unwilling, for some reason, to parade around with nothing on. 'You oughtta get some sleep now. We have to be up early, remember?'

He dropped dutifully back on the pillow.

'Si.'

But, as she went into the bathroom, sensed his mystification. The way his eyes followed after her.

He was just a kid maybe. But he was no fool.

★

They'd breakfast in the lounge. (She'd arranged, as promised, for Elise to get in later. So as to avoid any embarrassment, and to give them a little time together.)

He sat opposite her, at the smaller, drop-leaf table near the window. Immaculate, as always. His shirt as white as snow in the clear morning light. (Remembered how he'd draped it over the back of a chair before getting into bed, so it shouldn't crease. 'You're a bit of a dandy, you know.' At which he'd proudly admitted: 'Oh, yes. My mother said always to take care of my clothes. This was before my father rose from the ranks, you see, and was not as well paid as now.' He shrugged. 'It is a habit, I suppose.' But was amused by the unselfconscious way in which he spoke of his parents. No hint of rebellion, as with most young people today.)

Poised, self-assured (though not offensively so: for he remained, as at first, disarmingly respectful), he seemed somehow older than his age. She was very aware of this odd sophistication – which, she wasn't sure why, made her a little mistrustful of him. He was no longer her 'bambino' – pure, still, as a lighted candle – but a serious young *homme du monde*, who not only occupied her husband's place at table but had splashed himself liberally with his after shave.

And so, to hide her discomfort:

'What would your reverend gentleman say were he to see you now?'

'*Come?*'

'I'm sure he wouldn't recognise you.'

He looked at her a moment across the table. Then: 'Why?'

'Darling, you don't exactly look like a choirboy.'

Emphasised her meaning with her eyes. But suspected their message was also a mite resentful.

He took up a piece of toast, buttered it carefully.

'I am too old, in any case, for this.'

His rather dignified manner tempted her to pull his leg a little, but she refrained. She could, she knew, have cut him up in little pieces were she so inclined. (Kids, did they only know it, were so fucking vulnerable. As, of course, was she – for this very reason perhaps: that she'd never really grown up.) For the present, however:

'Yes, I know. I was just joking.' And, helping herself to marmalade: 'Were you ever in the choir? I mean, most Italians seem – '

'No. I never sang in church. But I was an altar boy – you know, with the censer, during mass. And I would have to swing it, so, or the incense would not burn.'

She smiled.

But the images these words of his brought to mind disturbed her. The Elevation; the Consecration; wine into blood. (Whether or not she was ever completely convinced of this, she wasn't sure. The idea, however, was attractive. If only because –) Her favourite glass – chalice shaped . . .

'You must have been very sweet. I expect your mother was proud of you.' And: 'Does she have any other children? – or are you the only one?'

'No: I have two sisters.'

'Oh.'

'Yes. But they are both younger. They are at school still.'

But . . .

Looked at him, and he was again different. But in a different way. The room, too. Everything. Like some sort of invisible influence – of a negative, even sinister nature – imposed itself upon her eyes, or all they saw. Not obviously. Insidiously, rather. But a definite shift. Accompanied by a sudden sense of panic.

She put her knife abruptly down. Her hand shook. Could feel the colour drain from her face.

And – like she was going to scream.

Was aware suddenly that he'd stopped talking and was staring at her.

'I – uh, yeah. Sure.' And, when he didn't reply: 'Wasn't that what you said?'

'No. It was not.'

But didn't see why she should have to apologise. Why she should allow him to embarrass her in this way.

She wanted a drink. And she'd damn well have one.

'I'm sorry. I was miles away.'

She got up. Went to the cabinet and poured herself a stiff whisky. (This was the sort of thing Hugh would say: 'You look like you need a stiff whisky.' But not of late.)

Had to hold the glass to the bottle to keep her hand from shaking. Spilled some anyway.

No sooner did the smell of the spirit reach her nostrils, however, when she was again mistress of herself.

He was shocked, naturally. Though why, she couldn't –

Relied on his discretion. (But that her room – this room, which she so loved – could, even briefly, have appeared so strange, so sinister, terrified her.)

She drank quickly. Took her glass with her to the window. Smiled. (As, indeed, she now felt able to do. Fire in her gut; fumes ascending, like incense, to her brain. The god in his temple . . .)

'What a beautiful morning. Be warm today, I bet.'

On a stand, there in the corner, the huge brass container with its profusion of yellow roses all alight like tallow candles on a paschal altar. Same soft effulgence. Same ethereal glow.

He looked at her a moment. Then:

'Yes.'

Put his napkin suddenly aside, rose from the table and came across.

Fixing her with his dark, steady gaze, he took the glass from her hand.

She feigned surprise. (Though, in fact, it was what she'd expected.) Like, really, she hadn't the vaguest idea what was going on – what he'd think of next.

'Is a little too early, Signora, for this sort of thing.'

His repeated use of the term 'Signora' rather than of her Christian name – the distance this implied – worried her rather.

But was angry, too. Ought, perhaps, to have given some indication of this. To have told him where he got off.

Shrugged, instead. Lightly, and in a conciliatory sort of way. But knew that she stiffened. That her expression froze. And that he of course saw this.

'Okay. If that's how you feel. But I don't see what's so unusual about it – or that it matters specially.'

Smarted, however. Was unable to shake off this sense of having been fairly chastised.

'Do you always drink at this time?'

She sighed. Rolled her eyes upward in mock exasperation.
'No. Of course not.' (Recently, yes.) And: 'But if I
did?'

But it wasn't like with Hugh. There was the Latin mach-
ismo – so much more difficult to deal with. And altogether
sterner: in fact, ridiculously so for his age. Obviously
thought he was doing the right thing (had, of course, seen
her drunk before: which gave him an advantage of a sort),
but was too openly alarmed, too critical.

He'd her glass in his hand still. Looked, now, into it, as
for an explanation.

'Is not, perhaps, for me to say . . .'

(Elise. Her very words.)

She nodded.

'Exactly.'

But kept her expression open, bright. In fact, too bright.
Brittle even. And her eyes, as always, too expressive. Not
intentionally; but because she was so damn mad.

Looked at her watch. (But like a nightmare – all in the
bright, the sacral light of morning.)

'Time's getting on. I ought – '

'What about your breakfast? – aren't you going to finish?'

'No. I've . . . had all I want.'

He set the glass carefully aside. His every move precise as
that of a chess master.

'You are not cross with me?'

'God, no. Whatever for? But I really ought to go.'

'Then I must, too.'

'Yes. I – I'll give you a ring.'

He took her hand. Looked a moment into her eyes.

'I will wait till I hear from you.'

Her heart beat like the wings of a humming bird. So light,
so fast, she hardly felt it. And so desperate now for a drink
she'd have crawled on her knees for it.

'Sure.'

He'd no sooner gone when she grabbed for the glass and
took it with both hands to her lips.

It was like a transfusion.

★

Two youths . . .

But –

Didn't know where she was even. (Or was it the tube?) Dimly but evenly lit. Like a sort of landing. Tiles. . . Aerosol graffiti. . . A further flight of steps. Beyond which . . . black.

Here, stink of disinfectant.

Two youths. Leering. Had her suddenly by the arm and – like she was a rag doll: seemingly weightless, and with no control over her limbs – threw her up against the wall, thumped her across the face, and . . .

No pain. Heard it only. Like somebody smacking cold meat.

Tried to speak. But like her mouth, inside and out, was just a jelly.

Something in her hand. (Her bag?) Which they tore now from her grasp.

And –

God!, they were going to kill her.

Must have screamed. But couldn't hear anything. One of them hit her again. Felt it this time. But distantly. Like, really, her head belonged to someone else. (Did not, in fact, believe this was happening to her. She was dreaming perhaps?)

Her hands . . . and, when she took them down, smothered in blood . . .

Threw up violently. And again.

But . . . gone. No one. Nothing.

Raining up there. Could hear the water shoosh . . . wheels of the occasional vehicle. Some traffic still.

The stairs . . .

But like they rush at her somehow, smack her in the face.

God, she was going to die . . .

'I must be dead.'

Instead . . .

The bathroom glass. Her image there.

But how . . .?

No idea. Some kindly soul perhaps. Saw the state she was in, and – (God, God . . .)

But what had they done to her? Black and blue. Literally.

Or not blue so much as scarlet, tinged with a funereal, a royal violet. One eye so swollen she couldn't open it. Lid drop like a broken blind.

Put both taps on full. Washed off some of the blood. Her lower lip open, like a surgeon's wound. Neat. Two distinctly separate lobes of flesh.

But could have been killed.

Turned. . . Endlessly, it seemed, upon some subtle axis. Straight into the wall.

No sound. Soft against . . . something. Not so much hard as firm. Firm but elusive.

Dissolve. . .

He stood at her door in the bright morning light.

It was past ten. But, because it was Sunday, there wasn't as much traffic as usual.

There were some half dozen names up next the door: each with its own bell.

At the bottom:

'Stone. Grnd. floor.'

He pushed it. Waited.

The bell sounds automatically in all her rooms. But not obtrusively. A leisured, musical chime, like that of a clock.

She thinks it must be Elise – though she isn't normally in on a Sunday. Has her story ready. 'Don't look at my face – it's a mess. I did such a stupid thing. You're never gonna believe this, but . . .'

Totally convincing.

But, when she opened the door:

'Enrico!' And, furious at this unexpected assault upon the paper walls of her fantasy: 'I – I've told you before: don't come unless I 'phone!'

'My God! – what has happened? Have you had an accident?'

'Look: I'm sorry. I can't talk to you now. I have to go out, and – '

'But . . . your face.'

'Well I'm certainly not going to stand here and argue about it.'

'Pardon me – but I was worried. I rang you three times last night, but could get – '

'Please: when I want to see you, I'll – '

But, about to close the door, found that she couldn't. He'd his foot in it: and it wouldn't budge another inch.

'Oh, for Christ's sake!'

'No! I must speak with you. *Per favore*, Signora – open the door.'

'I can't. I'm expecting my husband. He – '

'That is a lie. Your husband is away.'

'So? I've a right to privacy in my own home, surely? Now, get your foot out or I'll call the police.'

Could not, however, hold him off. Strength for strength, he'd the advantage. Put the whole of his weight now against the door, forced it open and walked in.

She was furious.

And a little afraid.

Turned abruptly, and went across to the lounge.

'Make it snappy then: I haven't got all day. And I absolutely forbid you to call like this again. Suppose my husband had been here? What in hell would I have done?'

He came in after her. Closed the door.

'What you always do. You'd have lied to him.'

About to light a cigarette, she turned suddenly.

'How dare you!'

He stood his ground, however.

'Forgive me Signora, but – unlike your husband – I am not easily deceived.'

Screamed at him now.

'You don't know my husband!'

'No. But – '

'You don't know me even!'

'Oh, yes. Better, I think, than you know yourself.' And, before she could start to argue: 'Please Signora: listen to me. At least hear what I have to say.'

She was silent a moment. Flicked her lighter at last; exhaled furiously through her nostrils.

'I don't know what makes you think you've the right to say anything.'

'Signora, I last called you at two this morning. Yet you were still not at home.'

She glared. Then, suddenly inspired, for she wondered if perhaps it was a matter rather of sexual jealousy – in which case it would be relatively easy to deal with:

'Okay – what's eating you?'

He approached at last. But stayed clear of her immediate vicinity.

'I don't want to upset you. But I would like to ask you something. I have this right, I think.'

She shrugged.

'You can ask what you like. But I don't guarantee I'll answer.'

'Well. . . But I don't actually need an answer.'

She picked at the butt of the cigarette with her thumbnail.

'What do you mean?'

'What I say. I have seen for myself.'

'Seen what for Christ's sake?'

Knew, however, what was coming next. Steeled herself, as for a shock.

'That something is the matter with you.' He hesitated. Then: 'Signora – why do you have this problem? What is the reason for it?'

She frowned. Turned her head a little away from him, but with her eyes fixed on him still. Turned her face away, rather. For it was an action with the face: at once aggressive and defensive.

'Problem? I don't have any problem.'

Again he hesitated. Until:

'You are worried perhaps about something?'

'No.' And: 'I don't understand you at all. I don't know what you're getting at. If you've something to say, then for God's sake say it.'

He stared.

'You frighten me . . .'

'What's that supposed to mean?'

'But I cannot believe that you are ignorant of what I am trying to tell you. If, however, you must have it in black and white – you drink too much Signora: and this concerns me.'

'What the hell are you talking about? I never heard such – '

'It seems a pity that someone like yourself cannot – '

'Look: what I do in my own time is my affair, and no way is it a problem. You've got a damn cheek if you think you can walk in here and – '

'Please: is not necessary to raise your voice. All I would like to ask is can I help at all? Is there something I can do? I should hate for our love affair to spoil because of this.'

She threw up her chin.

'Love affair! – some hope you've got. If I'd been in my right mind I wouldn't have had you here in the first place.'

'This is what I was afraid of. That when the effect of the drink had passed, it would no longer seem such a good idea.'

'Oh, for God's sake! – I didn't mean it literally. Though what I thought I saw in you I can't at this moment imagine. With your oiled hair and Goddam polished shoes you remind me of a small-time gigolo – which is about all you're fit for, so don't go playing Father Confessor with me!'

He drew himself up a little.

'Perhaps. But this is not the point, Signora.'

She took a deep breath.

'Okay. So you think I have a problem.'

Turned, went across to the window. Was deeply angry still. But felt, too, that – since he obviously had it all wrong (his approach was too simple by far) – she ought perhaps to put the thing in its correct perspective. (But . . .)

But the words were off her tongue already, like honey off a spoon.

'You're not,' she said, 'gonna believe me – but, really, there's nothing in it. I'm a busy person, and I need to relax sometimes. To work off tension, like anyone else. How I choose to do this is my own affair. I don't have any neuroses, any childhood traumas – that sort of thing. In fact the only real problem I have is convincing people like yourself – who find it either abnormal, or disgusting, or both – that, really, there is no cause for alarm.' She shrugged. Laughed a little. 'I enjoy a drink, that's all.'

'But is this not an abnormality of a kind – that you see it

in such a way? Look what it is doing to you: you cannot
now wake in the morning without you want a drink.'

She dropped her eyes. But this was not –

Or was it?

No. Nor did she have to subject herself to this type of
interrogation. She was not, after all, a child. She was a –

'Signora, please. This is a dangerous game you are playing.
Not only are you effectively cheating those around you, you
are also cheating yourself.'

She inhaled. Closed her swollen eye against the smoke.

'Rubbish. Either way, it's my choice. And for Christ's
sake stop calling me Signora.'

'No: you are wrong. You are no longer able to choose.
You will end by killing yourself. Each time I see you, you
are drunk already – or nearly so. And, in the restaurant, you
are so drunk you forget to take your things with you. What
kind of life is this?'

She swallowed hard. Her head – the whole of it – throbbed
still. Likewise her busted lip.

Had to get rid of him somehow.

'Now look: I've been pretty tolerant with you so far. But
I'm not gonna let you run my life. I appreciate your concern.
I just wish I could convince you there isn't any need for
it . . .'

He stared momentarily. Then:

'So what were you doing last night to get your face in
such a state? No: please. Answer me.'

Her heart thumped like a drum. Her throat was so tight
she could hardly speak.

'That's my business.'

'Is not, in any case, necessary that you tell me. I see it all
in your eyes. Either you have fallen somewhere, or you were
attacked. Easy prey for someone as desperate as yourself.
Someone who needed your money. So – what will happen
next? How much longer are you going to be able to deceive
those who are closest to you? Or – more importantly –
yourself?'

She crushed out her cigarette. Went to the door and threw
it open.

'You may leave. My maid will be here shortly – and I'm not gonna risk her finding you here.'

'I have heard this before. Or something very like it.'

'Get out!'

He came slowly across. Looked searchingly into her eyes.

'Please: don't be angry. I cannot leave while you are like this.' And: 'Did you go to the police? You ought at least to have reported the matter.'

'No. All I had in my bag, apart from cosmetics, was a purse. And there wasn't much in that.'

'And your face. . . Have you seen a doctor?'

She said nothing. Only looked at him. Again he drew himself up in that ridiculously pompous way he had.

'Obviously not. And for the same reason you have not been to the police: you were too ashamed.'

'Get out. Or I'll have you thrown out. And I'm not gonna say it again.'

He was silent a moment. Then:

'There is a reason for my concern Signora. My mother died of alcoholism in a Rome hospital when she was only thirty-three years old. My youngest sister was a baby still.' He paused. 'For your own sake, think about this.'

She watched him go.

Blinked.

It was like he'd slapped her across the face – only worse. Because now, of course, she understood. And, as he'd no doubt intended, felt at the same time terribly guilty.

But it was no good. She was not going to make herself responsible for something which – however sad – was not her fault. Could not allow him to interfere with her on the basis of what had happened to him in the past. Whatever his personal need. She was not, after all, his mother. Did not believe she was about to die of alcoholism. And, if he couldn't accept her for what she was rather than as a substitute for what he'd lost, then he must look elsewhere.

Could not, however, erase the interview from her mind. Remained both deeply disturbed by it, and deeply angry. (That he'd dared speak to her in such a way!)

Knew, too, that he haunted her.

Saw him on several occasions – which must have been more than just a coincidence. For how often, in the normal way of things, did one see the same person twice in a place as big as London? – let alone three times.

He made no attempt to speak, however. Only looked.

Or perhaps she'd imagined it?

No.

She called a cab in the Charing Cross Road, and. . . Across the street, his collar up against the rain.

And, a second time, in Selfridges. In the perfumery department.

And, again, outside her home when she got back late one night from work. His sallow features marked, as on each of these occasions, by an expression of miserable longing.

Suddenly afraid, she shouted out that if she saw him again she'd call the police.

He withdrew at once, like a disheartened hound. Vanished as mysteriously as he'd come. But left her feeling like she'd just woken from a nightmare. Or, at best, from a dream she couldn't explain. And unable at the same time to dispel a nagging sense of guilt over the whole affair – something entirely foreign to her.

Then – one evening, after a particularly exhausting day – she found a letter from him on the mat.

'May I come? I promise not to speak of what was said at our last meeting. I think of you all the time, and cannot bear to be so cut off from you.' And, somewhat selfconsciously: 'Ever your, Enrico.'

The idea of a night spent in his arms was in fact terribly tempting. The more so in view of his apparent contrition, his obvious deprivation.

Was on the verge of agreeing to see him when, the following night, she'd a call from Hugh. He'd booked the next flight, and was coming home.

'Fantastic! I can't wait. What's that? – this line is terrible: I can hardly hear you. Oh, yeah, fine. What about you? – you must be dog-tired.' And: 'Hurry back Hughie. I love you.'

Replaced the receiver.

Looked at it a moment, uncertain as to her actual feelings.

Mixed, of course. As always. Wanted him with her again, but resented the strain his presence placed on her. The constant deception, the evasive action made necessary by this living of another life right here under his nose.

Had done it, of course, before.

And would have, she supposed, to do it again.

She'd been to sleep already, but was woken by the 'phone.

Half-twelve. She'd been in bed just twenty minutes.

The lamp by her side was on still – she couldn't sleep without it. What light there was – low. Warm.

Hugh had his back to her. Was apparently asleep. Everything shadowy there: the coved ceiling, its corners arching over like the underside of a wave; the ivory walls; the window with its deep embrasures.

Phantom breeze lifts the net. She half expects to see someone step from out the folds.

But no. Only the 'phone.

Reached for the receiver.

'Signora. . .?'

Took it slowly down from her ear. Was sure Hugh must have heard. Stared at the mouthpiece like it was something totally alien – something invented on the spur of the moment by some invisible influence. His ludicrously reduced voice rattled on still: urgent, imploring.

Put it down at last.

Small click.

Looked again over her shoulder.

He hadn't moved. But:

'Who was that?'

'God knows. Must've been a wrong number.'

He, too, set the receiver back on its stand. Looked at it in much the same way.

So: his position now was clear. She wanted nothing more to do with him, and this was her way of telling him so. She was as cowardly in her handling of burned-out paramours as she was in her handling of more complex problems.

As far as she was concerned, he had ceased to exist.

Very well. If that was how she felt. But he was not going to stand aside and see her kill herself.

Evening. Late. Had worked on, as she often did, well past her usual time.

Let herself in at the front. The hall light was on. Not a glimmer even of daylight from the upstairs landing. The window black as, crossing to the lounge, she glanced up.

Played her usual little game of walking on the white squares only. Stones across the stream. . .

'Hugh?'

'Yes: I'm here.'

Knew, before she went in even, that something was wrong. He'd filled a pipe, and was setting it furiously alight. He only ever smoked a pipe when he was upset, or annoyed, or both.

She closed the door, threw down her things. Wanted a drink; but sensed that this was not the right moment. Lit a cigarette instead.

'Something wrong?'

He looked acutely at her. Acutely, because there was something extreme about his expression. Something which, in all the years she'd been married to him, she'd seen only twice. Once, when a business colleague had betrayed him. And now.

'I'm not sure.' And: 'Only you can tell me that.'

She dropped the cigarettes back into her bag. Came across. 'What do you mean?'

He took an envelope down from the mantelshelf and held it out to her.

She frowned. Felt the blood first drain from her face as she recognised the writing, then flood suddenly back till even her ears burned.

'What is it?'

'What does it look like?'

'A letter. But. . .'

'Go on. Read it.'

Forced herself, before taking it from him, to look into his eyes. They were full of a terrible suppressed rage. And, worse perhaps, were deeply shocked. Their expression that of one recently involved in a near fatal accident. Or of a man brought in off the battlefield. A man so seriously wounded his body temporarily withholds this information from his brain lest he go mad.

She took the envelope from him.

'All right. But really, I – '

'Read it.'

In a small voice:

'Yeah, well, okay.'

Dear Sir,

I must apologise first for writing to you in this way. You do not of course know me, and it may seem that I am taking a liberty in addressing you at all. We have, however, one thing in common: a shared admiration for the lady who happens to be your wife.

I will spare you an explanation as to why I feel I have as much right as you in this matter. But would like to say that I remain her friend – though obviously, after what I have to say, I cannot expect that she will continue to regard me as such.

I don't know if you are aware that your wife is an alcoholic. Perhaps not. For I understand that you are away for long periods at a time, and are only recently returned from another such trip. I am, however. And it makes me very sad. Especially since, when I spoke to her about it, she seemed determined not to admit to it. Like my mother, who was similarly afflicted, she has developed a deliberate blindness to her condition, and it makes me sad to see this in one who is otherwise extremely intelligent and who has my highest regard. I hope, as a result of my letter to you, that you too will speak with her. And that you will have more success than I.

Please rest assured that I have no motive other than a sincere wish to see her free of her dependence before it is too late. I am aware that she will not like me for what I have done. And, as a result of my having confronted her with the truth, obviously wants nothing more to do with me. If, however, my having interfered in this way will have contributed toward her return to health, then it will have been worth my while.

Again, I beg that you forgive me.
Yours very sincerely,
Enrico Muraro.'

Could not at first take her eyes off the page. Was shocked.
Furious. Had he been present now, she'd surely have killed
him.

Dragged, instead, at her cigarette. Her eyes part closed
against the smoke.

In effect, she was going to have to defend herself on two
counts: his accusation of alcoholism, and his intimations as
to the exact nature of their relationship. Though whether it
might not be better to admit to this last – in order to blame
the other on his disappointment at her having terminated
their association – she wasn't at this stage sure.

She turned the page. Scanned the opening paragraph again
before, handing it back:

'Some kinda nut. That's all I can say.'

He took the letter from her. His eyes, however, never left
her face.

'Who is he?'

He'd made, of course, one mistake. Had omitted – perhaps
deliberately – to write in an address. So that, to all intents
and purposes, he was a name only in any number of names.
Faceless. A crank like any other crank. She alone knew of
his whereabouts, both on a personal and on a business level.
Which gave her – for the present, at least – some sort of
advantage. There was no way Hugh could hope to find out
more about him – not from the directory even. For – resi-
dent, as he was, in a hostel – his name would not appear.
Whether he was prepared to check him out by other means
– the Home Office, or whatever – depended on how she
handled this thing now.

She shrugged. Exhaled through her nose.

'How should I know?'

'He appears to think you should.'

Attack, she decided, was her best method of defence. It
was vital she convince him. (But. . .?)

'You mean you actually believe all that?' And, when she
saw that he hesitated: 'You know what I'd do? – hand it in

to the police. Tell them what happened. I mean, it amounts after all to defamation of character. If we could find out who this guy is, he'd be in real trouble. What address does he give?'

'There's no address.'

'Oh, well. Goes to show. But there must be some way we could find out who he is. Some guy I forgot to tip maybe – a cab driver, or a waiter. Well, I mean, you never know.'

Was sticking her neck out perhaps in naming his actual occupation, but adopted this ruse deliberately. Like a hare which – hunted by a dog, and with no immediate cover – will suddenly sit absolutely still while the dog, confused, will fail to locate his former quarry and, assuming he has escaped, will give up the chase.

'How, then, does he know so much about you? – your name, your address, and so on?'

'Search me. I imagine, if one were determined enough, this wouldn't be too difficult.'

'Viv: look at me.'

She obeyed. God knows how. Her expression must have passed through as many phases as a strobe lamp.

'Is he your lover?'

'No.'

There was, however, a technicality here. Aware of which, he switched at once to the past tense. Had her now – or so he thought.

'Was he ever your lover?'

'Strictly, no.'

'Strictly?'

'Yeah.' Waved her cigarette around. 'I mean, God knows what sort of fantasies he may have dreamed up about me.'

He tried, as a last resort, to stare her out. But, amazingly, she stood her ground. Felt, in fact, strong. Convinced of her untruth – of its validity.

'Like I said, he's probably a waiter or something – that's what it seems like. And I've been into the restaurant; and I've upset him in some way or other. Or, he developed some sort of fixation on me. Why don't you do like I said: take it to the police? Ten to one, if he's the nut he seems to be, they'll have a file on him already.'

'You've really no idea who this man is?'

'Hughie: no. What more can I say?'

'What makes you think he's a waiter?'

'Well. . . The name.' And, flippantly: 'Aren't all Italians waiters?'

'But this accusation he's made against you . . .'

'What accusation? – oh, that. Well, I guess he had to think of something. Maybe, at the time he saw me, I'd had a few drinks, and, well, he just assumed . . .'

But like her mask started to slip. This was somehow more difficult. Felt, suddenly, like when she was a kid and used to play this scary little game – used to walk around with her eyes closed and imagine what it would be like if she was blind.

'Assumed what?'

She laughed. Not altogether convincingly.

'God alone knows. The whole thing is ludicrous.'

He was silent a moment. Then:

'It does seem rather odd though.'

'What?'

'That he should hit on something which concerns me as much as it apparently does him.'

She stared. Thrust her fingers into her hair.

'I don't believe I heard right. What was it you said? – implied rather? That this guy may have a point after all?'

'It can't just be coincidence.'

Tossed her head.

'What in hell are you talking about? I mean, what really are you – ?'

'What I'm trying to say is, I was on the verge of discussing this with you before I went away. Now, suddenly, I get a letter from a total stranger which would seem to prove that my suspicions were not unfounded.'

'Now look!'

'Yes, yes – all right. Just listen to me a moment. I feel sure this man is telling the truth. That he is, or was, your lover. And, more importantly perhaps, that there is as good a reason for his concern as there is for mine.'

Felt that she was going mad. Was frightened half out of her wits.

'Then you're as crazy as he is! What's got into you for God's sake? Or is this some sort of dream I wonder?'

'It's my belief you've been living in a dream for longer than you'd care to admit. It's in your eyes: in everything you say and do.' He put the letter to one side. 'Now: I want the truth. I want to know what the matter is – why you're behaving in this way.'

She threw down her cigarette.

A shower of sparks in the grate.

'Why I'm – ? Why are you doing this to me? What right have you to treat me like some sort of – '

'Because, this letter apart, I know that something is very wrong – and has been for a long time. Now, please: for both our sakes, I want the truth.'

Threw herself at him suddenly. Beat at his chest with her fists. Tears of rage sprang up in her eyes, blurred her vision. All she saw was the hot blood inside her head.

But he was apparently prepared for some such demonstration. Caught hold of both her wrists and held them firmly.

'Stop that! Stop it at once!'

'It's a lie. A Goddam lie I tell you!'

But had driven him, she realised, too far. At his wits' end, he slapped her sharply across the face.

Unable at first to believe what had happened, she gasped. Never before, in their entire married life, had he laid hands on her in such a way. And now, at last, the fragile fabric of lies and half truths blew suddenly away. And she felt like in a dream. Like she was in the supermarket or something and, looking down, saw that she was naked.

Covered her face with her hands.

'What have you done? What have you done to me . . .?'

'Drink is a devil Viv! – you must understand. You worship at your peril.' And, less vehemently: 'Now – we'll get you booked in at a clinic or something, and see what they can do for you.'

'No – please. Just let me – '

He took her hands down; smoothed the tears away.

'Darling, I'm sorry. It has to be done. You've got to help

yourself – got to want to help yourself. No one – not even
me – can do it for you.'

She swallowed hard.

Nodded at last. Bit in her lower lip.

'Okay. Just give me a day or two to sort myself out. And
I'll – I'll – '

Burst again into tears.

'God! Oh, God!'

He took her into his arms.

'Now, darling. You've got to do it now. But remember:
whatever happens, you can rely on me.'

No, no, no. He had it all wrong . . .

She was going at first to ring Enrico. To pull him apart.

But soon saw the futility of any such move. Of further
argument. He was, besides, innocent. Hugh had been right
when he guessed his concern to be genuine: she couldn't
blame him for that.

Was, in any case, too shaken to act positively at any
level. Didn't seem able to think for herself at all. Or didn't,
perhaps, want to.

'I'll leave it to you,' she told him at last. 'You fix something up for me, an' I'll do whatever you say.'

He worried, however. She could tell.

'You do want to get better . . .?'

She dropped her eyes.

'Sure. Yeah, I – '

(But what did he mean, 'better'?)

He waited. Searched her face.

'I – I'll do whatever you want.'

Grabbed for her cigarettes. But her hand shook so, he had
to light it for her.

Same at the office. Totally unable to concentrate.

Was drinking still – more heavily than before even. Why
not? Her secret was out: it didn't matter. But drank only
irreligiously. No more ecstatic ceremony.

Would just walk in, with what he called 'that silly look
on your face'. He had not, however, understood; and she

no longer cared. As a result of which new bravado, he distanced himself a little.

Well. . . Okay.

But then, when the euphoria passed, her nerves so raw she could have screamed. Didn't know what to do. Jumped half out her skin at the slightest sound. Or was so withdrawn she heard nothing at all. Not when he spoke to her even.

It was like – quite suddenly and dramatically – everything was just slipping through her fingers. Both figuratively and literally. Everything she picked up she dropped. And her hold on reality, on her day-to-day routine, equally shaky. She'd get to the office, and find she'd forgotten to shower . . . Passed up opportunities she knew were there but hadn't the zip to follow.

How long before her boss told her where she got off? Everyone, she knew, saw the change in her. The accelerated downward slide. It was like she was on some sort of fair-ground ride gone crazy.

But didn't want to stop.

Was booked to enter a private clinic on the tenth October.

'But, really, I can't understand why the fuss . . .'

'Darling, you know as well as I that this has to be done.'

'Yeah. But. . . I mean, it's not like there's some reason for it.'

'But there must be.'

'But there isn't. And if some shrink or other is gonna grill me, looking for clues which just aren't there, then all I can tell him is I enjoy getting pissed – that's all. An' they're gonna think I'm frivolous: that I'm wasting their time.'

Saw at once that her words alarmed him. It just didn't fit in with what he knew – or thought he knew – about alcoholics. Began now to think he must be right. No longer knew whether she was telling the truth or not. Whether there was in fact some reason which – consciously or unconsciously – she chose to ignore. Felt – like when, at convent school, she went to confession and had to rack her brains for something to confess – that there ought to be one. That she must be wrong in thinking there wasn't. But, however hard she tried, could come up with nothing remotely convincing.

Other than that it was just the way she was made. Which, for a doctor, was perhaps too glib.

'Darling, wait and see. I'm sure they'll be able to help you. Or, if you feel they can't, then we must think of something else.'

A bright, beautiful autumn day.

Had lunched with a prospective client, and . . .

Was now in the Strand, the time around two. Amazing. She'd thought it was much later. Imperfect sense of time . . .

But good. A really good feeling. Like she'd just been to a priest, and was now absolved. Purged of sin. If only she . . . so Goddam woozy.

Would get a cab at the station for sure.

Charing Cross. A huge crowd here.

Station forecourt.

Everyone in such a hurry. (But they stare so. Like she's some kind of leper or something . . .)

'Taxi!'

Stepped forward. But the cab was occupied, pulled abruptly away. Another . . . into its place.

Slam!

Didn't feel anything . . . exactly. But like –

Somebody screamed.

Screamed . . .

'My wife,' he said, 'died yesterday in hospital. She was knocked down by a car.'

(Siren. Ambulance. Blue lamp flashing. Police. Young fellow chalking round her broken form; her head awkwardly to one side in the gutter. Eyes wide open: astonished. Their expression fixed forever. Awed crowd in the shadow of the huge façade. Testimony, avariciously offered. She was drunk: the driver was not to blame. Another statistic.)

The young man stared. Did not, however, seem surprised.

'I – I'm terribly sorry . . .'

'What,' he asked, 'is your name?'

But knew, before he answered even.

'My name is Muraro. Enrico Muraro. I – '

'You wrote to me, yes.' Then: 'My wife was due to enter a clinic at the weekend. But now . . .'

The young man looked at him a moment. Morning light reflected back off his features.

'Yes. I understand.' And: 'If there is anything I can do . . .'

'There is nothing now that anyone can do. But thank you all the same.'

The young man nodded.

'Goodbye then. I am sorry to have troubled you at a time like this.'

'Not at all. Goodbye.'

Was half way across the hall when he stopped suddenly. They ought perhaps to have a talk sometime.

Went quickly back and opened the door.

But he'd gone.

Instead . . . Moyses Stevens, with the yellow roses.